REPRISAL

SPACE COLONY ONE BOOK 9

J.J. GREEN

These soldiers had done what they had done, and been done unto in return. This was how it went. In the cycle of the world, reprisal begat reprisal, forever.

— LAINI TAYLOR

1

Seeds, tubers, corms, bulbs, spores, rhizomes, cuttings—everything needed to replenish Concordia's biome was stacked deck to overhead in the Ark. Wilder walked the aisles, past refrigerator units, shelves full of boxes and thick packets neatly filed, and glasshouse areas sectioned off by transparent plastic curtains moist with condensation. The growing tanks that had kept the crew fed on their long voyage had been dismantled months ago, yet she could still remember where they'd been and the crops that had grown in them. She'd worked the 'fields' for years, after all, along with everyone else.

The scientists said the seeding material carried fungal spores, bacteria, and other micro-organisms that would subtly promote its growth. These were missing from her home planet, as well as the many species the Scythians' biocide had destroyed. Their absence was the reason things struggled to grow. All were required, apparently, for a healthy ecosystem. She didn't doubt the scientists were correct. Her crew mates weren't exactly her best buddies, not after living in close quarters with them for so long, but they knew their stuff. Kes had picked only the best for the trip.

She halted.

Tall shelving units stacked with containers flanked her. A faulty light flickered above, casting the space into chaotic darkness.

She checked her surroundings again. Everything was different, but she was sure it was here she'd found Cherry, flat on her back on a deck swimming with water. Her friend had slipped and sustained a severe concussion. She'd been lucky she hadn't been electrocuted.

Cherry.

"It was good knowing you, Wilder."

Those had been her parting words. Now she was on Earth fighting the Scythians, and it was up to the remaining personnel of the *Sirocco* to continue the fight on Concordia.

For the aliens would return one day, perhaps soon. They knew that their biocide hadn't wiped out the humans. They knew the colony had survived, and they knew of its plan to restock the planet with life from Earth.

She walked on.

A comm arrived.

"Where are you?" Niall asked. "It's time to jump."

"Already? Sorry, I'm on the Ark."

"What are you doing there?" His tone was cold, impersonal, irritated.

"Just reminiscing."

"Right." A touch of scorn. "Vessey's going to blow her lid if you don't get over to the jump chamber in the next five minutes."

"All right. Tell her I'm coming."

"Tell her yourself."

The comm cut out.

Swallowing her anger, she sent a message to the captain to apologize and say she was on her way. Then she stomped toward the exit.

Niall had been cantankerous and distant toward her ever since a Scythian had snatched her on the Makers' island on Earth. She hadn't pushed him about his attitude. She knew what his problem was. Kes had given her an insight into what was probably going on with Niall, and she thought the older man had been right. She was sympathetic, but it was no excuse to treat her so badly.

When she reached the chamber, a few people remained outside

their capsules, chatting. They side-eyed her as she walked in. She ignored them and walked to the nearest empty capsule. There was no point in placating them. Her rep had never recovered from the failed jump that had taken them decades off course, and it never would. Everyone had expected to be gone from home for a few weeks. Instead, with the effects of time dilation, they had been absent for decades. Even if their loved ones had survived to old age on the crippled planet, they were probably long dead. It was hard to forgive something like that.

"Jumping in two minutes," Vessey announced over comm.

Wilder stepped into her capsule and lay down, sinking into the spongy seat. She fastened her harness. They no longer had the gel that was supposed to cocoon the jump passengers. A leak in a supply line had allowed air in and the gel had dried up. But they'd jumped safely without it several times. This time should be no different.

What would Concordia be like? Was anyone still alive? If the colony had failed, was there any point in re-seeding the planet, especially considering the Scythians were bound to return? Maybe it would make more sense to go back to Earth and try to make a life there.

Her stomach sank at the idea. Earth was beautiful but it wasn't home.

"One minute," Vessey announced.

The shell closed over her.

A voice sounded in her ear. "Wilder?"

"Hey, Miki. Everything okay?"

"Yeahhhh..." Silence.

"Are you worried about what we might find when we arrive? You're not alone. But don't be too concerned. The Scythians don't have jump drive. It will take them years to reach Concordia."

The young girl's breathy sigh came down the line. "I feel bad for telling them everything."

"You didn't have a choice. If you hadn't they would have killed Nina. No one blames you. Besides, the Scythians would have returned to Concordia anyway sooner or later. It's their origin planet. They have a sentimental attachment to it. It doesn't matter that they can't live there anymore."

"I guess so," Miki replied doubtfully. "I just can't help feeling that Dad would be disappointed in me."

"No, he wouldn't. He would have been proud of you for protecting your sister. And, anyway, he loved you so much I don't think anything you did could have disappointed him. You don't need to concern yourself about that."

A pause.

"Thanks, Wilder."

The computer countdown began.

"See you in Concordia orbit," Wilder said.

The numbers counted down. She'd endured many 'jumps' now, journeying to Earth and returning home. She should have become accustomed to the sensation, yet she still tensed as the countdown neared its end. Traversing spacetime in a manner at odds with the natural movements of the human body was something that could never feel familiar, she guessed.

Three.

Two.

One.

Zero.

Reality shifted.

She could no longer feel where she was in space. Her view beyond the transparent shell of her capsule stretched wide and then squashed in, folding in many pleats. At the same time a piercing whistle assaulted her ears. Then it was all over.

Her capsule opened.

Excited voices filled the chamber.

"Home," someone said. "Finally!"

"I can't believe it," said another. "It doesn't feel real."

"I wonder what we'll find down there," said a third. "I wonder what's left."

The tone turned somber and the voices quietened.

Vessey cut through the conversations. "At your stations, everyone. You all know what you should be doing. Zapata, where are you?"

After a preliminary check of the state of things on the planet surface, the captain would go down with a small team. Everyone else would follow later. The *Sirocco* was not to be abandoned entirely. A skeleton crew would remain on duty but on a regular rotation. It would not be right to condemn anyone to spending long periods of time aboard the vessel after everything that had happened.

Wilder sat up. People were climbing out of their capsules. She gave Miki and Nina a wave, trying to look positive though inside she felt quite different. She was all the girls had left in terms of a parent and she felt utterly unequipped. She barely had her own life in order. How was she supposed to be a mother to two recently bereaved orphans?

"No!" Niall was standing at the interface near the chamber entrance, staring at the screen. "Dammit! Captain, you have to see this."

"Is it what we thought?"

"Yes."

Vessey's features tightened. "Right. Then I don't need to see it. Plan B, everyone. Back in your capsules. Niall, do the honors."

Wilder's heart sank deeper than her body into her seat as she resumed her position in her capsule. The shell closed over her again, and the countdown started up. It would be shorter this time, the minimum the engines needed. They could only make a small jump, using up the remainder of their power.

The question was, would it happen fast enough?

An alarm blared out. A split second later, the ship shuddered.

They'd been hit.

Groans and exclamations of fear leaked from the surrounding capsules.

She prayed the jump drive hadn't sustained any damage. If it had, they were screwed.

This time, the countdown seemed agonizingly slow. She willed the numbers to decrease faster. The alarm continued to sound, loud and urgent, as if the ship was begging her crew to do something, fast, before it was too late. But there was nothing they could do. They'd used most of their power getting here. There was too little left to operate the Parvus's weapon *and* jump. It was one or the other, and until they understood the situation better, getting the hell out of Concordia's system was the safer option.

The *Sirocco* lurched, and she was pressed tight up against the side of her seat.

The assault seemed to have come from the port side this time.

Not the jump drive. Not the drive!

The countdown was only just audible over the alarm. It whispered tantalizingly.

Two.

One.

She held her breath.

2

"Someone turn off that damned alarm," Vessey ordered.

The cover of Wilder's capsule opened, but this time she didn't sit up. Though they'd only completed two jumps and she was fully rested, exhaustion had settled on her. Lifting her head felt like too much effort. Or was it only dread of what she was about to discover?

They'd known it was a possibility. The alternative scenario to what everyone had been anticipating had been the great unmentionable subject of the return voyage.

She lay still, waiting for the motivation to rise. Others were moving around and talking. The earlier excitement had disappeared and been replaced by grim resignation.

"Any ships within range?" Vessey asked.

"The scanners aren't picking anything up," Niall replied. "We're safe for now."

For now.

A face appeared in Wilder's vision, long red-black hair hanging down.

"Why aren't you getting up?" Miki asked.

Wilder smiled thinly. "Just taking a minute. Want to give me a hand?" She unfastened her harness, and Miki helped her climb out.

"The jumps make me feel sick too," said Miki. "What's going on? Vessey said something about Plan B. Have we left Concordia?"

"Yes, but we've only gone a little way. We're at its closest neighboring star."

"How come?"

"Uh..."

Miki really didn't know? Wilder hated to be the one to break the news. "Didn't you feel the hits?"

"Hits?" Miki's eyes widened. "I thought there was something wrong with the ship. We were under attack?!"

"Where's Nina?"

"She's gone back to our cabin. She always needs an hour to recover from a jump."

"In that case, come with me. Let's see what the scanners picked up."

Miki was going to have to deal with what faced the returning Concordians, despite her young years. It was better that she knew what they were up against. It wouldn't be fair—or even possible—to keep her in the dark.

They walked to the bridge. Zapata was already at the pilot's controls, probably moving the ship to the optimum spot in the new system to avoid detection. They couldn't be too cautious. Vessey stood with Niall, assessing the scanner data. They looked up as Wilder and Miki walked over.

Vessey frowned. "Miki, I'm not sure this is the right place for you at the moment."

"She needs to know what's going on," Wilder retorted. "She's a member of this crew the same as everyone else. Hell, she and Nina grew up on this ship. And their father sacrificed his life—"

"Okay, I get it. Take a seat. Niall, put images up for us all to see."

While the captain was sitting down, Wilder asked, "Did you get the damage report yet?"

Vessey grimaced. "The Ark took a hit that breached the hull. I've sent in a team. Hopefully, we haven't lost too much."

"I felt two impacts. Where was the second one?"

"Just above the jump drive. We had a lucky escape. My guess is they don't know exactly where it is. Otherwise we wouldn't be here."

"The data has rendered," Niall announced. "I'll put up the images of Concordia first, followed by what's in orbit."

The bridge lights dimmed and the center brightened with a holo of the planet surface.

Miki gasped.

Wilder's hands tightened on her armrests. She'd been expecting to see something like this, but the extent of it was shocking.

Scythian domes dotted a dusty plain under a clear blue sky. It was hard to estimate the area the scanners had captured but if the domes were the same size as the ones on Earth, they stood only a few kilometers apart. The surface of Concordia was thick with aliens.

"But I thought they didn't have jump tech," Miki blurted. She turned to Wilder, eyes wide. "How could they have got here so fast?"

Niall tutted irritably. "They were already here, of course."

Wilder studied the holo more closely. It showed a Scythian in mid-air between the domes—unusually, considering it was daylight —wearing the same breathing apparatus they'd used on Earth. That was somewhat of a relief. At least they hadn't managed to reverse the 'poisoning' of Concordia's atmosphere with oxygen.

Miki asked quietly, "Is anyone still alive down there?"

Vessey got to her feet and strode into the holo. "These look like human figures, don't you think?" She pointed to a patch of land greener than the rest. Small, upright shapes could be spotted among the vegetation. Were they people? It was hard to tell but it seemed likely. Other macro-organisms had been wiped out by the biocide.

"What are they doing?" asked Miki.

"Tending crops, I'd say," Niall offered, "probably to feed themselves and perhaps the Scythians too."

"I think that vegetation must be crops," Wilder said. "It looks homogeneous and there's precious little else around. I can't see any trees or scrub. The place doesn't look much better than how we left it."

"But I still don't understand how the Scythians..." Miki paused. "I get it. They didn't come here due to what I told them on Earth. They'd already returned to Concordia anyway. What I said didn't matter." Tension seemed to leave her body. "That's a relief, though this is still a…a…"

"Disaster?" Vessey suggested. "What do they have in orbit, Niall?"

The landscape vanished and black space took up the central position on the bridge. Within the star-speckled darkness hung three crescent-shaped ships.

"The largest is the one that fired on us," Niall said, consulting his screen. "It was quick off the mark. I don't know about the other two, whether they aren't armed or if they didn't manage to fire before we jumped."

"They're all Scythian military," Vessey said grimly, "not transports. I'd lay money on it. We got a good look at their colonization vessels while we were on Earth."

"I can make a detailed comparison," Wilder offered. "We have plenty of information on both types of vessel."

Vessey waved dismissively. "Depressurization in the Ark and a damaged hull near the jump drive tell us all we need to know for now. There's no question in my mind that, A, Scythians arrived at Concordia many years ago and, B, they know a starship carrying humans had departed the system and was expected to return. Those ships were waiting for us."

"But how could they know that?" asked Miki.

"Probably the same way they found out you were from Concordia."

The young girl put her head in her hands.

"The colonization attempt succeeded here," Niall said. "Unsurprisingly. The place was in a weakened state when we left. The Scythian attack had destroyed its defenses, their biocide had wiped out most living organisms, human civilization was on its knees. We thought Earth was in a bad position to defend itself, but compared to Concordia it's a well-stocked fortress. Those poor bastards."

"Maybe it isn't such a bad thing," said Wilder.

Niall stared. "How the hell do you figure that?"

"It might have been the Scythians' return that saved the colony. You remember what things were like when we left—food stores were running out, crops would barely grow, and insect swarms were making being outdoors intolerable. If there are people down there, it might only be because the Scythians enslaved them. They need humans for labor on a planet where they can't breathe the atmosphere. They would have had to fix the environment sufficiently for humans to survive."

Vessey gave a snort. "The Concordia Colony only continues to exist because it has alien overlords? That's rich. I wonder what Aubriot would have said."

"He must be spinning in his grave," Niall muttered. "But wondering about what happened isn't going to change anything."

"Exactly," said Vessey. "I have some thinking to do. We need a way forward but at the moment I'm not seeing it."

The minimal data the *Sirocco*'s scanners had gleaned in the short time the vessel had been in Concordia orbit painted a dire scene. If colonists remained on the planet they were in thrall to Scythian masters. The aliens were somehow aware that an armed vessel belonging to the humans could appear one day, and they were on guard against it. And, aside from crop plants, the environment didn't seem to have recovered on its own. The planet desperately needed the seeding material in the Ark to replenish its ecosystem.

But how were they to get it there? How could they defeat the military vessels? Any small element of surprise they'd had previously was now entirely gone. How could they help the colonists, descendants of the people they'd left behind?

Miki lifted her head from her hands. "Things might be even worse than we think."

"I'm not sure that's possible," said Vessey, "but I guess I need to hear it. Fire away."

"Dad told me and Nina lots about Concordia while we were growing up. I could only just remember it, and Nina couldn't remember it at all. He told us all the good stuff—how determined, brave, and hardworking all the colonists were, what they'd endured and come through, despite the challenges. But he also told us something else, something I...I think you might have forgotten." She looked up at Vessey timidly.

"Forgotten? Well, I've certainly had a lot on my plate during this mission. Don't worry. I'm not Aubriot. I don't think I'm perfect and I'm not going to bite your head off for pointing out a flaw."

"Umm..." Miki glanced around the group on the bridge.

Zapata looked over his shoulder.

"Dad said the colony needed fresh genetic input. Otherwise, over the long term it was doomed. He said we needed to bring people from—"

"Holy shit!" Wilder clapped a hand over her mouth. "Miki, you're right! I'd forgotten. We've all forgotten. The original mission was to bring back the seeding material, but we were also supposed to be introducing new human DNA to the colony eventually. If not people, then donor eggs and sperm. Or else inherited diseases would start to appear and the population would weaken and in the end it would die out. Kes mentioned it at the meeting in the Town Hall, but that was so long ago."

"We were fixated on the main task," said Niall. "The delay pushed everything else to the backs of our minds."

Vessey shook her head. "And to think I was set on not taking any Earthers with us."

Miki said, "If I hadn't gone to the surface with Nina I might have remembered in time and been around to remind you. I'm sorry."

"Don't worry about it," Vessey reassured her. "This mission has been crazy for all of us. We've made plenty of mistakes. I'm certainly not blameless in that regard. But it's time to move on and look ahead. Zapata, have you brought us within range of the star to begin energy harvesting?"

"In another few minutes."

"Niall or Wilder, could you please do the usual? I'll be in my office. I have a lot to think about. If anyone has any suggestions, feel free to disturb me."

3

When Miki arrived at her cabin Nina had woken from her nap.

She sat up in bed. "What's happening? When are we going down to Concordia? I'm so excited to see it. I know it won't be for the first time but that's how it feels. I was only a baby when we left. I don't remember home at all." Her lips twisted downward. "I wish Dad was here. He could have taken us back to our old house. Only maybe it isn't there anymore."

Miki sat next to her sister and put an arm around her shoulders. "We won't be going to the planet surface any time soon, sorry." She gave her sister the news.

Nina gasped. "We were being *fired* on?!"

"I didn't realize either. I felt the hits and heard people's reactions, but it was all over so quickly I didn't get much time to think about it."

"I thought the jump drive had gone wrong again." Nina rested her head on Miki's shoulder. "Are they going to force the Scythians to leave? How long will we have to stay on the ship?"

"Captain Vessey is trying to figure out a plan. I'm sure she or one of the other adults will think of something." She was trying to reassure herself as much as Nina, but the impression she had from the discussion on the bridge was that going home was going to be very difficult and dangerous.

Nina asked in a soft whisper, "Should we have stayed on Earth?"

The same idea had occurred to Miki. They'd left Dad behind, and Cherry too, and for what? She'd thought Concordia would be safe, that she was taking Nina away from the Scythians, but it had sounded like the aliens were more established on their home planet. The defenses would be stronger, and the *Sirocco* was alone, without any other human military force to help her. On Earth there had been helis, weapons, and a big population. There was none of that on Concordia.

A heavy feeling settled in her stomach. Dad was gone, and it was down to her to protect Nina. She'd done a terrible job so far. "I don't know," she replied equally quietly. "Maybe."

"But Concordia's our home, right?"

"It is, but..." In truth, if any place was their home it was the *Sirocco*. They'd spent most of their lives on the ship, growing up aboard her, and for a very long time her crew were the only people they'd known. They'd met some Earthers in the Scythian domes and after escaping, but they spoke a different language, making it nearly impossible to communicate. "I think Dad would say Concordia is where we should be. That's where we were born, and that's where Mom is. I was dumb when I pulled that stunt and we snuck off to Earth."

"You're not dumb."

Nina was being kind, but she felt dumb. Dumb and powerless.

"Did they say if there's anything we can do?" asked Nina.

"Nope. I think we can be most helpful by staying out of everyone's way." She bit her lip. "Or maybe not. The Ark took a hit and depressurized. We lost some of the seeding material. We could help by figuring out what we lost. I'll ask if that's okay."

"Sure. I'll get ready."

Nina climbed out of bed while Miki comm'd the captain. She felt a little bad bothering her when she had a lot on her mind, but Vessey's response was positive. She only asked her to double check the Ark was completely safe before they went over.

THE PLACE WAS A MESS. The crew had fixed the hull, but roughly. Thick lines of solder ran over the plain metal surface like barely healed scars. They had fixed the interior first and were now working on the hull. An acrid scent from the work remained in the atmosphere. Circulation fans whined as they sensed the remaining particles of contamination and strained to draw them into the filters.

The crew had done nothing to address the devastation to the seeding material. The hit from the Scythian ship had penetrated an area with a diameter of about thirty centimeters. Whatever was gone had squeezed through the gap. The shelves nearest the breach were empty, naturally. Their contents had exploded into space, the internal pressure forcing them out.

Miki read the labels. Seeds of plants that grew in alpine regions had been stored here. She'd nursed a vague hope that some of the material might not be entirely lost, but there was no hope of recovering these. The cold and vacuum of space wouldn't harm them in the short term, but the packets that held these seeds had been tiny, smaller than the palm of her hand. Locating them would be impossible.

"Oh well," Nina said. "Concordia's mountains are going to stay bare for a while."

"Or overrun by one species. Dad said some things had grown rampantly, covering hundreds of square kilometers because nothing that used to eat them or compete with them had survived." She had a faint memory of a swarm of insects biting her, but she didn't tell Nina about it. The image of the humans toiling in the fields on Concordia sprang to her mind. What were the people there going through?

The effects of the breach on the material outside its immediate vicinity was less calamitous. Plenty had been dragged from its storage place, smashed against shelving units, thrown against bulkheads, torn apart, shredded, and jumbled up, but it hadn't been lost.

The situation here seemed more salvageable. She and Nina had spent long hours cataloging and storing the samples the crew had collected on Earth. They were familiar with many of the items by sight, so identifying them shouldn't be too hard, and they could confirm their identification with DNA analysis. Then it would only be a matter of re-packing everything. The task would be lengthy and painstaking, but it would help to take Nina's mind off everything else that was going on.

"What a mess!" her sister exclaimed in dismay, surveying the destruction.

"It isn't as bad as it looks." Miki stooped to pick up a tuber. "This is one of the roots mountain dwellers eat, remember? Wilder said it tastes floury and sweet." They hadn't tried it. Everything the gatherers had brought up had gone straight into the Ark.

Nina's brow wrinkled. "Yeah, I think I remember."

Miki pushed up her sleeves to her elbows. "Let's get started. First, we need to separate it all out. We can use the empty area next to the site of the breach."

"Ugh, this is going to take *forever*," Nina complained, but she squatted down and began to scoop up detritus.

Miki joined her, relieved they would be doing something useful as well as staying out of everyone's way. The last thing she wanted was to cause more trouble.

4

The Scythian vessel lay in pieces over the holding bay deck. Wilder, Niall, and Dragan had recently spent every spare moment investigating the alien spacecraft, while the *Sirocco* had leapfrogged across the galaxy. What they'd discovered didn't seem helpful for tackling the current crisis, but Wilder had returned to the bay nonetheless, hoping to find something they'd missed.

The major disappointment had been that the small, two-seater ship appeared to be only for traveling within a planetary atmosphere. As far as they could tell it didn't possess a-grav—though, to be fair, that had been a recent introduction to intelligent galactic species in this sector, courtesy of herself. More pertinently, the craft wasn't airtight. They'd guessed the Scythians who flew them must have worn breathing apparatus, and Miki and Nina had confirmed.

After discovering Earth's location from the android, Faina, they had sent attack ships to bombard the planet, and then swiftly followed them with transport vessels for colonization. Despite their haste, the journeys had taken years. Concordia's greatest superiority against the Scythians was the jump drive. But how could they deploy their advantage for the best outcome?

The Scythian planetary craft were driven by a compact engine core and battery powered turbines. The remaining components comprised predictable devices: an altimeter, gyros, a compass, and so on. Some items remained a mystery, but most of the differences between the alien vessel and a heli were superficial. The crescent shape Scythians favored seemed to be only a style preference. The oddly shaped seating and flight controls that made it impossible for a human to pilot the vessel were perfectly suited to Scythian anatomy. The aliens clearly reclined, their wings folded to their sides, and operated the controls with their prehensile feet.

Overall, the ship's technology was surprisingly similar to something humans might invent. Or perhaps not so surprisingly. There had to be a limited number of ways to achieve and maintain flight.

Wilder gazed at the heavily studied parts of the dismantled ship, feeling she was at a dead end. Even if they managed to figure out the functions of the remaining mysterious parts, she didn't think the revelation would help.

Maybe it was time to try a different avenue of exploration. She should leave her comfort zone and venture into that cryptic discipline —biology.

She comm'd Vessey.

"Wilder," the captain answered with a note of hope, "what can I do for you?"

"Can you tell me who's been working on the Scythian cadaver?"

"Ryan mostly. Why?"

Ugh.

"Has he sent in a report?"

"Yes, but..." she sighed "...it's mostly gibberish to me. I'm no scientist. Perhaps you could understand it better?"

"I doubt it, but I'm willing to give it a try."

"Anything you can suggest that might help us—*anything*—I'd be happy to hear it. I'll send you the report."

"Thanks." She felt sorry for Vessey. The captain had only signed up for a short voyage to Earth. Instead, she'd found herself in command of a ship years off course, whose crew verged on suicidal. She'd sunk under the pressure, but lately she'd rallied. She'd given up the booze and was trying her best with her mediocre skill set. She was no Aubriot but her heart was in the right place.

The report arrived and Wilder began to listen to it, but many of the terms were unfamiliar. She found a wall interface and opened the file on the screen. Reading the information made it more understandable, but it was quickly apparent that she needed to speak to the author himself.

This was going to be tricky. Ever since the incident where they'd tried to kill her, she'd avoided members of the Final Day Five, except for Dragan, who had ended up saving her life. Avoiding Marcus, whom she'd blinded, was easy. He rarely left his cabin. Durbin and Goslin kept out of her way too. Ryan, on the other hand, seemed to cope with embarrassment over what he'd done by pretending it had never happened. After recovering from the injuries she'd inflicted to his knees, he'd tried to interact with her as if she was just another member of the crew. He'd never apologized or even acknowledged the attack.

She wasn't sure she wanted him to, but she'd wished he would read the room and leave her alone. The memory of nearly being hanged by her shipmates wasn't something she wanted to dwell on. She tried to never bring it to mind, though the event invaded her dreams. In some, she didn't manage to get away. In others, she made it to Dragan's cabin but he didn't experience his epiphany and defend her.

So if Ryan appeared she would leave, and if he was someplace she needed to be she would delay going in until he left, whenever possible. What made it worse was the fact everyone seemed to want to move on from the attempted murder, like it was just one of the many crazy things that had happened on the ill-fated voyage. She understood how that was the most convenient reaction. Trying her would-be assassins for their crime would have been difficult, considering the circumstances, and it would have deprived the mission of desperately needed specialists.

But how was she supposed to 'move on'?

She'd reached Ryan's cabin. She hesitated, her hand halfway to his door chime. Did she really want to do this? She set her jaw and pressed.

"Wilder! Great to see you. It's been a while."

"I want to talk to you about—"

"Take a seat. Can I get you something to drink?"

Ryan's cabin was neat and bare, almost pathologically so. His bed was made, his desk empty, the walls unadorned. It looked like he'd only just moved in, not lived here for over a decade. The only sign of occupation was a faint scent of antiseptic. What had he even been doing before she arrived?

"This won't take long. Vessey said you've been working on the Scythian corpse. I was wondering what you could tell me about what you found. I read the report, but…"

He lifted an eyebrow. "Gobbledygook, right? Don't worry, I feel the same when I look at anything to do with engineering or physics. I tell you what—why don't you come with me to have a look at it? I can give you an illustrated explanation."

"Uhh…" She hadn't anticipated viewing one of the creatures up close, but when she woke up today she hadn't anticipated a chat with the man who'd tried to kill her either. She might as well go all in. "Sure."

"Actually, I'm glad you came to see me," said Ryan as they stepped out of his cabin. "We haven't had the chance to talk about what happened when…you know…"

"We haven't had the chance to talk about it?" she echoed. *I haven't given you the chance, asshole.*

"I just wanted to tell you, I forgive you."

She halted, hard, as if she'd walked into a wall. "You *what*?"

"I understand you were scared and reacted in a panic. I know if you'd been in your right mind you would never have done what you did. You wouldn't have hurt me." From the mild expression on his face he didn't seem to be registering her shocked reaction.

"We…we are talking about the same incident, right?" she spluttered. "You do mean the time you, Marcus, Goslin, and Durbin tried to string me up? You mean *that* time, right?!" Her tone had reached almost screeching pitch.

This wasn't how she'd wanted things to go. The last thing she'd wanted was to get distracted by past events, especially considering no one could do anything to change them. They needed to focus on present problems. But she couldn't let this twisting of the truth slide. Her entire body rebelled at the notion.

"I believe you might have misinterpreted our intentions," he said.

"Oh, I don't think so," she snapped, setting off down the passageway at a speedy pace. "Take me to see the Scythian. Let's get this over with."

He trotted to catch up to her. "If you would just let me explain…"

"What you did doesn't need explaining. I don't know what's gone on in your head since then—what mental gymnastics you've performed to convince yourself you didn't do anything wrong—but *my* memory is clear. And, frankly, attempting to persuade me I misunderstood what you intended is disgusting."

"But—"

"Not another word. Show me the Scythian."

"If I could just—"

"Show me the Scythian!" She glared at him until he could no longer meet her gaze.

His shoulders slumped. "It's this way."

Understanding her fellow humans had never been her strong suit, and the effort got harder day by day. People could excuse anything to themselves, even the most abhorrent behavior. Ryan obviously had some weird mental thing going on, with his surgically clean cabin and rewriting his heinous act in his mind. Niall was another weirdo. He was mean to her because he liked her. How stupid was that?

Maybe she would have better luck understanding the aliens.

"I PUT IT BACK TOGETHER, kind of," said Ryan, dragging a body bag out of a freezer.

Wilder hadn't included a mortuary in the *Sirocco*'s plans. In the rush to design and build the vessel, there simply hadn't been time for non-essential facilities. It was one of the reasons they had buried Kes on Earth rather than bringing his body back to Concordia. People who had died during the voyage had been given a space burial. But the Scythian's remains could provide crucial information, and so the post-autopsy corpse had been placed in a food freezer—to many grumbles from the crew. Storing food alongside an alien cadaver was far too dangerous a risk to take.

"Want to help me lift it up onto the table?"

"Are you sure it's safe to open it up?" Wilder asked, the thought suddenly occurring. "Maybe you could show me slides instead."

"It's been tested for all known toxins and pathogens, I didn't come to any harm dissecting it, and it's frozen solid. There's nothing in here to concern you."

Ryan probably knew what he was talking about. She took one end of the bag while he took the other and, together, they lifted it up.

"It's so light," Wilder commented.

"Typical of an aerial species. Its bones are thin for its size and mostly hollow, like a bird's." Ryan pulled on surgical gloves. "Just a precaution." He pulled the zipper the length of the bag and pushed down the sides, revealing the contents.

Compared to her memory of the Scythian who had grabbed her and carried her aloft, the creature was almost unrecognizable. (This was not that one, this was its partner that Strongquist had killed on the rocks, but the aliens looked extremely alike.) A stiff, slightly frosted, dull, cut-up mess lay within the bag's folds.

Ryan chuckled. "I thought I did a better reconstruction job." He prodded a convex structure. "That's its skull." His fingers traced a line along thin, translucent membranes. "Those are its wings. The external structure is already familiar and somewhat predictable, given what we already know about the Scythians. The skin is sensitive to ultraviolet light. No surprise there. We know they prefer to move about at night. My guess is, when they lived on Concordia they were either nocturnal or the planet was heavily swathed in cloud cover. We know the climate was very different in the past. CO_2 was the main atmospheric gas. So either conjecture could be correct."

He dug around deep within the anatomical mess. Meat grated against bone and, despite the frozen state of the corpse, a faint whiff of the creature's nauseating odor wafted upward.

Wilder put a hand over her mouth and nose. "What *is* that smell?"

"It's quite something, right? I got used to it in the end. It comes from glands either side of the creature's anus. Possibly a territory-marking or sexual advertising hangover from its evolutionary past." He grinned. "The Scythians must either tolerate or enjoy their scent, otherwise they would go to greater lengths to cover it up." He dug deeper. "The most interesting part for me was its insides." He lifted a set of dry, deflated bags, like shrunken balloons.

It was the most repugnant thing Wilder ever recalled seeing.

"Can you guess what these are?" Ryan asked.

"Surprise me."

"Stomachs."

"Stomachs, plural?"

"Plural. It has three, possibly four. One of the attached structures was hard to identify. I knew these had to be stomachs because they were filled with partially digested material, and they led to the afore-mentioned scent-producing anus."

"And because a tube leads to them from the mouth?"

"You would think so, but, no. As far as I can tell, they only use the mouth in their heads for breathing and speaking. They have another mouth in their abdomen for ingestion. It's covered by a flap and has only rudimentary grinding structures that look like modified scales. Hence the three stomachs."

Her confusion must have shown in her face.

He replaced the stomachs within the cadaver. "In human diges-tion, food is ground up in the mouth, mixed with saliva, and swal-lowed. In the stomach, acids mix with it, breaking it down further—"

"I studied human biology at school."

"I'm sorry. I don't mean to be patronizing..."

Like you didn't mean to try to kill me.

"...I'm only giving you a comparison to make my point. Scythians employ an entirely different digestion method. First, the food is some-what broken down by grinding within the mouth cavity. Then it passes into the first stomach, where small stones get to work on it."

"Stones?"

"That isn't so strange. That's typical of a bird's digestive system, as I discovered on Earth. In the second and third stomach, bacteria complete the process. I haven't managed to identify any of them, which indicates they're all from the Scythian planet. It could be that Earth bacteria wouldn't work for them—there are animals that use bacteria for digestion—and would give them an upset stomach."

The feeling of being at a dead end rose up in Wilder again. Finding out about the details of Scythian anatomy seemed to be a waste of time. "I'm sure this is all very interesting for you, but did you discover any information that we might be able to use to defeat them?"

"Nothing springs to mind, I'm afraid, but the news about their digestive process was reassuring in a way."

"What way?"

"Well, I believe it's long been speculated that the Scythians might want to not only use humans as their slaves, but also to farm them, so to speak."

"You mean eat us?" Wilder asked bluntly.

"If you insist on not putting a fine point on it. My investigations revealed that's extremely unlikely."

"Why?" She couldn't see what was stopping the aliens from putting pieces of people into their mouth flaps.

"Because they're vegetarian."

"They're...?" She paused. "That can't be right. Miki said she saw immature Scythians eating each other."

"I'm aware of Kes's daughters' reports. I can only tell you what I discovered. There was no animal DNA within the subject's stomachs, and everything about its digestive system screams vegetarian."

"But the rest of their anatomy is like a predator's, isn't it? Forward-facing eyes, grasping appendages, claws for cutting and slicing..."

"That's correct. Yet their digestive structure tells a different story. I agree it's counter-intuitive, knowing what we know, but it isn't impossible. Life forms can pass through several apparently mutually exclusive stages before achieving maturity. It's feasible that Scythians begin life as carnivores, preying on each other as Miki suggested, but end up as plant-eaters."

"Peaceful, docile, passive vegetarians?"

"As we know, unfortunately not."

5

Miki surveyed the section of the Ark they'd been working in, she realized only a small amount of material remained. Their work was running out. She needed to think of something else for them to do, especially since no one seemed to be coming up with a plan to fix their problems. As far as she could tell, the *Sirocco* would remain in orbit around the star neighboring the Concordia system for the foreseeable future. It was like the journey to Earth all over again.

What she needed was a big distraction, something focused far away from the ship and the current circumstances. She wondered what Dad would have suggested, and immediately the answer came. "Nina, I have an idea. When we get back to the cabin, we can re-start our history research."

Her sister, who was crouching to reach under a shelving unit, straightened up. "No, thanks. I'm tired. I'm going to watch a vid."

"You must have watched all the vids in the database by now. Aren't you bored of them?"

"Not as bored as I would be studying *history*." Nina emphasized the final word as if it was the most ridiculous suggestion she'd ever heard.

"But we were interrupted in our studies when we jumped to

Earth, and we never went back to them. Dad would have wanted us to finish." Miki felt guilty using Nina's feelings about their father as leverage, but it was for a good cause.

"I suppose you're right," Nina replied resignedly. "Do you remember where we were when we stopped?"

"The Second Scythian Attack, I think."

"All right, let's start there. But can we skim the stuff about the bombardment? It's too sad and I don't feel like being sad right now."

"Sure, we can do that."

THEY WERE IN THEIR CABIN, reading about the early days of the Concordia Colony, when the door chime rang. It was Wilder.

Miki hugged her. It had been days since she'd seen their friend, who felt like an older sister.

"I want to give you a heads up," Wilder said, "so the general announcement isn't going to be the first you hear about it."

"Oh." Miki sat down and invited Wilder to do the same. "What's it about?"

"We're going to jump back to Concordia and attack the Scythian ships."

Nina sucked in air. "But that's really dangerous! Last time, they fired on us first."

"I know. There's more to it than that, but you're right, it is very risky. That's why I wanted to come here and tell you myself. We'll do everything we can to keep you and the ship safe."

"Can't we go back to Earth?" Nina asked.

"It's been discussed as an option. The decision was made to stay on mission. Captain Vessey will make the announcement at 0700 tomorrow, and the jump will take place at 0900. Needless to say, you must be in your jump seats well before 0900."

Miki nodded and she said with more confidence than she felt, "Thanks for telling us. We'll be there. Right, Nina?"

Nina didn't reply. Her head was down and her hands lay listlessly in her lap.

"While the battle's in progress," Wilder continued, "you must remain in your capsules. That'll be the safest place, and we will be jumping out again with little or no notice. You might not have time to get back to them if you leave."

"Isn't there anything we can do to help?" asked Miki.

"The best help you can give is to stay where you are so no one has to worry about you."

"All right." Miki sighed, but then she said more brightly in an effort to take her sister's mind off the upcoming battle, "Wilder, you were around in the early days of the colony, weren't you?"

"I was, but I was quite young. About your age, in fact."

"Did you know Ethan? We were just reading about him."

"Only by sight, mostly. I did meet him face-to-face once or twice." Wilder smiled, and the worry etched into her features faded. "I had to ask his permission to build a tree habitation outside Sidhe."

"A *tree* habitation!" Miki lifted her eyebrows.

"You never told us about that," said Nina.

"I never had any reason to. So much stuff went on in those early times, it wouldn't surprise me if little of it was recorded. Ethan seemed nice when I met him, but distracted. He must have had a lot on his mind. Cherry knew him much better than me. They were friends."

"Cool," said Miki. "It's hard to imagine you guys were around all those years ago, right at the beginning."

"Did Dad know Ethan too?" asked Nina.

"He must have. They were all together at the start. But I don't think Kes was close with him like Cherry was. Ethan and Cherry were Gens, while your Dad was a Woken, one of the scientists. There was hostility between the two groups in those days."

"We've been reading about that," said Miki. "Ethan brought everyone together and gave them hope to carry on."

"Yeah," Wilder said wistfully, "he really did. I can't tell you much more. I wish I'd known him better. He was a great man. But I didn't see him much after I built the tree village, and then he died very soon after I returned from the Galactic Assembly." Her expression turned thoughtful, but then she focused on Miki and Nina again. She rose to her feet. "I'm sorry, but I have to go. I have things to do before tomorrow."

"We understand," said Miki. "Thanks for taking the time to come and see us."

"It's a pleasure. I wish I had the leisure to do it more often. Maybe when this war with the Scythians is over we can spend more time together. I could teach you physics," she added, her tone brightening as if the happy idea had only just occurred to her.

"Uhh, okay," said Nina, giving Miki a look. "That would be great."

Wilder chuckled and leaned down to give them a hug in turn. "See you in the jump chamber."

6

Wilder swallowed and gazed at the overhead above her capsule. The countdown had begun but it barely registered. Should she have argued harder with Vessey when she'd announced her decision? The attack seemed rash, hasty, and desperate. Should they have taken the time to think things through better? They had plenty of supplies. They could last months in this uninhabited system.

On the other hand, the Scythians knew the *Sirocco* was back. They might have already dispatched reinforcements. The longer the delay, the stronger and better prepared the aliens would become.

Perhaps it wasn't such a bad decision. Perhaps it was the only one possible.

Yet she couldn't help feeling it was wrong.

At least this time the Ark was protected. They had detached it from the main ship and would leave it behind when they jumped. Naturally, that meant they had to make it back to collect it, or their entire journey to Earth would be wasted. Concordia would never be reseeded.

She had never liked Aubriot. At times, her feelings about him had bordered on hate and disgust. He'd been arrogant, obnoxious, callous, and overbearing. But when it came to battle strategies he'd known his stuff. If it hadn't been for his insistence that the *Sirocco* be fitted with its devastating weapon, they would be helpless against the Scythians. He'd been their best military tactician, and his death had left a vacuum Vessey was in no position to fill.

The overhead stretched wide, multiplied into myriad versions of itself, and was instantly normal again. The shell of her capsule popped open. The jump was over.

She and Niall had programmed the ship's scanners to determine the largest vessel in Concordia's orbit and transmit the coordinates to the Parvus's weapon, which would lock onto them and fire. Everything would happen at computing speed, orders of magnitude faster than human capability.

As she sat up, the ship shuddered. The weapon had discharged.

A cheer rose from the surrounding capsules. She understood the sentiment. They were finally fighting back, striking a blow for humanity, getting revenge for the countless deaths and injuries humankind had suffered.

She climbed swiftly out. Though none of the crew could work as fast as scanners and armaments, they could perform in ways chips and circuits could not. Breach teams had to be at the ready to seal the hull against depressurization, medics were needed to treat injuries, Zapata had to pilot the ship through regular space, she and Niall had to interpret scanner data to inform the captain, and Vessey had to make decisions on the fly.

A second shudder passed through the ship. The *Sirocco* had either locked onto a second target or fired, or she had repeated fire on the first after concluding it remained in action. The battle had taken place without human input so far. That situation couldn't continue.

Wilder sprinted to the bridge, dodging the rest of the crew running to their stations. Niall beat her there and was already assessing the stream of information pouring in. Vessey was white and her facial muscles were rigid as she sat in the captain's chair.

"Looks like four ships," Niall said as Wilder reached his side.

"One more than before?"

"It might have been around the other side of the planet. We scored a hit on the biggest, but it's still—"

His words were drowned out by the alarm. He might have said *Shit!*

They'd been hit.

Vessey silenced the alarm.

Wilder read the data. "Deck Two port side dorsal," she told Vessey. "No indication of a breach."

"The biggest Scythian ship is still moving," Niall said, "but that wasn't the one that fired."

"Return fire on the one targeting us," said Vessey. "Maybe we took out the other's pulse cannon."

"On it, Captain," said Niall.

The *Parvus*'s weapon could be devastating, but it was not particularly maneuverable. It would take precious seconds to reorient to the new target and lock on.

Data flooded Wilder's screen. "Another hit. Deck One, port side."

"Bring us around, Zapata," Vessey ordered.

She was presenting another side of the *Sirocco* to their attackers, reducing the chance the same place would be hit twice, causing a breach. The ship's dorsal faced toward Concordia, protecting the jump drive.

"Firing," said Niall, quickly followed by "They're coming for us, Captain. Three ships. The other one's staying in orbit."

Wilder had seen the alert too. The Scythians were speeding toward them, trying to close the distance separating the vessels to increase the impact of their pulse cannon. Why had one remained behind? Did the aliens anticipate the arrival of more hostile ships? The idea that had occurred to her while she was talking to Kes's daughters resurfaced.

"Take us away, Zapata," Vessey said, "but remain within our weapon's range."

The pilot had already begun to sweep the ship around in response to her first order. Now, the *Sirocco* jerked forward.

Wilder gripped her panel, hoping Miki and Nina had obeyed her instruction to remain in their jump capsules. "We've been hit again."

As she spoke, Niall said, "We got that ship. It's dead in the water." He consulted his screen. "But they're gaining on us."

"Zapata!" Vessey urged.

"She can't go any faster."

The Scythian ships' engines would beat the *Sirocco*'s regular drive.

"Is the biggest one heading toward us, Niall?" asked Vessey.

"It is. I don't know why. I'm pretty sure we took out its cannon."

"Focus on the dangerous one. Wilder?"

"The hit was on the starboard dorsal, ten meters from our gun."

Vessey uttered a curse. Protecting the already damaged areas of the ship had exposed their weapon to attack.

More data arrived. "Hull breach," Wilder reported.

"I know," said the captain. Her expression was strained as she listened to her ear comm. There must have been casualties. She dispatched another breach team.

Meanwhile, Niall had fired on the second Scythian spacecraft that had operational cannon.

Wilder tightened her grip on the panel. Zapata was flying them from the Scythians at maximum speed. She managed to squeeze out, "Maybe they intend to capture and board our ship. They don't have jump tech, but now they know we have."

"*That's* why their biggest vessel is coming for us," said Niall.

"Holy shit," murmured Wilder. "Imagine what they might do if their ships could jump."

"We're running out of juice," Niall said.

Wilder checked her screen. Firing the Parvus's weapon had heavily depleted their energy stores. Zapata's maneuvering was also draining them. They had to return to the other system, and soon.

"Another hit!" Wilder exclaimed. Their attack on the second Scythian ship had been ineffective. "Hull breach, Deck—"

"Fire again, Niall," Vessey ordered.

"No. We won't be able to jump."

"If we destroy the second ship and the biggest one's cannon are dead—"

"It could be a ploy. Wilder's right. They must be slavering for the jump drive, prepared to sacrifice a lot. And they still have a vessel in orbit."

"We have to jump," Wilder urged. "We can't out-fly them and

another hit could take out our regular engines. Then if we don't have power to jump we'll be paralyzed. When the Scythians get here they'll slaughter us." The crew had pulse rifles, brought along in case of problems with Earth natives, but it was not military. The scientists would fall like flies under determined assault.

"But the breaches..." said Vessey. "What will happen if we jump when the hull isn't intact?"

Wilder's throat constricted. "I don't know."

She and Niall shared a glance. He shook his head. He didn't know either, and there was no time to contact Dragan, the only other person who might have a valid idea.

Vessey's lips drew to a thin line. She opened a general comm. "Jumping in fifteen seconds. If you won't make it to a capsule in time, secure yourselves as safely as possible."

Wilder was already activating the drive. She checked the energy stores. The ship would only be traveling a short distance in galactic terms, but it would be close.

Very close.

As well as not knowing what would happen if they jumped with a breached hull, she also didn't know what might occur if the jump drive lacked power to complete its function. Would it only stall, or do something else?

Niall said, "Shutting everything down except essential life support."

The lights died, replaced by an eerie red glow, and a sudden force threw Wilder against her panel. The loss of power to the regular engine had halted their acceleration, and the inertia dampeners hadn't quite managed to deaden the effect. She groaned from the impact, square in her middle.

The emotionless computer voice began the countdown.

"Are you okay?" Niall asked.

Swallowing hard to force down vomit, she shook her head.

He pulled her to the deck, and they crouched together under the console. Wrapping his arms around her, he held her tightly. The computer voice droned on.

She closed her eyes and tensed.

7

Wilder's gut was a ball of pain, eclipsing all other sensations. She opened her eyes. The bridge remained intact. Vessey was gripping the armrests of her seat. She looked how Wilder felt—about to throw up.

"We made it?" Wilder whispered.

"I think so." Niall released her and stood up before awkwardly looking away. "Are you hurt?" His gaze remained averted.

"Yes." Now was not the time for heroics. The ship was no longer under attack, and her stomach hurt like a bitch.

"I'll comm a medic."

Wilder gently lowered herself to her side to wait. From her new vantage point, she noticed the deck was grimy. She also had an excellent view of Vessey's shoes.

The captain walked over. Squatting down, she put a hand on Wilder's shoulder. "Someone should be here soon, but there have been several casualties. You might need to wait a while."

"Okay." She couldn't say anything more. Lacking anything to distract her, the pain seemed to be growing. Or maybe it really was growing. Maybe whatever the blow to her stomach had done, it was getting worse.

"I'm sorry," Vessey said, "I would wait with you but I have things to do."

Wilder squeezed her eyelids closed and nodded.

The captain left.

Where was Niall? Had he gone too? She gingerly scanned around.

He was sitting near her feet, head down, elbows on raised knees.

Willing the pain away, she managed to utter a few words. "You don't need to stay."

He shook his head and placed a hand on her ankle. His hair had grown out while they were on Earth, and it hung down, obscuring his features.

Miki ran in. "What happened to you? I came as soon as I heard you were injured."

Wilder wanted to reassure her that it wasn't that bad, but she actually couldn't speak.

"She needs a medic," Niall said tetchily. "Don't bother her."

"I *am* a medic." Miki held up a medical scanner. "For now, anyway. I'm supposed to be assessing injuries so the worst get priority treatment. What happened to her?"

After Niall explained about the accident, Miki asked Wilder to lie on her back. It was all she could do not to cry out as she complied. Miki ran the scanner over her stomach and transmitted the results to the sick bay. The answer that returned within a few seconds caused Miki's mouth to drop open and her eyes to fill with tears. "You need urgent care. Someone is on their way." She held Wilder's hand. "You're going to be all right."

Wilder vaguely heard footsteps.

Niall was leaving.

THEY HAD LOST one crew member, Wilder discovered when she woke up from her operation. When the *Sirocco* had jumped a member of a breach team hadn't managed to secure himself, or at least that was what everyone supposed had happened. On the other side of the jump he was found to be missing. The only possible conclusion was that he'd been forced out of the ship. Whether he was torn to pieces during the evacuation or he died of asphyxiation when his suit ran out of oxygen, it would have been a horrible death.

When she found out the missing person was Ryan, even *she* felt a twinge of pity.

Otherwise, the ship's personnel had survived the battle mostly unscathed. Wilder had only one companion in sick bay: Maddox, Aubriot's partner when Cherry had found out he was cheating. Maddox had broken her leg during the abrupt deceleration. Wilder didn't have a lot to say to her and Maddox seemed to feel the same.

She read Vessey's report again. The ship was in a worse state than her crew. She had sustained two major hull breaches and severe damage to her exterior from other hits. However, the Parvus's weapon remained operational and the jump drive and regular engines were intact. Her bones were strong even if her skin wasn't in the best shape. And they'd inflicted significant harm to the Scythian fleet. All in all—Ryan's death aside—the attack had been a success. What was more, the Ark had never been at risk. Their plan to reseed Concordia could still go ahead, if only they could drive the aliens from the planet.

The sick bay door opened, and two flashes of color darted in and ran to her side. Wilder found herself in the grip of a fierce hug.

"Let her go!" Miki remonstrated. "You'll hurt her."

Nina relinquished her grip. "I'm so glad you're okay, Wilder. You *are* okay, right?"

Her eyes were watery as she stared anxiously.

"I'm fine. Really. Don't worry. I'm not going anywhere."

The girls had lost their father and Cherry, who had become some-what of a mother to them, as she had herself. She understood Nina's fear. The loss of their remaining parental figure would be devastating.

Miki perched on the edge of the bed. "What was wrong with you? The only thing I understood from the scanner was that you were bleeding internally."

"Ruptured spleen."

"That sounds serious!" Nina exclaimed.

"It was, but it's been fixed. I won't have any lasting side-effects according to the doctor. I only need to rest for a few days to give it time to heal."

The sick bay door opened again. Niall appeared, took a quick look at the girls, and ducked out before Wilder even had time to say hi.

"Who was that?" Nina asked, regarding the closing door.

"It doesn't matter. I'm glad you two didn't come to any harm during the battle. You stayed in your seats, right?"

"Of course we did," Nina replied petulantly. "We always do what we're..." Her words trailed to silence and she flushed deep red.

She was thinking of the time they'd stowed away on the shuttle to sneak off to Earth.

"We always do what we're told *now*," Miki corrected.

"Speaking as someone who rarely did what she was told at your age," Wilder said, "all I can say is sometimes you have to follow your heart, right or wrong. It's just what you have to do. You don't have anything to be ashamed about. And, don't forget, if you hadn't gone to Earth and been captured by the Scythians, no one would have known how they raise their offspring. That's valuable intel."

Nina's features brightened.

"What's going to happen now the battle's over?" Miki asked. "I heard we didn't get all their ships."

"We didn't, but we got some."

"Are we going back to finish them off?" Nina's tone was hopeful and excited.

"It isn't as simple as that. We did inflict some damage, but the *Sirocco* didn't come off unscathed. And we lost a member of the crew."

"And you were hurt!"

Wilder smiled. "And I was hurt. Captain Vessey will have to do some thinking before deciding what to do next. We can't keep exposing our ship to attack. We were lucky last time. We might not have the same luck again. One thing..." she hesitated, reluctant to reveal too much and give the girls more to worry about.

"You can tell us," Miki said. "Whatever it is. We want to know what's going on and no one ever tells us anything."

Though her years of adolescence were long past, Wilder recalled vividly the feeling of being excluded from vital knowledge due to her youth. She wouldn't inflict the same experience on Kes's daughters. "One thing in our favor is the fact that the Scythians probably want to capture the *Sirocco* with her jump drive undamaged. Aside from us, the only other species who can jump across galactic space is the Fila, who are aquatic. Their anatomy has properties that allow them to survive the effects of jumping. Niall and I invented a new system that mitigates those effects to a level human bodies can tolerate. As far as we know, every other atmosphere-breathing intelligent species still uses regular interstellar engines."

Miki said, "So now the Scythians know we have jump tech they want it too."

"You got it. And that means they won't go all out to destroy our ship. I suspect that might be one of the reasons we survived the battle. The Scythians were holding back."

"They will be waiting for us to return," said Nina. "They will be preparing to take the *Sirocco* away from us."

Without any regard for the human life aboard. "You see why Captain Vessey has a lot to think about? I expect we'll hear from her in the next few days."

Miki and Nina stayed with her for an hour or so, chatting about more pleasant subjects, such as the work they'd done in the Ark and what they'd learned in their studies of the history of Concordia. Miki in particular seemed fascinated by Ethan, and Wilder regretted she couldn't tell her much more than she already had about the great man. She'd been a teenager when she'd known him, and not part of the inner circle of decision-makers in the colony. To her, he'd mostly been a remote and imposing figure, even though he'd been friendly and down-to-earth when she'd met him.

"Is it true he was a farmer at first?" Miki asked.

"I don't know. If that's what the history files say..."

"If he was only a farmer, how did he become Leader?"

"In those days anyone could be Leader. You just had to stand for election."

"I wonder who's Leader now?" Nina mused.

Wilder very much doubted the surviving Concordians had a Leader at all. She yawned.

"You're tired," Miki said. "We should go."

"You don't have to. It's nice to chat."

"No, you need to rest." Miki got up from the bed. "Come on, Nina. Let's see if we can be useful somewhere." She added, to Wilder, "The ship's a mess. And we're going to rejoin to the Ark soon. I want to check over the reseeding material."

Wilder relaxed on her pillows after they'd gone. Maddox was asleep. Not that she had anything to say to the woman anyway. Wilder turned over an idea in her mind, an idea that had been niggling at her for days. It was hopeless, stupid, and desperate. But she couldn't see how it could do any harm, and ideas to help them in their predicament were scarce.

She comm'd Vessey.

8

"It's a waste of time." Niall had that look on his face he frequently wore when Wilder suggested something out of the ordinary. She knew from long experience it was only the beginning of his typical mental process: skepticism, doubt, a closer examination, analysis, acceptance. Nevertheless, his initial reaction irritated her more than usual.

"What's the harm?" she snapped. "It's minimal effort. We might as well try, and if nothing comes of it, so what? At least we'll know we did everything we could."

"I'm sure that'll be a major solace as we're being eaten by Scythians. *Oh well, at least we did everything.*"

"They don't eat people. They're vegetarian. Or...herbivores? I don't know. Anyway, they don't eat meat."

"What makes you so sure? Just because Miki and Nina didn't see them eating meat, it doesn't mean—"

"Ryan told me, before he...you know."

"Got sucked out of the ship."

"Couldn't have happened to a better person," said Dragan.

"Uhhh," said Vessey. "If we could stick to the subject? I can't see a reason not to try Wilder's idea."

They were in the captain's office, debriefing post-battle. They'd gone over the breakdown of the engagement, ship's damage report, and casualties. After assessing the scan data, no one had been able to determine with any certainty the status of the enemy's largest ship. It had taken a hit, but they had no detailed knowledge of Scythian military vessels. It was impossible to say if its armaments had been destroyed.

The *Sirocco* could have been in a worse state. The jump drive and regular engines remained fully operational. But it was clear that she might not survive a repeat battle. What was more, materials to effect hull repairs were in short supply. It wouldn't take many more breaches before they couldn't patch her up anymore.

"I can see two very good reasons," said Niall. "One: morale is already at an all-time low. When we don't hear anything back—I say *when* not *if* because, seriously, what's the likelihood of getting a response after all this time?—it will tip the crew over into despair. Or, two, it will stop people from trying. They will give up, imagining some great galactic power is going to come to our rescue. We need to find a solution ourselves. We need to figure out a way to get to Concordia without being blown to pieces, and we need to do it soon, before the Scythian defenses grow stronger."

"You think we should fight back at them from the surface?" Dragan asked. "Not try to destroy their ships?"

"In order to reach the surface we have to destroy their ships. I thought that's what we were attempting as a means to an end. Destroying their ships isn't an end in itself because they will just send more ships. But if we can mobilize the existing human population, attack the Scythians from within, make Concordia an uninviting place to live—"

"They give up and blast the place with biocide," Wilder interjected. Two could play at shooting down others' ideas.

Niall faced her, eyes ablaze. "Then what to you suggest we do? Give up? Kill ourselves?"

"I already made my suggestion. I haven't heard you offering up anything concrete lately. Unless I missed something?"

"Please," said Vessey, rubbing her temples, "let's not argue among ourselves. I have enough to do keeping the peace among the rest of the crew. Wilder, what form exactly would this message take?"

"It would be similar to the Mayday we sent out not long after the first jump failed, when we were decades from Earth. Do you remember?"

"Vaguely. That seems a long time ago now."

Wilder suspected the captain had also begun her descent into alcoholism. "We have to send it in English. The only other galactic language we know even remotely is the one the Fila speak, though 'speak' isn't the right word." The aquatic aliens communicated via water movement, thus their language was virtually impossible for humans to learn or use.

"They must have used electronic communication too," said Dragan. "Otherwise how could they comm the Galactic Assembly? It was the Fila who arranged for Concordians to go there, right?"

"It was, and you're right, they spoke to us using electronics. That must have been how they contacted the Assembly. But if anyone discovered exactly what they did and how, I certainly never heard about it." A sudden pang of wistfulness hit as she recalled her Fila friend, Quinn, who she'd considered one of her closest friends. "We don't have any other option except to broadcast high energy transmissions and hope someone picks them up. I know it's a long shot, but we don't know what receivers the Assembly might have, where they are, or how they work. We didn't ever learn anything about how Assembly members communicate. The Fila always took care of that kind of thing for us."

"What's the point?" Niall asked. "It didn't work before, when we were delayed. It won't work now. We need to focus on ideas that are likely to bring results. The Galactic Assembly isn't going to come to our rescue at the last minute like it did last time. That's ancient history. If by some miracle our message is picked up and the Assembly still exists, it will have forgotten all about Concordia and humans."

"The *Sirocco* was in an area of galactic space that isn't inhabited by Assembly members," Wilder retorted. "That's why our Mayday wasn't picked up."

"You don't have any evidence to support that assertion! You can't possibly know that."

"You can't prove I'm wrong!"

"Guys," said Dragan, lifting his hands, "cool it."

Wilder folded her arms over her chest, fighting her growing anger. Niall was correct, of course. She had no idea why the Mayday hadn't been picked up. She hated it when his stubbornness made her irrational.

In a more moderate tone, Niall continued, "My major doubt isn't that sending a message would be pointless—though it is—it's that it will give the crew false hope. Everyone knows or remembers the Assembly arriving to head off a Scythian attack. If we give the crew even a hint the same thing might happen again, everyone will want to down tools and wait indefinitely to be rescued. We've been through significant hardship since we departed Concordia. People don't need much of an excuse to hand responsibility over to someone else and relax."

"Then the answer is simple," Vessey said. "We don't tell them."

Niall opened his mouth as if to speak but then closed it again.

As his frustration at being unable to think up an objection filtered over his features, Wilder smirked. "I think that's a great idea, Captain. We send the message as a repeat transmission, but we keep it between ourselves. I don't think anyone else has access to systems that would allow them to detect it except we four. How does that sound, Niall?"

He glared at her.

"Glad you agree. I'll draft a message and submit it for approval before sending it out."

"Now that's decided," said Vessey, "I want to turn to more pressing issues. As Niall was saying, the key to driving the Scythians from Concordia lies on the planet surface, not in space. That's what I've come to accept. We can't defeat them in orbit but there's a chance we can change their minds about living there."

Dragan said, "If they can't live there they don't want us to either. They've made that clear. Humans must serve them or be annihilated."

"I don't know what the answer is, but if we can make it to the surface we can understand the situation better. Maybe a solution will present itself. That's all I'm saying."

"So our new goal is to land the shuttle planetside?" Wilder asked. "Kind of...sneak it in? Nothing springs to mind, but I can work on some ideas."

"We all can," said Dragan.

Vessey's features relaxed into relief but instantly tensed again as she lifted a hand to her ear. "What? Say that again." The comm, silent to everyone except her, must have repeated. "Slow down! I can't understand you." Another pause. "*Ugh!* Okay, don't interfere. I don't want anyone else getting hurt. I'll be there in a few minutes."

Her attention returned to Wilder and the others. "I have to go and break up a fight. Who knew a captain's duties would be so varied and entertaining?"

"A fight?" asked Wilder. "Who's fighting?"

"Marcus and Belvedere. It's something to do with Maddox." The captain slowly rose to her feet. She didn't seem in much of a hurry.

"Maddox?" Dragan gave a short laugh. "I think we all know what *that's* about."

"We do?" Niall asked.

Wilder also didn't have a clue. Neither she nor Niall got involved in ship scuttlebutt.

"Oh, you know. Marcus must have found out Maddox is cheating on him."

"With Belvedere, presumably," Niall said.

Wilder frowned. "I thought Maddox had a thing with Aubriot. She moved on fast."

"He was never exclusive with her," Dragan explained. "It used to drive her crazy."

As well as telling them the ship's gossip, he was revealing a whole new side of his character. Despite their years of friendship, Wilder hadn't known he was so deeply enmeshed in the goings-on aboard the ship. It explained how he'd been drawn into the Final Day Five cult.

"This is fascinating," Vessey said dryly, "but I have to go."

As the captain departed, Wilder said, "But Marcus is blind and spends ninety-five percent of his time in his cabin."

"Makes him easy to find," Niall quipped.

Wilder continued, "And Maddox has a *broken leg*." A horrible image leapt into her mind. "Do you think Marcus caught her and Belvedere..."

"Doing it?" Niall asked. "Who knows? At least he would only have heard rather than seen them."

"I'm not sure that's better," said Wilder.

The three engineers chuckled.

9

Aside from the stories about Ethan and the battles, the history of Concordia's founding was boring. It was all about construction, farming, food supplies, the developing health care infrastructure, setting up schools and so on, and on, and on. There was a bit about the difficulties the first colonists had faced transitioning from communal child rearing to nuclear families that was mildly interesting, but not much else. Miki sighed, rested her elbow on the table and her chin on her upturned palm.

"I'm tired of this too," said Nina. "Shall we do something else?"

Miki was loath to agree. As the eldest of two orphans, it was her responsibility to do the hard stuff—to set the tasks a parent would have set, the tasks she also would have complained about doing. Yet she didn't think *she* could take another data set of harvest statistics from the colony's first five years. "Maybe just another fifteen minutes? Then we can stop for lunch."

It was way too early for lunch, but it was a convenient excuse.

"All right," Nina agreed, though in a grumbling tone.

Miki blinked and refocused her attention on the brain-numbing figures. No patterns or meaning emerged, and the numbers seemed to dance and meld as if they were alive and confusing her deliberately.

She yawned and stretched her arms and back. "I'll tidy up the cabin while you finish."

"Hey! If I have to do this, so do you."

"Just another fifteen minutes."

Nina rolled her eyes as Miki stood up, but she bent over her work again. She'd always been ridiculously obedient.

Miki fussed around the room, moving items from one place to another, putting things that seemed vaguely related into groups, hiding stuff behind the sofa. She heard a soft *tut* and turned to see Nina giving a little shake of her head. In order to escape scrutiny, she walked into their shared bedroom. Here, she discovered something useful to do. Their bedding hadn't been changed in weeks. Neither of them bothered making their beds when they got up. Without Dad around to chide them there didn't seem much point, and no adults ever never came into the inner rooms. The grubby, wrinkled sheets and covers seemed to reproach her for her slovenliness.

She pulled the bedclothes off her bed and pushed them into the laundry chute. She would have to remember to collect fresh ones from the laundry room after lunch.

"What are you doing?" Nina called out.

"I told you. I'm tidying up." She stepped to her sister's bed and picked up her pillow, and gasped.

"Don't touch my—" Nina was standing in the doorway, flushed. She strode to Miki and snatched the pillow from her hands. "Leave my bed alone! I didn't tell you to change it. I can do it myself." She put the pillow on the bed and pulled up the cover, roughly straightening everything.

"Nina..." Her sister might have hidden the evidence, but the image remained clear in Miki's mind. A pile of long, black hairs had been secreted under the pillow. Nina's hair, unmistakably, and far too much to have fallen out naturally.

"I'm going to finish my work," Nina declared. "Then we can go and eat. I'll change my bed later."

Miki's gaze followed her as she left the bedroom. What was wrong with her sister? Was her hair falling out? If it was only a medical problem, why was she hiding it? Why hadn't she told someone?

Miki watched Nina from the doorway as she bent over her interface once more. "Nina, is something wrong? You can tell me. You know I won't judge you."

"Nothing's wrong."

But fat tear drops landed on the screen, and Nina was only staring downward, not working.

Miki realized her sister had recently begun to always wear her hair in a ponytail whereas before she'd worn it down. And she used to take great care with it while now she only brushed it quickly before putting it up.

"Can I look at your hair?" Miki gently asked.

Nina gave a firm shake of her head.

Her reaction told Miki all she needed to know. Without seeing them, she could guess Nina's head had bald patches where she'd pulled out her hair. Why was she doing it? It had to be a reaction to the stress they were under. A lead weight settled in the pit of Miki's stomach. Though logically she knew the current situation wasn't her fault, she couldn't help feeling it was. At the very least, she'd failed in her primary duty to keep her sister safe and happy. Nina certainly didn't feel safe and happy if, in the quiet of the night, she was wrenching out her hair.

Miki moved to her sister's side and tried to hug her, but Nina pushed her away. "Leave me alone! I don't know what you're making such a big fuss about."

Miki hesitated. How could she help if Nina wouldn't accept it? But maybe she was right. A hug wouldn't make anything better. What Nina needed was for this whole, torturous experience to be over. She needed a home and a life free from fear. How could she give her that? They were both powerless, overlooked, a burden on the *Sirocco*'s crew. They were an additional complication in an impossible situation.

She had to *do* something. She had to make a positive difference. She had to *act*. How else was she supposed to live with herself? How could she live with the knowledge that she'd let Dad down and his confidence in her was misplaced?

She marched to the outer door.

"Where are you going?" Nina asked.

But Miki didn't answer as she left.

THE CAPTAIN'S office was on the other side of the ship. By the time she reached it Miki's determination had weakened and she was muddled about what she wanted to say. Then the imagined image of Nina's head flashed into her mind. She gathered her resolve and walked in.

Captain Vessey had always employed an 'open door' policy, saying any crew member was free to come and see her at any time, to talk to her about anything. So Miki had been expecting she might see someone else in the room when the door automatically slid to the side.

What she hadn't been expecting was a dead man.

Aubriot?!

The man's deep, voluminous voice burst out at her as she walked in. He was standing in his usual arrogant pose, hands on hips, chest prominent, jaw slightly upturned so he looked down his nose at whoever he was addressing.

She screamed and clutched the door frame as her legs lost their strength.

Wilder—who she hadn't even noticed—was instantly at her side. "It's a holo, Miki. It's just a holo."

Aubriot disappeared. Captain Vessey, sitting at her desk, must have turned it off. Wilder led her to a chair.

Sitting down, Miki gasped, "I'm sorry. I thought—"

"We know what you thought," said Wilder. "Are you okay?"

"I think so." The tingles of shock were beginning to dissipate. "What was he saying? I didn't catch it. How come we have a holo of Aubriot?"

"It isn't important," the captain replied.

It clearly was important. Otherwise why would she and Wilder be watching it? What Vessey meant was *she* wasn't important. Not important enough to be told what was going on anyway.

"How can I help you, Miki?" Vessey asked impatiently.

She sat up straight. "I heard there's going to be an attempt to land the shuttle on Concordia. Is that right?"

"What if it is?"

"I want to go along."

"You want to...?" Vessey chuckled uneasily.

"I want to be one of the away team."

The captain's features grew serious. "Absolutely not. The mission is insanely dangerous. It's the last place for a young girl. You're only fifteen!"

She'd been anticipating the refusal. On her way over she'd thought up the reasoning to back up her proposal, but then forgotten it. Now it all came flooding back. "I might be almost the youngest person on the ship, but I'm also one of only two people who have had close contact with the Scythians. Unless you're suggesting Nina should go in my place?"

"That's even more preposterous."

"Nina and I fought our way out of a Scythian dome. Do you have anyone else who has done that?"

"You know I haven't but that's beside the p—"

"Who else on this ship has had conversations with Scythians?" The 'conversations' had actually been interrogations, but stretching the truth made her sound more convincing.

Vessey glowered.

Wilder was watching, arms folded over her chest, smiling.

Miki continued, "Can you name a single person under your command who is better suited to going to Concordia and figuring out a way to get the aliens to leave?" She arched an eyebrow. "Hm?"

"Your argument might have some weight," Vessey replied, "if you weren't a child. More than anyone on this ship, you have been entrusted to my care. I have a responsibility to your late father to keep you from harm. Assigning you to the mission to land on Concordia would be the very antithesis of that. I'm sorry. I admire your bravery and I can't deny you make some very good points, but the answer is no. However, if you can offer the away team any suggestions or advice, you would be very wel—"

Miki sprang to her feet. "But you aren't keeping us from harm! We aren't safe here. Not in the long run. We could have died in the last battle. And no one tells us anything. We don't know what's going on. We're slowly going crazy, living in this make-believe world where everyone pretends everything is normal, while in reality we're one wrong step away from death. Every day, the inevitable creeps closer but no one acknowledges it, not to our faces."

She swung around to stare at Wilder and turned back to Vessey. "You all pretend to care but you don't. Not really. No one knows what really goes on with us. You want us to stay quiet and keep out of the way, to be good, and as long as we do that everything will be all right. But it isn't all right. Nothing is all right. Nina's..." Her emotions choked away her words and she thrust her face into her hands.

An arm descended over her shoulders, but she shrugged it away. Talking into her hands, she said, "I want to help. You have to let me help. And I *am* the best person. I really am. If you don't recognize that then you're a pair of idiots."

10

*N*o one knows what really goes on with us.

Miki had left Vessey's office but her words continued to echo in Wilder's mind. The girl had been distraught, almost hysterical. *No one knows what really goes on with us.*

What had she meant? Wilder had thought she knew Kes's daughters pretty well, but the surprise trip to Earth had blindsided her. She hoped she'd helped to fill the hole left when their father died. Had she really done any good at all? She had no idea how to parent adolescents. She'd never been parented herself. The attempts of the couple she'd been assigned to in the underground settlement, Sidhe, had been farcical. Kes's friendship had come close but he'd been more like an older brother.

Was that why Miki had been so fascinated by stories of Ethan lately? Did she crave a father figure, or maybe only someone who had known her father?

"Are you ready to continue watching?" Vessey asked.

Wilder snapped back to the present. "Yeah, sorry."

Aubriot reappeared.

The recording had barely begun when Miki had burst in. Vessey had returned it to the beginning.

Wilder's customary, visceral reaction to Aubriot flared up: dislike, bordering on hatred. She'd never forgotten the months she'd spent in close confinement with the disagreeable man aboard the *Opportunity* on the journey to the Galactic Assembly. What had Cherry ever seen in the man?

Vessey had said she discovered the holo while going through his files. The file was entitled 'To be played in the event of my death' so Wilder hadn't had any qualms about invasion of privacy when Vessey had invited her to watch it. However, why the captain had been going through the man's data at all was a question that remained unanswered. Wilder guessed she'd been looking for inspiration and guidance.

Good luck with that.

Aubriot glared at the camera as if angry about his potential demise. Wilder was reminded of the holo of the Maker, Steen, full of bitterness and rage. The men's desire to live had been strong.

"So I'm dead," Aubriot spat. "I hope I went down fighting. I'm guessing it was the Scythians. If it wasn't, if some stupid accident killed me or a disease got me like Kes, that's a crying shame, and I'm glad I don't know about it."

His arms fell to his sides and he strode a couple of paces before turning to the camera again and jabbing a finger at it. "You're all going to be worse off now I'm gone. You might not think so. A fair few of you hate my guts and you aren't afraid to show it. But I'm right. You need me. You need someone to tell you what's what and make the hard decisions. That's why I'm recording this—so you get the benefit of my wisdom and experience even though I'm no longer around. I might be dead, but I still want the colony to succeed. It's my legacy, my gift to humanity."

Wilder rolled her eyes. Aubriot was even managing to annoy her from the grave. She signaled to Vessey to pause it. "Have you watched this already? You could give me a summary."

"It's my first time too. I find him just as irritating as you, but perhaps he says something useful." She started up the recording again.

"Right. I'm going to make this simple. I have one message for you. Just one thing for you to remember." He said two more words slowly and with emphasis: "Never compromise. There are to be no half measures, no negotiation. Cherry, I know you beat yourself up about rejecting the Scythians' proposal when they wanted to enslave the colony. Even now, you think it was a big mistake because it caused them to launch the biocide. But you were right."

His hands returned to his hips. "If there's one thing I learned running my businesses, it's this: the minute you show weakness, your enemy will go for your throat. Believe me, I saw it again and again. So you have to stay strong and never back down. Remember that, Vessey. As soon as you start to give ground it's the beginning of the end. You've lost." He paused and his expression turned pensive.

"Better no future at all for humanity than a future where we've been brought low. Who wants to live in shame? That isn't the way of humans. That isn't the spirit of the people who left Africa hundreds of thousands of years ago, leaving behind everything they knew, journeying into unknown lands without knowing what dangers lay ahead." He jabbed a finger at the camera again. "You *cannot* give in to the Scythians, not on anything, or before you know it, it will be all over. Don't give up who we are. A human being controlled by another species isn't human anymore."

His rigid posture softened. "That's it. I could say more but it would only confuse you, so that's all I have to say. It's a pity I'm dead, but I've lived an amazing life. I was there at the founding of humanity's first deep space colony. I flown on starships. I've fought battles in space. I've loved. I've hated. I've *lived*. At the end of the day, I suppose I can't complain. Good luck, you lucky bastards. Don't let me down."

He disappeared, but his final look before the recording ended struck Wilder's core. The sadness and yearning in his eyes were emotions she'd never seen in him before. His lust for life and sorrow as he imagined his death were almost palpable. Maybe his drive and vitality were what had attracted Cherry.

"Well, that was disappointing," said Vessey.

"I'm not sure what you expected. It was Aubriot, after all."

"A revelation or tactical advice would have been nice, something to help us defeat the Scythians. Something other than telling me not to negotiate with them. As if I have the opportunity! Their go-to response at any encounter is to try to kill us. And the situation is similar to how it was at Earth—more of their ships must be on their way, if not due to Miki informing them she was from Concordia, then in response to our arrival at the system. They might have guessed where we're hiding too. Their reinforcements might stop to check around here on their way over."

The captain's spewing of her worries was clearly rhetorical. She needed a friendly listener while she got it all off her chest. Wilder was sympathetic but she had no answers. "It isn't Miki's fault she—"

"I know, I know. I'm not saying it was. She's just a kid. She couldn't be expected to stand up to the Scythians. I can't imagine what she endured in that interrogation."

Wilder recalled the sensation of long, scaled Scythians toes gripping her tightly around her middle. She shuddered. What must it have been like for the girls living in those domes, not knowing if they would ever get out alive, surrounded day and night by the nauseating Scythian stench?

Yet Miki and Nina had escaped, albeit with the help of other captives. When it came down to it and their courage was put to the test, neither had quailed.

"What are you thinking?" Vessey asked. "Have you thought of a way of getting the shuttle to Concordia in one piece?"

Wilder smiled sardonically. "Still working on it. I was thinking about Miki's request."

"Request? It was more like a demand. An outrageous one, I might add. Just the thought of how Kes would have reacted to even the mention of endangering his daughters' lives strikes terror into my heart."

"As Miki pointed out, they're already in danger. Dire danger if, as you guess, the Scythians are on their way to this system. I mean, we could jump at the first sign of approach, but where to and for how long? Unless we figure out a way to free Concordia we're screwed. As Aubriot would have put it, we need to piss or get off the pot."

"You think you're telling me something I don't already know?"

"What I'm saying is, Miki's request isn't so outrageous. She and her sister do have the most experience of Scythians of anyone on this ship. And they've demonstrated they can be brave and resourceful."

Vessey's mouth fell open. "You aren't seriously suggesting...?"

"It's worth thinking about."

"No. Absolutely not. What would everyone say if I assign a teenager to the mission? They would think I was either crazy or desperate, or both."

"Maybe it's time you stopped caring about what people say. Aubriot didn't."

"And look where that got him."

Vessey's retort didn't make any sense. Aubriot's death hadn't had anything to do with his indifference to others' opinions of him. The captain was being defensive, grasping at straws in an effort to win the argument. Few things annoyed Wilder more than irrationality. Through a clenched jaw, she replied, "Dislike him or hate him, Aubriot knew how to command."

"And I don't, I suppose?" Vessey looked about to rise from her seat with indignation.

Wilder allowed silence to be her answer. After a pause, she added, "Miki should go on the mission, along with me and Niall. You need resourceful people, not only brawn, on the surface. Shall I give her the good news?"

"Do I have a choice?"

Another rhetorical question. Wilder got to her feet, somewhat giddy from what had just transpired. "I'll let you know when we figure out a plan."

She made her way through the *Sirocco*'s passageways, heading for Miki and Nina's cabin. Vessey's face had been a picture as she left— partly shocked, partly outraged. But something needed to be done, and though the captain meant well, she lacked the brains and decisiveness to pull them out of the deep, dark hole they were in.

Wilder's understanding of the truth of the situation had seemed sudden initially, but she realized it had simmered below the surface for weeks, perhaps months. Her preference was to remain on the sidelines, working on interesting projects. She wasn't comfortable with ignoring the captain's seniority but it was necessary. She would have to take a more active, assertive role in the future.

When she arrived at Miki and Nina's cabin, Nina was hastily scraping her hair into a ponytail and Miki stood behind her with a brush. The girls seemed to have been doing some kind of hairdressing, which was utterly unlike them. Even Wilder, who seldom noticed such things, had observed the two girls' hair resembled the nests of Earth birds lately.

Nina was flushed and wouldn't make eye contact.

"Is something wrong?" Wilder asked.

"No," replied Miki, adding bitterly, "Have you come to tell me off for getting angry at the captain?"

"Stars, I'd hoped you knew me better than that. When I was your age…" She paused, realizing she sounded like an old-timer. "I'm not here to tell you off. I'm here to let you know Vessey agreed to you joining the mission."

"She did?!"

"What mission?" Nina asked.

"To go to Concordia. I'm going on the shuttle to fight the Scythians on Concordia!"

"You can't!" Nina leapt to her feet and faced her sister. "You'll die."

"I won't. I'll figure out a way to make the Scythians leave. You'll see."

"You'll be killed, and I'll be all alone." Nina collapsed into her seat and began to sob.

Wilder watched awkwardly. She'd thought she would be the bearer of good news. She hadn't anticipated Nina's reaction, even though it was entirely predictable.

Miki was comforting her sister, whispering, "I'll be fine. The Scythians will leave, and then you can go home. Maybe we can find our old house."

Wilder watched on, feeling like an outsider. The two girls were enclosed in their own small world of despair.

11

"Holy shit!" Wilder exclaimed. "We're morons. Morons!"

She was with Niall and Dragan, eating dinner. They'd spent the day trying to figure out a way to get the shuttle to the surface of Concordia without everyone aboard being killed. The *Sirocco* might survive the brief time she would have to spend in Concordian orbit before she could jump out again, but the shuttle would be a clear and obvious target for Scythian attack. They hadn't managed to come up with anything concrete, and now that Miki was coming along the imperative for caution was even stronger.

Niall eyed her irritably. "Interesting that you include me and Dragan in your character critique."

Raising her voice had attracted the attention of their crew mates in the refectory. The chattering had paused and heads turned toward them. Wilder waited until the audience grew bored and returned to their conversations before leaning over the table to speak to her companions more quietly. "The answer has been staring us in the face. Hell, we've been *working* on the answer for weeks."

When Niall and Dragan looked back at her blankly, she asked, "Have you finished eating?"

Dragan nodded.

Niall put down his knife and fork. "I'm so keen to hear your suggestion I've lost my appetite."

"I'm not going to tell you. I'm going to show you, and then you'll agree we're all dumb as a sack of rocks." She got up from the table and, without waiting to see if Niall and Dragan were following, walked out of the refectory.

She marched to the holding bay, the only place sufficiently large for the work they'd been focused on for so long. If anything, her fellow engineers had spent longer on it than she had. They'd started while she'd been on Earth, trapped by Vessey's cowardly attempt to leave her behind along with Cherry, Aubriot, Miki, and Nina.

The bay doors slid apart, revealing the items lying on the deck in their various groups: sections of hull, engine, controls, interior, and so on. The dismantling had been meticulous. Even the nuts, bolts, and rivets had been removed and carefully examined. Reconstruction would take time and concentration, but it would be worth it. In fact, now she'd thought about it, she believed it was the only sane option.

"Yeah," Dragan conceded. "We're morons."

Niall's gaze roved the dismantled Scythian ship. "You're seriously suggesting we fly *that* to Concordia?"

"You're seriously suggesting we fly the *Sirocco*'s shuttle, a human-built vessel, into airspace controlled by the Scythians? It wouldn't last a second."

Dragan said, "I have to admit that's our biggest problem. Even if we're lucky enough that they haven't created air traffic monitoring systems, the shuttle is so easy to distinguish by sight—"

"Yes," Niall snapped. "That point has been made several times today. There's no need to repeat it."

"This does seem the obvious answer," Dragan said mildly, gesturing at the aircraft parts.

"It gives us our best chance," Wilder urged. "The vessels the Scythians used on Earth were pretty much identical, and they weren't designed for an oxygen-rich atmosphere. The aliens had brought them directly from their planet without bothering to refit them. It stands to reason they've done the same on Concordia, which means this aircraft won't be distinguishable from the others they're already using. All we have to do is strengthen the hull and make it airtight. If the Scythians miss its launch from the *Sirocco*, we'll be home free. And if they notice it, well, they might lose it among their regular air traffic."

"But the cabin will only accommodate two people," Niall countered. "We planned on sending more on the mission."

"The cabin fits two *Scythians*. We don't need the internal fittings except for the controls. We can leave them out and the aircraft will look the same from the outside. I reckon it would fit four people, five at a squeeze."

Niall's expression remained doubtful. "No one knows how to fly it."

"Zapata can figure it out, I'm sure. We know the design isn't that different from an aircraft built by humans."

"But we discovered it needs a Scythian's skin print to open it. The same is probably true for operating the controls."

"We have the Scythian cadaver in cold storage. We can take an imprint from its skin and make some gloves."

"It will take forever to put it back together again."

"We itemized everything when we took it apart. It shouldn't be too hard to reconstruct it, and it won't take *that* long, considering we're only rebuilding the bare bones of it." She folded her arms over her chest and tilted her head. "Any more objections?"

Niall was silent.

"Go on, admit it. You know I'm right."

He glared at her, turned, and strode down the passageway.

She watched his retreating back with amusement. When she saw Dragan's look, however, her smile faded. "What's wrong? Don't tell me you're having doubts too."

"Not about your idea, no. You're right. It's the only way anyone stands a chance of making it to Concordia alive, and it's ridiculous it took us so long to think of it."

Wilder was about to remind him that *she* thought of it, not them, but it seemed churlish.

"I just think you could be gentler with Niall," he continued.

She blinked. "*Me* be gentler with *him*?! Are you sure you've got that the right way around?"

"I know he's being even more combative than usual, but he's suffering. He wouldn't want me to tell you this, but he was nearly demented with worry while you were on Earth. He was the one who figured out what Vessey was up to and forced her to go back to pick you up."

She hadn't known that, not exactly. She hadn't made many inquiries about what had gone on during her absence from the ship. She'd been too sad about leaving Cherry behind and concerned about Miki and Nina and what the future held. "I guess I should thank him," she muttered.

"He doesn't want your thanks. Rescuing you is sufficient reward, I'm sure."

"I know he cares, but he's so relentlessly negative toward me. So prickly. It's hard to tolerate."

"I know. I honestly don't think he can help it. It's just how he is. But maybe you could try..." Dragan struggled to finish his sentence. He seemed embarrassed.

"I could try what? Tell me. I'm a big girl. I can take it."

"You could try being more understanding. I hate to say it, but you're often...cold. I mean, I get it. With the stuff we do, we're in our heads a lot of the time, not aware of other people's emotions or reactions. We can get into a certain way of thinking where everything has to make sense, and we apply the same expectation to people. We find it frustrating if they aren't logical. But people aren't logical, not even us. You have to allow for that. You have to allow other people to be flawed, irrational, inconsistent, whatever."

His gaze drifted to the bulkhead. "It wasn't until I accepted I'd lost my wife forever that I realized she'd been doing that for me, for years, and I hadn't reciprocated. I'd always made out I was the logical one and she was ruled by her emotions. I didn't know, then, that it wasn't a difference of intellect or rationality, but a difference in compassion. Not comprehending that until it was too late is one of my greatest regrets."

Wilder inhaled sharply. She'd vaguely known that Dragan had left his partner behind on Concordia but she'd never asked him about her. Not even once. She reached out and touched his arm. "I'm so sor—"

"It was a long time ago. I can't say I'm over it, but it is what it is. Talking about it won't make it better. All I wanted to say is, don't make my mistake."

She looked down.

When she didn't answer, Dragan said, "I'll talk to Niall. We can begin work on the Scythian ship tonight."

12

It had taken way longer to rebuild the Scythian ship than anyone had expected. Miki had spent weeks in grueling anticipation, the ache in her stomach and insomnia growing greater, waiting to hear from Wilder that they were finally ready to attempt landing on Concordia. At the end of every active shift, Wilder had come to see her and Nina, her hair an unkempt halo, shadows under her eyes, looking thinner than ever, only to announce again and again that the ship wasn't quite finished.

The snags the engineers had encountered while reconstructing the vessel weren't the only source of delay. The man most familiar with the frozen Scythian cadaver had died the last time they'd jumped to the planet. Someone else had been tasked with making the gloves the pilot would wear to fly the ship. Miki heard down the grapevine that their early attempts were unsuccessful. It had taken a while to figure out that it wasn't only the print of the creature's skin that was required to activate the controls, but the underlying bone structure too.

All the while the preparations had been taking place, her doubts had grown. Who was she to think she would be anything other than a hindrance and liability in the mission? What did *she* have to contribute? She wasn't a scientist or an engineer. She didn't possess a fraction of the knowledge or skills of the rest of the crew. She'd grown up on a starship without even a proper education.

When she'd gone to see Captain Vessey to demand to be included, it had been a spur-of-the-moment decision, a knee-jerk reaction to discovering that Nina was so anxious she was pulling out her hair. In the captain's office, she'd exaggerated her knowledge of the Scythians to try to persuade Vessey to agree. In reality, she knew hardly anything about them, very little more than anyone else. The captain had either been kind or desperate to allow her to join the mission.

She was an imposter. A fraud. She'd done something stupid, and Nina was right—she was going to get herself killed.

Yet she hadn't been able to bring herself to back out. Was she too embarrassed to admit her mistake? Was she simply ashamed of being a coward? She didn't know, but day after day, when Wilder had arrived to give an update, her mouth stubbornly refused to utter the words *Sorry, but I changed my mind.*

Now it was too late.

Wilder sat across from her in the cramped interior of the Scythian vessel, knees drawn up, her features obscured by the reflective visor of her EVA suit. Niall crouched by her side. The other engineer would remain on the *Sirocco*. Someone was needed to oversee the jumps. Next to Miki, so close they were squashed up against each other, was someone she didn't know very well—a woman called Maddox. She'd taken part in the first attack on a Scythian dome on Earth, with Cherry and Aubriot, so she had a little experience of the aliens. Between the four mission members was Zapata, the pilot, wearing his outlandish gloves.

The tiny space would have been claustrophobic in the best circumstances. As it was, with five people in bulky suits crammed in, about to embark on what amounted to a suicide mission, it felt stifling. What was more, though the seats had been removed, the interior reminded her of the time she'd flown with a Scythian for hours, not knowing whether her sister was alive or what lay ahead. It was as much as Miki could do not to panic, thrash, and scream, begging to be let out.

The countdown to jump was comm'd into their helmets. As it

neared zero, Wilder gave Miki a thumbs up. She couldn't return the gesture. She couldn't move. Her breathing was loud in her ears, louder than the countdown, louder than the thrum of her racing heart. She was painfully aware she was depleting her suit's oxygen at a dangerous rate but she couldn't help it.

The *Sirocco* jumped.

The too-familiar blending of reality shifted back to normality.

"One good thing about being jammed in here," Maddox remarked over helmet comm, "we can't get thrown about."

As if defying her words, the ship lurched violently. Naturally, the second the *Sirocco* had arrived in Concordia orbit, she would have come under attack. But she might not have been hit. The plan, as Miki understood it, was to create as much of a distraction as possible so the Scythians might not notice the tiny craft launching into the upper atmosphere. Captain Vessey intended the aliens to think the *Sirocco* had returned to attack their ships again. Also, without Zapata at her controls, the stand-in pilot might be flying erratically anyway.

Even in the small space, the *Sirocco*'s movements threw them into each other. Except it wasn't the *Sirocco*'s movements. Zapata was flying the Scythian vessel out of the bay. The overhead, visible before through the overhanging transparent shell, had switched to black faintly speckled with stars. They'd left the ship and she hadn't even noticed.

Then the sky exploded.

Maddox's screams echoed around Miki's helmet, but she was silent, dumbstruck by the spectacle. Her retinas retained an imprint of a blinding flash, now faded to dull red. Brilliant stars zoomed past, almost too fast to register. Except they could not be stars. What were they?

Maddox continued with her deafening screams. The world upended. Miki caught a glimpse of a curving planet surface—yellow land and cobalt ocean—before space appeared again. The background stars had gone. Ebony had lightened to glimmering, dark blue-gray. Fiery objects rained down.

Clang!

A shock ran through the deck and shook Miki's bones. Something had hit the wing. The craft shuddered, drooped to the right, somersaulted again. Another scene of yellow and blue flew by above.

Miki shut her eyes. She couldn't look anymore. She was about to throw up, and ensconced in her suit that would be very nasty. Feeling for the straps of her safety harness, she clung to them for all she was worth. The sickening maneuvers went on, or perhaps they were not maneuvers. Perhaps Zapata was no longer flying them but was also trapped in the awful descent, helpless.

What had the explosion been? Had the *Sirocco* blown up? Had the Scythians destroyed her? Was everyone else dead?

The sensations were chaotic, but then they began to repeat. The ship was spinning, and the pull of gravity came from above. She risked a peek. A horizon raced around them, blurred due to speed. They were falling, whirling hopelessly out of control. They would plummet nose first into the ground, and that would be it. She would never see Nina again. Was Nina even alive? She'd left her aboard the *Sirocco*, which must have blown up.

Black misery and grief descended. She should never have left her sister. They should have been together at the end.

Above Maddox's screams, someone was shouting. Miki couldn't stand it. She turned off her comm, bent her head, and waited.

There was jostling, agitation. The whirling converted to a swoop. Her stomach rebelled and she couldn't control herself any longer. Bitter, acid vomit spurted up her throat and out of her mouth. She didn't care. She retched again and more vomit came up, soaking her front and smelling vile.

An impact threw her into Maddox. Another impact threw her the opposite way. *Thunk! Bang!* The Scythian vessel was turning over and over, each time it came down sending a teeth-rattling judder through the cabin. She was going to be killed, but it didn't matter. If Nina was dead she didn't want to live on.

Something slammed into them, and all movement stopped.

Something hadn't slammed into them. Their vessel had hit something and finally come to rest.

She was still alive.

She took no joy from the realization. Dispiritedly, she took a look at her surroundings, revealed through the veil of vomit on the inside of her helmet. An EVA suit filled the area immediately in front of her. It moved slightly. Whoever was inside it hadn't been killed in the crash, but their weak motion indicated they were injured.

She prodded her belly until she felt the lock of her harness and unsnapped it. The effort did little to increase her freedom of movement. Something was crushing her side, forcing her against the bulkhead, and before her was the injured person. She squirmed, pushing up, but her hands met something solid. She tried moving sideways, easing Maddox—she presumed—out of her way.

Breaking through, she came up against the shattered remains of the transparent shell, mixed with rocks and sand. She backed up, but the two mission mates had closed in behind her, blocking her exit. The stench of her own vomit thick in her nostrils, she felt the urge to throw up again but managed to ignore it. There had to be a way out. She was hesitant to move the people blocking her in case she hurt them, but—

A body shifted out of the way and sunshine poured in. Sand stretched to the edge of her view, broken only by the legs of someone in an EVA suit, hauling the second person from the crashed vessel. When he or she reached in to grab her too, she waved the hands away and crawled out.

What a mess.

Twisted, crumpled sections of hull lay scattered on the desert. She looked back at the vessel and was amazed she'd exited it alive. Only a smashed-in shell remained, driven into the sand. How had anyone survived?

Knuckles rapped her helmet. She looked up. The person gestured at their head. She didn't understand. Had she hurt her head? Had they hurt their head? She'd barely begun to accept she hadn't died.

The person thrust their helmet against hers.

"Have you turned off your comm?" Wilder asked, her words muffled but intelligible.

"Oh, yeah." She turned it on. "Sorry."

"My helmet's jammed," Wilder said. "Can't remove it. Are you hurt anywhere?"

"I don't think so."

"Take off your suit. We need your help."

Miki got to her feet, hastily removed her helmet, pulled apart the EVA suit straps, unzipped, and stepped out. Hot, dry air hit her, sucking the moisture from her skin, and the rays of a merciless sun bore down.

Two figures lay on the ground, one with a leg at a strange angle. Wilder and someone else were getting them out of their suits. The wreckage of the Scythian craft dotted the immediate area but otherwise the landscape was bare and lifeless.

She was finally back in the place she could hardly remember, the place she'd left so many years before. She was on Concordia.

She was home.

13

Niall approached with a knife.

"About time," Wilder said, though she knew he couldn't hear her.

Miki must have found it among the survival equipment they'd stowed in the Scythian vessel's curved wings. She'd been a real trooper, rising to the occasion after the crash. Initially, Wilder had the impression the girl was nearly comatose with shock. She'd been white as a ghost when she'd taken off her helmet—and yellow with dried vomit—and her gaze had been unfocused, but she'd quickly snapped into action as soon as she was given a task. She'd been searching the desert for the remains of the aircraft's wings and come up trumps.

Niall was saying something.

Wilder cupped a hand to the side of her helmet and shrugged. He'd taken off his suit. Unless someone spoke to her via comm she was locked in a world of silence. "Hurry up. It's getting hot in here."

He slipped the knife inside her suit near her neck and began sawing.

As well as jamming her helmet into the neck ring, a crash impact had damaged her suit's cooling system. Its insulating material protected her from external temperatures but it also trapped her body heat, and she'd been growing steadily warmer ever since crawling from the wreckage. She'd managed to open the front of the suit but it didn't make a whole lot of difference. If things got really bad she supposed she could take off the suit but her head would remain inside the helmet, and what good would that do? She could hardly travel around Concordia like that.

Niall didn't seem to be making much progress. It wasn't surprising. The suit was designed to protect against penetration by sharp objects.

"Let me try." She gestured to him to hand over the knife.

He said something.

"I can't hear you!" She gave an exaggerated shrug and held out her hand.

Scowling, he gave her the blade.

She groped for the opening. Wearing gloves didn't help. Which way around was the knife? She didn't want to hold the sharp edge against her skin. She lifted it to check. After turning it over, she felt for the gap in her suit again. She pushed the knife in.

"Ow!" She poked her chest with the tip.

Giving up, she handed the knife back. Niall snatched it angrily and spoke to her again, no doubt telling her off.

"Yeah? Well let's see if you can do any better."

It was going to take him forever to cut through sufficient material to allow her to pull off the suit and slide her head out of the helmet. She hoped she *could* slide her head out of the helmet. EVA suits fit pretty snugly around the neck.

When she was finally free, what then? Zapata was in a bad way. His broken leg looked nasty, jagged bone protruding through his calf. He wasn't shouting about it, but he had to be in agony. How would he go anywhere? They would have to leave him here in the middle of nowhere. At least, she guessed they were in the middle of nowhere. She had no idea where they'd flown—looped and spiraled—after the impact. Their plan was already severely awry.

Maddox was in better shape though also injured. She seemed have broken some ribs and, in contrast to Zapata, was whining about it plenty. Not that anyone was paying any attention to her. Zapata was in too much pain, Niall was concentrating on getting her out of her suit, and Miki had set off again to search for more wreckage.

She'd been against bringing Maddox along, and now she was regretting the decision even more. But Vessey and Niall had overruled her and that had been that. Her objection wasn't only over loyalty to Cherry, though she suspected they thought it was, she also didn't understand what Maddox added to the team except for being an extra person. More wasn't always necessarily better, and someone could be more of a liability than an aide. Maddox's attitude so far seemed to be proving she was the former.

A burst of fresh air hit her collarbones. At last, Niall was having some success. She couldn't see the area he was working on but he must have sliced through an area of material.

She tapped his shoulder. "Can I take it off yet?"

He held up a hand. *Wait.* His head bent down as he continued to work.

"Come on!" There was so much to do and they were under threat of being captured by Scythians.

As if sensing her agitation, Niall looked up. He mouthed something that looked like *Nearly there* before continuing to work. A few minutes later he put the knife down and pulled the front of her suit apart, allowing more air to rush in.

"All right. I can do it." She felt for the cut edges and tugged at them.

Together, they forced the material over her shoulders. At the same time, she stepped out of the suit's legs. Though the desert air had to be hot, its movement on her sweaty skin was a wonderful relief. She'd been soaking in a sauna of her own sweat for ages.

She pushed upward on the edges of her helmet. Her head slid through the stretchy material of the neck ring's interior, and finally she was free. "Phew!" She dropped the suit to the ground. There was a thunk as the helmet she'd come to despise hit the desert sand. "Thanks. I thought I was going to boil alive."

"You're drenched," said Niall. "Was your cooling system out too?"

"Uh huh. Where's Miki?" She scanned their surroundings.

The area they'd crashed in wasn't entirely devoid of life but it came close. Spine-covered shrubs and a lone, twisted tree with needle-like leaves clung to life in the harsh environment. The remains of the Scythian vessel's cabin lay close by, barely recognizable, and shattered fragments of the strange hull with its whirling, irregular pattern could be spotted here and there.

"She's looking for the other wing," Niall replied.

"The one with the rations? Gee, I hope she finds it. I'm parched already. It was a mistake to split the equipment up like we did. We should have put the same things in each wing, not all the food and water in one of them."

"No one anticipated this scenario."

"We should have anticipated all possible scenarios. Still, no point in wasting time on regrets."

Maddox cursed as she turned onto her side. "I hope the girl finds the water too. Zapata and I will need extra shares as we're injured. I wish I'd never come on this mission."

"You're not that badly injured," Wilder snapped, "and you could have always said no." *I wish you had.*

"You don't know how I feel. I'm in agony."

Her comment as she lay next to Zapata, who really was in agony, was so outrageous Wilder couldn't think of a reply.

"You might be lucky," Niall said. "We all might be the lucky ones."

He didn't say more. There was no need. All present knew what he meant.

What had been the explosion that occurred soon after they'd launched from the *Sirocco*? Had the ship blown up, destroyed by the Scythians? It seemed the only logical explanation but if it were true the implications were too enormous to grasp. Was everyone else dead? All the people they'd lived with, suffered with, and toiled with to survive for years, were they all gone?

Not only was the concept hard to bear, it also meant there was no going back. There was no way off the planet. They were doomed to live like the rest of the Concordians, enslaved to alien masters unless they could think of a way to overthrow them.

"There she is," Niall said.

In the distance a small figure could be seen slowly dragging something through the sand. She disappeared into the shade of the tree momentarily and then appeared again, blurred by the heat haze.

Wilder and Niall set out to meet her.

THE RAGGED METAL was hot in Miki's hands. It had been baking in the sun until she'd found it, and the strong rays had continued to warm it as she hauled it over the ground. Should she stop and leave the boxes here, returning to the crash site to tell the others about her discovery? In this lifeless place, nothing seemed likely to take them or disturb them while she was gone. But the supplies were precious, their only source of water and sustenance. Leaving them out in the open even for a short time was too risky.

Grasping the torn piece of wing tighter, she walked on. The scrape of the metal on the sand and stones was the only sound. No animals seemed to live here, not even insects. Where was she? Captain Vessey had explained they would be going to a country called Suddene, but that didn't mean anything to her. This wasn't how she remembered Concordia. Where she'd lived there had been houses and fields. She couldn't remember much else, but she could remember that much.

She hoped Wilder had managed to get out of her suit, and that she and Niall had been able to do something for poor Zapata. The pilot's face had been rigid and wet with sweat when she left the site for the second time. But what could anyone do? They had no medics.

The sound of water sloshing in the container on the broken wing brought her a little comfort. Now Zapata could at least have a drink.

Edging out her fears for the pilot was a black, thick cloud of worry ballooning from the back of her mind. She forced the thought away, blinked back tears, and trudged on.

"Miki!"

She looked up. Wilder and Niall were walking toward her.

"Wait there," Wilder shouted. "We'll help you."

She was out of her suit, thank the stars.

Miki released the piece of wing and sank to the ground. Her shoulders ached from hauling the supplies. She'd found the other wing about a kilometer away. She wasn't sure how it had ended up so far from the rest of the vessel. It must have broken off when they were still high up.

"You're an absolute star," said Wilder as she arrived.

"There's more. This was all I could fit on the wing."

"Fantastic." Wilder squatted down and began going through the packages.

"I didn't drink any of the water."

"Why not?" asked Niall, joining Wilder. "You must be thirsty."

"I thought we should ration it, save it for Zapata and Maddox."

Wilder huffed with contempt. "Maddox is fine, but you're right, we need to make sure Zapata has everything he needs, even if we have to go without."

Niall straightened up. "We should all drink when we need to. Dehydration makes people confused and disoriented. Did you spot any medical supplies?"

"There *is* more stuff there," Miki replied. "I'm not sure what it is. I thought it was important to bring back water and food first of all."

"You were right," said Niall. "You did a good job. Wilder and I will pull this the rest of the way."

"Should I go back and get the rest?"

"No, come with us."

As Wilder grabbed the edge of the metal, she asked, "Did you see any Scythian domes?"

"I don't think so. Nothing that looked like a dome to me anyway, but the air is hazy. It's hard to see well into the distance."

"Maybe we have something in our favor at last and we were right in thinking the Scythians aren't interested in Suddene. It's too barren for them."

"We can't be sure of that," said Niall. "Let's not get ahead of ourselves. First, we need to try to make Zapata comfortable. Then we figure out what to do next."

14

"I don't want to stay here," Zapata said. "I'd rather take my chances with you." He spoke through gritted teeth, his face a mask of pain despite the medication Wilder had given him. "I'm sorry. I'll slow you down, but if those things find me..."

Underlying his physical discomfort, Miki read another discomfort in his features. He hated being a burden but his fear of the Scythians and what they might do to him was greater.

What *would* they do to an injured human? None of the people she'd seen in the Scythian domes had been injured. They'd all been put to work by the aliens, tending their young or performing other tasks. Zapata was no use to them in his condition, except perhaps as a subject for anatomical study. If they found him they would either leave him, kill him, or experiment on him.

Wilder and Niall exchanged an enigmatic look.

Maddox said, "You'll be safer here than trekking through the desert with us, out in the open."

"For how long?" Zapata asked. "We only have limited supplies of food and water. How much can you leave me? Three days' worth? Four days? Then what? I guess you could give me a gun to finish myself off before I die of thirst," he added bitterly, immediately followed by, "I know I'm asking a lot."

"You're not asking a lot," Miki murmured, touching the man's shoulder.

"No, you're not," Wilder echoed.

Niall said, "You've been there for us since the beginning, man. If you don't want to stay here you're not staying, and that's it."

"That's right," said Wilder. "We'll figure it out somehow."

The sun was going down. They'd been at the crash site four or five hours, and they'd found just about everything they were ever going to find in terms of the supplies they'd brought along. There had been a medical kit in with the rations and water. Maddox's chest was strapped and Zapata had received a dose of painkillers, but Miki didn't know what else they could do for him. She couldn't see how he could walk, and he wasn't a small man. He was the largest and heaviest of all of them. If they had to pull him on the piece of wing she'd used to transport the food and water, they would travel very slowly.

"We need to start moving soon," said Wilder. "The Scythians will be leaving their domes. Some might fly overhead and spot us by chance. Or they could be looking for debris from the...incident...after we left the ship."

"In the dark?" Maddox asked.

"Especially in the dark. They see infrared. It was one of the things Ryan discovered from examining the cadaver."

"*Shit.*" Maddox's shoulders slumped. Instantly, she winced.

"What does that mean?" Miki asked. "That they see infrared?"

"They can see the heat from our bodies," Niall explained.

"Oh." Miki looked up into the twilit sky, suddenly feeling naked and exposed. It was strange to imagine that the coming night wouldn't hide them, yet at the same time she could see through Scythian eyes five figures crouched next to twisted wreckage, glowing in the dark. Her gaze turned to the shattered remains of the cabin. "Could we hide in there?"

"We won't fit," Wilder replied, "and even if we did our body heat would radiate out of the holes. We could cover them up but then we would swelter all night." She glanced at the pilot. "Our best chance is to keep moving."

Niall grimaced. "I'm sorry, Zapata, but we have to set your broken bone. It's the only way you'll be able to move at all."

"I know," he replied quietly.

Again, Miki was unsure what they were talking about but from everyone's expressions it was clearly something awful.

"Count me out," said Maddox. "Not with these ribs."

"If you can find something for me to hold onto..." Zapata offered.

Niall shook his head. "Once we start pulling you're not going to be in a condition to hold onto anything."

"Then..." Zapata looked at Wilder.

She lifted her thin arms. "I'll do what I can, but..."

"Miki," Niall said. "You have to help too."

"Of course, but I don't know what you want me to do."

"You have to help Wilder hold onto Zapata while I pull his leg. We're going to straighten it."

Her jaw dropped. What they were proposing had to be incredibly painful. "I can try."

"Good," Niall said. "Let's get it over with."

Zapata's pants were cut from where Wilder and Niall had examined his wound. The man's leg was bare, the bone shard poking horribly through torn skin, bruised purple and oozing blood. Miki could hardly stand to look at it.

She moved to his right shoulder as instructed by Niall, while Wilder sat on his left.

"Hold him really tight under his arm," Wilder told her. "When Niall starts pulling, whatever you do, don't let go. Dig your heels in for traction." Her eyes said more, things like *If we don't manage to do this he's going to die.*

"I won't let go." Miki grabbed Zapata around his armpit. She began panting even though Niall hadn't started yet.

"Take it easy," said Wilder.

"Okay," she squeaked.

Niall sat at Zapata's feet. He rubbed his hands. He and Zapata held each other's gaze. "Are you ready?"

The pilot tensed under Miki's hands.

"I know it's gonna be hard," Wilder said, "but you should try to relax your muscles as much as you can. It'll make the job easier."

His shoulder softened a fraction. "Do it."

Niall grabbed Zapata's heel in one hand and the rest of his foot in the other. He pulled. The pilot screamed and slid across the ground.

"Hold on, Miki!" Wilder yelled.

She gripped the man's shoulder with all her might, thrusting her heels into the slippery sand. Zapata was wriggling, squirming, unable to control himself in his agony. She dug her fingers into his skin as she struggled to hold onto him. Every fiber of her being rebelled against what she was doing. She was hurting him, but he needed to be hurt. He had to suffer this terrible ordeal if he was going to survive.

Her chest heaving, she turned her head away. She couldn't bear to see what was happening. All she could do was focus on stopping Zapata from moving. Why was it taking so long? Did straightening a broken bone take a long time? No one had told her how long it would take. Her muscles were nearing exhaustion from the effort.

The pilot's screaming resounded in her ears. It encompassed her entire world. All she knew was the sound of the man's pain and her determination to cling on.

Zapata jerked backward and she fell down, sprawling on her back.

"You can let go," Wilder said.

She sat up. Zapata's eyes were closed. His skin shone wet in the failing light. Niall's hunched form remained at his feet. The jutting bone had gone. Only the open wound remained.

They'd done it.

Wilder leaned over the pilot. "I'll clean you up and make a splint."

He didn't seem to hear.

NIALL HAD BROKEN a branch from the twisted tree, and Wilder had wrapped material around the thicker end to make it into a crutch while Zapata recovered from his ordeal. As they worked, Miki stowed their supplies into three of the backpacks she'd recovered from the wreckage. Maddox was adamant she couldn't carry anything and naturally no one expected the pilot to burden himself.

As she stuffed the backpacks with rations, Miki regularly checked the skies. They had guns. If one or two Scythians attacked they might be able to kill them, though no doubt more would soon be on their way.

The plan was to reach a place Wilder was confident still existed, a hidden place where they would be safe and from which they could launch an effort to turn the tide against the aliens. Miki didn't know the location of the place or how far away it was and she wasn't sure anyone else did. But at least they would be moving. That was something.

"All set?" asked Niall, looming up out of the dark.

"I divided the rations and water up like you said. Equal amounts in each in case we get split up."

He reached down and lifted a pack experimentally. "Are you sure you can carry one of these?"

"It's the water that's making them heavy. They'll get lighter as we drink it."

"If you're sure you can manage..." His gaze turned to Maddox, who sat alone some way off, staring into the night.

"I can manage."

Wilder arrived. She'd been helping Zapata to his feet and given him his crutch. "The sun went down over there..." she pointed "...so we have to head that way." She swiveled so she was pointing in the opposite direction.

"Toward the coast," Niall said.

"When we hit the ocean I should be able to figure out if we go north or south."

"You remember that well?"

"Well enough."

Niall stooped and picked up a backpack, handing it to her. "Maddox, we're leaving."

Miki shouldered another pack.

Wilder and Niall walked in front as they departed the crash site. Miki walked next to Zapata, who hopped along slowly on his crutch. Maddox brought up the rear.

The temperature had dropped fast after the sun went down, but the exercise staved off some of the chill. Miki's backpack straps dug in hard and she struggled along, only just able to keep pace with the injured pilot. The terrain didn't make for easy going. Her boots sank into the sand and the additional weight of her new load only made the problem worse. She kept quiet, however. Compared to the man trekking next to her she had little to complain about. His grunts of effort put her troubles to shame.

Everyone walked in silence except for Maddox. Her grumbles and curses accompanied them from a distance. After a while, Niall turned and noticed she was dropping behind. He signaled to the group to wait until she caught up.

"I can't go any faster," she whined when she reached them. "I'm in agony here."

Zapata said nothing, and Miki marveled at his restraint.

"I know you're hurt," said Niall, "but it's hard for all of us. You aren't carrying a pack, so—"

"You're not going to make me feel bad about that," she snapped. "I wish I'd never come on this goddamned mission. I must have been out of my mind to agree."

Wilder said, "You're not the only one who wishes you didn't come along."

"Cool it," said Niall. "Arguing isn't going to get us anywhere. Maddox, do your best. We have a long way to go to reach the coast."

It was hard to make out faces in the dark, but Miki caught a glimpse of Maddox's sullen glance. Niall told Zapata to lean on him, and the two men set off again. Maddox slowly followed them.

Wilder had hung back to walk with Miki. "How are you doing?"

"I'm fine. It's not too bad. Only…"

"What?"

She swallowed. "Do you know what happened…before?"

"You mean before the crash?"

"Uh huh. Is…" her voice dropped to a whisper "…is everyone else dead?"

Wilder didn't speak for a long while. "I'm sorry, Miki, but I don't know. I just don't know."

15

They walked through the night and into the dawn. As Wilder felt the sun's rays hit her back she looked behind her. Niall and Zapata walked as a three-legged pair, the taller man's arm over Niall's shoulders. At each step the pilot wobbled precariously and Niall struggled to keep him upright. Miki trudged not far behind them, her backpack incongruously large on her small body. In the distance, silhouetted against the rising sun, was the slim figure of Maddox.

As the night had worn on, first Wilder and then Niall had given up on exhorting her to walk faster or calling a halt to allow her to catch up. Sure, her ribs had to be painful but she was unburdened. Zapata, who was in far worse shape, was putting in his best effort. And Miki had been a trooper, hauling a pack that didn't weigh much less than her without complaint. In the trying circumstances it was hard to not be resentful about carrying Maddox's food and water.

The place they'd crashed seemed like paradise compared to this new region. Not a stick or leaf of vegetation grew anywhere as far as the eye could see. A thin layer of sand overlay stony ground, and there was no sign that water had flowed or rain had fallen here for a very long time. The air temperature was already rising in line with the sun. The day promised to be brutal.

Wilder drew to a stop, unfastened the catch on her waist strap, slipped off her shoulder straps, and let her backpack slide to the ground.

Niall appeared to register the sound, looking up and asking, "We're taking a break?"

"We should call it a day—or a night." She gestured at a group of boulders protruding from the ground. "They will give us a little cover and shade. There's nowhere else suitable in sight, and he can't go any farther." She jerked her chin toward Zapata, confident he was either past registering what was going on around him or too exhausted to care.

Niall glanced at the pilot. "No argument about that. Come on, buddy. Just a few more steps and you can lie down." He guided the exhausted man to the boulders and in among them before easing him to the ground.

Wilder waited for Miki. Her head was down and her hair obscured her face. When she reached Wilder she almost passed her by without noticing, but Wilder reached out to touch her. "We're stopping here."

Miki lifted her head, revealing drawn features and a sagging mouth. "Huh?"

"We're stopping." She pointed at the boulders. "Take your pack off over there. We'll eat and drink before resting."

Without reply, Miki plodded along the new course. Wilder turned her attention to Maddox, still distant. While waiting, she scanned the sky. If any Scythians had passed overhead during the night they must have not spotted them or not bothered with a small group of humans wandering the desert. None of the aliens' domes were visible in the surrounding land.

Maddox was progressing at a painfully slow pace. Wilder gave up on waiting, hauled her pack onto one shoulder and walked to join the others at the boulders. Maddox would figure out for herself where they'd gone.

Zapata was already out of it, flat on his back in the growing shade.

"I got some water and rations into him," Niall explained, "and I dosed him with painkillers. He zonked out immediately after."

"I'm not surprised. It's a miracle he made it this far. He must be completely beat if he can sleep while his leg is in that state."

The wound in the pilot's calf had puffed out and turned a deeper shade of purple. They had no antibiotics. The last of the supply they'd brought on the *Sirocco* had been used up years ago and the ship lacked the facilities to create more. If the Earthers had them, Vessey's abrupt departure had put paid to any chance of a request to replenish the ship's stocks.

Miki was sucking water from her bottle.

"How are you doing?" Wilder asked.

"I'm good."

Everything about her said otherwise. From the shadows under her eyes to her limp arms and slumped posture, it was clear that Miki was at the end of her strength too.

"When you've eaten," Wilder said, "try to get some sleep."

"How long are we going to stay here?"

Wilder checked the sky again. Not a cloud was in sight. "What do you think, Niall?"

"At least until after midday. The heat will be unbearable by then, even for us let alone Zapata."

"How much farther do we have to walk?" asked Miki.

Wilder replied, "I'm not sure, but we seem to be heading in the right direction at least. Maybe only another day or two."

In truth, the topography told her they'd crashed far from their intended destination. They shouldn't have had to cross a desert to reach it, which meant they were closer to the center of Suddene than she wanted. Depending on how close, they might have two days' or two weeks' walking ahead of them. How could the pilot do it?

"I can manage another few days," Miki announced. "No problem."

"You're a great help," said Niall. "We couldn't do without you."

His comment sparked energy in her features. She reached into her pack and drew out a ration package.

Wilder gave Niall an appreciative look but he turned away to get himself some food. She rolled her eyes. Dragan had accused her of being cold. How was she supposed to be any different when Niall rebuffed every attempt to be nice?

Between mouthfuls he asked her, "When were you in Suddene?"

"A very long time ago." She took a swig of water.

"Did you live here? It's so long since we were on Concordia I can't remember."

"I visited for a short time after the biocide attack."

"You were only here a few days?!"

"How long did you think I'd been here?"

"Longer than that. Long enough to be confident this is the best place for us to go."

"Did you have a better idea?"

"If we'd gone to Lyonesse we would be sure of finding people."

"And thousands of Scythians too. You saw the images of the surface."

"Who the hell would choose to live in this desert?" Niall grumbled. "And now we've lost the aircraft we have no way of crossing the ocean."

"There are people here, people the Scythians don't know about."

"How can you be so sure?"

"I just know, okay? If Concordia had been invaded while I was here, Suddene would be the place I would go."

He didn't reply, only chewed his food forcefully.

Maddox appeared between two boulders. "Thanks for waiting for me, guys."

"We *were* waiting for you," Wilder replied. "Here."

Ignoring her, Maddox rummaged in Miki's pack. Wilder was tempted to tell her off. They had a strict schedule for using up the supplies. But the more Miki's pack could be lightened the better. Wilder wasn't confident she could make another long trek.

SOMETHING HAD CROSSED THE SUN. Somewhere deep in the depths of Wilder's subconscious, her mind registered the fact. Very briefly, something had cut out the light blasting her skin from the hot desert sky. Blearily, she opened her eyes.

While she'd been sleeping, the shadow of the boulder she was lying next to had moved away and the high sun shone directly on her. Her exhaustion after the long night's trek had made her oblivious to the increased heat and her burning skin. Another realization had dragged her to wakefulness, a realization that something more dangerous than sunburn threatened.

What was it?

She sat up.

All her companions were sleeping. Zapata remained in the shade. Maddox was exposed to full sunlight but unaware. Niall and Miki's upper halves lay in shadow but their legs had to be roasting.

She touched her face. The skin was hot and sore, and her clothes were uncomfortably warm and sweaty.

That wasn't it.

The brilliant sunshine dimmed for a fraction of a second.

That was it.

She turned her gaze upward.

High above, two winged shapes were circling.

Scythians out in the open in the middle of the day?

"Holy shit! Wake up! Wake up!" She roughly shook Niall's shoulder. "Wake Zapata." She crawled to Miki and Maddox. "Scythians! We need to hide."

They moved deeper into the group of boulders, huddling in a central space where they only barely fit. Zapata grimaced with pain as he was forced to bend his broken leg. They gripped the three backpacks on their laps. They couldn't afford to leave any trace the aliens might notice.

Miki whispered, "Will they see our body heat?"

"I really hope not," Wilder replied.

Would it have been better to lie on the baking sand where the infrared might confuse the Scythians' sight? But the act of lying in the open in order to hide felt so counter-intuitive. Her first impulse had been to conceal themselves as if hiding from other humans. It was a mistake that had almost been the downfall of Sidhe. The first colonists had removed all visible traces of the settlement from the surface only to discover the Scythian spiders worked by tracking scent.

But it was too late to move out from the boulders. If the aliens hadn't seen them yet, they would almost certainly discern movement in the lifeless scene.

"Where have they gone?" Maddox asked.

The sky was empty.

Wilder pulled out her gun and the others did the same except for Zapata, who was slumped against a boulder, his eyes shut tight. Her gaze flicking between the narrow entrances to the cramped spot, she strained her ears for sounds of the aliens approaching. There was nothing, not even the noise of the wind. The air was utterly still. Sweat coating her palm made her weapon slippery in her hand. She gripped it tighter.

"Have they left?" Miki whispered. She had crouched into the tiniest ball and her eyes were wide.

No one answered.

How long should they wait before concluding it was safe to come out? Wilder wished they had a better view of their surroundings. If the aliens had flown away they would see them in the distance. But here the tall boulders blocked their sight of everything except the sky immediately above.

The faintest whiff of an odor crossed her nostrils. Instantly, every nerve in her body was alive, an instinctive, visceral reaction prompted by a horrifying memory. She was being carried aloft, an alien's long, scaly toes crushing her chest and stomach, its revolting stench enveloping her.

She hissed, "*They're here!*"

Miki had smelt them too. She'd turned deathly pale.

"We have to kill them before they find us," Wilder murmured, "before they get a chance to send out a comm. If the rest of them know where we are we're dead meat."

Niall nodded grimly.

Twisting to ease herself out of the packed bodies, Wilder rose to a crouching position and leaned through a gap between the nearest boulders. Their former resting site lay before her, the sand disturbed but with no sign of the aliens.

They had to be approaching from—

Miki screamed.

Wilder whirled 180 degrees. A Scythian was leaning in, its head encased in its breathing apparatus, wings outspread. Something was different about it, but she didn't have time to think more before firing. Her and Niall's pulses caught it square in the chest and it toppled backward.

"Two!" Wilder yelled. "There are two. We have to get the other one!" She darted to the opening, stepping on bodies. The Scythian lay on its back, moving weakly, the ribs of its massive wings twitching. She fired another round, aiming at its helmet. Though it was out of action they couldn't risk it comming its friends.

There was the other one!

It was running, and its wings beat. It was abandoning its partner, heading for the skies.

She aimed, fired, and missed. She leapt over the downed alien, trying to get closer, hoping for a better shot. An iron grip fastened around her ankle, and suddenly she was on top of the wounded Scythian. It had grabbed her as she jumped. Its burned flesh and noxious odor surrounded her, and the helmet she'd fired at was in her face. She'd only scored it. The thing still wasn't dead.

The other one was getting away. She had to do something before it alerted the rest of them. But the one holding her wouldn't let go and at this close range, struggling with the creature, she risked hurting herself if she fired at it.

With her free hand, she reached behind the helmet and grasped the tube that led to its CO_2 pack. She gave a hard yank. That did nothing. She fumbled at the base and felt a snap lock. She flicked it open, the tube came out, and finally the thing released its grip. She scrambled to her feet.

Where was the second one?

It was flying, but beneath it stood Niall, aiming. He got off two shots in quick succession. The first pierced the alien's wing, disrupting its flight. The second bright pulse round seemed about to go astray but the creature turned into its path and caught the round in its throat. It tumbled from the sky and landed heavily on its back.

As Niall finished it off, she checked the alien that had grabbed her.

It held the tube she'd pulled out in one of its feet, but it was still. Either it hadn't managed to replace it before it suffocated or it had expired from its wounds in the process.

Both the Scythians were dead, but had they managed to tell others about the humans in the desert?

16

In a flurry of haste, they made their departure. Niall helped Zapata to his feet, the older man grimacing and blanching in pain. Miki quickly pulled on her backpack. Maddox was already out in the desert, striding away from their useless hiding place.

Wilder called her back. She was heading in the wrong direction. As she returned, she complained loudly that no one had told her which way she was supposed to go.

They set out once more for the coast.

It was early afternoon. The sun was barely past its zenith. Wilder was already burned from her exposure to its rays while sleeping. She pulled her hat lower and rolled her sleeves down from her elbows. Better to swelter than burn.

Glancing back, she assessed the trail they were leaving. The looseness of the sand made their footsteps indistinct but they remained visible to a sharp-eyed observer. There was nothing to be done about it. No one in their party had the energy to cover their traces. All they could do was hope the two Scythians hadn't managed to get word out about their discovery or their location, and that it would be a long while before their bodies would be found.

"Wilder." Niall had Zapata's arm over his shoulder again while the pilot struggled along with his crutch under the other one. Niall's features were sweaty and strained.

She dropped back a few paces to draw level with them. "Yeah?"

"Did you think those Scythians looked different from the ones we saw on Earth?"

"You noticed that too? I thought I might have imagined it." Her only close encounter with a living Scythian had involved it nearly killing her, and the second time she'd seen one it had been cut up and frozen.

"Their visors were darker," Niall said, "and so were their bodies, right?"

"That's right. I guess it makes sense. They usually come out at night so ultraviolet light must hurt them. They're getting around it by protecting themselves."

"I wonder if it's an old practice or if they've only recently started doing it. Either way, it spells trouble for Concordians. They aren't able to escape the aliens day or night."

"I'm more worried by the fact that we saw two here on Suddene. I'd been hoping they wouldn't bother with this continent and it might be a safe haven for people who could make it over the ocean."

Zapata stumbled and Niall grunted as he struggled to keep him upright. "I think Scythians have been here a lot longer than they were on Earth. They've spread to inhospitable places and they've adapted their strategies to deal with a harsh climate—at least, it is to them. When you said that our colony could have survived only because the Scythians arrived and enslaved them, you might have been right. The aliens could have been here for decades, but if that's so, things might change soon."

"In what way?"

"They're figuring out ways they can travel around during daylight. Why? Why bother if they have humans to do that for them?"

"So they can capture more colonists?"

"I doubt it. They seem to have the local population under control. A few stragglers who lack the technology to hurt them won't make a difference one way or the other. No, it's more serious than that. I think they're moving to the second stage of reclaiming their home planet.

They're planning to eradicate their need for humans entirely. Eradicate *humans* entirely."

Her stomach clenched and she stuttered, "You-you really think so?"

"What do you think? This is where the Scythian species originated. Why would they want a bunch of illegal immigrants living here when they could have the place to themselves?"

She was silent.

"I don't know for sure, of course," he said, as if trying to soften the blow. "It's just supposition."

"Makes sense, though."

Shit. How long did they have before the slaughter began? Had it already begun?

Zapata stumbled again, crashing all the way to the ground this time. He yelled as he hit, impacting his broken leg. He lay still, panting and cursing under his breath. Niall stooped to help him to his feet.

"Leave me," said Zapata. "Leave me here and go ahead. I'll take my chances."

"Don't be dumb," Niall admonished. "We're not leaving you. Come on, let me help you."

Zapata batted his hands away. "Leave me, goddammit. I've slowed you all down enough already."

Wilder went to his other side. "Seriously, Maddox is more trouble than you, Zapata." The woman had already dropped behind. "Niall's right. There's no way we're letting you stay here while we go on. Besides, if we find another Scythian aircraft, who's gonna fly it? We need you."

The pilot's shoulders sagged. "I can't do it. I can't go on. I thought I could make it but I was wrong."

"No," Wilder said, "you were right. You *can* make it. We'll take it one step at a time, okay? First, we get you upright. You can do that. Just focus on standing up."

As she'd been talking, Zapata's head had been down. He lifted his gaze to meet hers. Holding eye contact, he grasped her hand.

"That's it. You can do it."

Together, she and Niall hauled him up. Niall pushed the crutch under his arm and lifted the other one to put it over his shoulder.

"I'll help him this time," Wilder said.

"You're too weak. You won't manage."

"Let me try."

Let me in.

He looked at her uncertainly. "Okay, but the minute you get tired out tell me about it. We need to keep him on his feet. You saw what happens if he falls."

It seemed rude to talk about the pilot while he was right in front of him, but in truth he acted as if he was oblivious to anything except his pain and the question of whether he should go on.

She took over from Niall, taking Zapata's free arm. "Next step."

They moved forward.

While she was helping the pilot she had little energy for anything else. Her backpack became a leaden weight and the man's arm pressed down heavily on her shoulders. She relied on Niall to check the skies and what Maddox and Miki were doing. When Zapata had fallen Miki had continued walking. She probably hadn't noticed. And in all the time it had taken to get the pilot to his feet Maddox hadn't caught up. She was positively dawdling, like she was passively aggressively punishing them for the situation. Wilder had a silent vision of a Scythian swooping from the sky and carrying her off.

They walked on, and soon it became a matter of not only Zapata forcing himself to put one foot in front of the other—or rather one hop after another—but her too. Yesterday night's walk seemed like a pleasant stroll compared to this forced march through the heat of the desert day, not knowing if the Scythians were already on their trail.

Time and again she was tempted to ask Niall to take over, but he had to be beyond exhausted. He'd helped Zapata all the previous night.

In the midst of another miserable internal debate, as she exhorted herself to walk just another hundred meters, a breath of cool air hit her, accompanied by a salty tang.

Was she imagining it?

Had extreme fatigue made her delirious?

"Does anyone else feel that?"

The others either didn't hear her or were too tired to reply.

Perhaps she had imagined it after all.

There it was again. Unmistakable, a waft of refreshing air had moved over her skin.

The realization energized her. "We're near the ocean! We're nearly there."

Niall looked back at her and then turned his gaze ahead again. His footsteps slowly drew to a halt.

The landscape rose in front of them, sandy hillocks mounting higher until cut off by a cobalt, cloudless sky. Thick clumps of tough undergrowth dotted the slopes.

Niall lifted his backpack straps and allowed it to slide to the ground.

Wilder halted. Without a word, Zapata stopped alongside her. Miki walked on, heedless of everyone else.

Niall walked ahead. Wilder watched him staggering through the low hills, disappearing beyond each and then rising into sight again.

He disappeared beyond the farthest slope.

Miki finally noticed what was going on. She stopped, dropped her pack, and turned to look at Wilder questioningly.

But she was more interested on what was happening on the horizon.

"Wilder!" Miki called. "What's going—"

Niall popped up on the ridge, waving excitedly.

"We made it!" Wilder called back. "We've made it."

17

They hadn't made it.

When Niall had announced they'd reached the ocean, that it lay just another few hundred meters' march over the sandy hills, Miki had thought they'd nearly reached their destination. But it turned out that wasn't the case.

She'd trudged the remaining distance to the water and then dropped onto the beach, too tired to remove her backpack. A little later, after her legs had ceased thrumming and the sea breeze had cleared her head, she snapped the waist catch open and gingerly slid her shoulders out from under the straps. The pack fell backwards onto the sand and she left it there.

Where was the place they were supposed to be going? The shoreline ran for kilometers to the right, and though the view to the left ended in a high bluff, there were no signs of people living here. No footprints marked the beach except their own. There were no buildings or roads, nothing that indicated a human presence.

She waited.

Niall had gone back to help Wilder with Zapata. Maybe she should try to help too, but now she was sitting down she found she couldn't get up. Her legs simply refused to work. Instead, she watched the water. She'd seen Earth's oceans but only from afar. Now she was up close to one, the sheer amount of water all in one place was hard to take in. While she'd been growing up on the *Sirocco* water had been a precious commodity, to be measured out and conserved. The presence of so much of it seemed wasteful somehow.

A scuffling sound behind her, louder than the gentle waves, drew her attention. She started. She hadn't checked the sky for Scythians in a while. But it was only Niall and Wilder arriving with Zapata. Helping the man down the slope was hard. The sand gave way every step they took, but eventually they made it and lowered him to the beach. He lay down, instantly out of it. Even at a distance his leg wound looked awful.

"How are you doing?" Wilder asked, approaching.

"When you said we'd made it, I thought you meant we were at the end of our journey." Miki hated the petulant tone in her voice but she couldn't help it. "But we aren't, right?" She squinted as she looked up at Wilder, who stood over her, her back to the sun.

"Right. Sorry, I should have explained. The site we're aiming for isn't on the coast. It's—"

"Is it much farther?" She wasn't sure she could walk any more, at least not today.

"Uhhh..." Wilder took off her pack and dropped it. Then she put her hands on her skinny hips and gazed up and down the beach.

"Do you know where we are?"

"It'll take me a little while to get my bearings. It's been a long time since I was on Suddene."

"Are we going to rest for a while?"

"Yeah, I need to figure things out." Wilder looked pensive but she didn't have that look of deep concentration she wore when she had hard thinking to do. Her expression was more one of concern or worry.

Niall had splashed sea water over his head and chest and was walking over. "Got your bearings yet?"

Wilder bit her lip. "Let's rest, drink some water, and eat. I need to think."

Miki decided to follow Niall's example to refresh herself. She pulled off her boots and socks, clambered to her feet, and slowly stepped down to the ocean's edge. A wave surged close and washed up to her knees. She gasped. The ocean was colder than she'd anticipated, but it wasn't unpleasant. She waded in deeper. As another wave retreated she stooped and gathered water in her hands to splash on her face. As the water hit some of it leaked into her mouth. "Ughhh!" She spat to get rid of the taste.

"Too salty?" Wilder asked.

Miki hadn't noticed her arrive. "I wasn't expecting that. Do all oceans taste of salt?"

"All the ones I've encountered, but that isn't many."

Miki gazed into the murky waves. "I remember Dad saying that an intelligent species called the Fila lived in Concordia's waters. Did you ever meet any of them?"

"*Meet* them? Humans and Fila co-existed happily for quite a time." Wilder's expression turned sorrowful. "A few of them traveled with us to the Galactic Assembly. I got to know one of them well. We were friends. He helped me a lot. His name was Quinn."

"What happened to him? Did he die in the biocide attack?"

"No, he survived, but then he left with the rest of the Fila survivors. They didn't have a vaccine and their anatomy was too different from ours for us to manufacture one. Concordia wasn't safe for them, so he left, and then not so long after I left too. I don't know what happened to him."

"It's been so long..." Miki said softly.

"Fila don't die of old age. Unless something else killed him he's probably on another planet, living out his life. I hope so."

The water didn't feel so cold now. Miki bent down to splash it on her upper body, taking care to keep her mouth closed. But as it soaked through her shirt sharp pain jabbed from her shoulders and she gave a small scream.

"What's wrong?" Wilder asked.

"I don't know." Miki pulled her shirt away from her collarbones. The straps of her backpack had rubbed her skin raw.

Wilder peered in too and sucked air through her teeth. "It's the salt. It makes wounds sting. I think we have some ointment in the medical kit."

Before they settled down to sleep, Wilder had walked to the distant bluff. She'd gone alone. A capable adult had to stay on the beach in case the Scythians spotted their party. So Wilder had made the trek by herself. Miki had watched her leave and seen her return at dusk, the dim light not disguising her troubled look.

A whispered argument between Wilder and Niall followed. She only caught a few phrases, all from Niall, whose voice was deeper and louder: *I thought you said* and *Then what do you propose?* and *Zapata will never make it.*

Were they lost? Or only very far from where they needed to be?

There was clearly a problem yet she found it hard to care. Every part of her body ached, especially her shoulders, waist, and feet, which had borne the brunt of the day's exertion. She wasn't sure *she* would make it to whatever destination tomorrow held in store, let alone Zapata. He looked ready to lose his leg like Ethan.

More than her physical pain, she was heartsick, dreading the possibility she might have lost the only remaining member of her family. If Nina was dead was there any point in going on?

Despite her inner and outer discomfort, despite Niall and Wilder's quarrel, despite Zapata's soft groans and Maddox's snores, she drifted into slumber.

Dad was here. She knew it even before she saw him. She sensed his presence, calm and strong. She felt his love.

"Miki, I've missed you." He hugged her tightly.

"I've missed you too." She had a vague memory of him being ill. "Are you better now?"

"Yes, I'm better. How are you? What have you been doing?"

Looking into his amber eyes, she found she couldn't remember. She chuckled. "It's weird. I don't know what I've been doing. But I'm fine. It's nice being here with you." She rested her head on his shoulder like she had when she was a little girl. A deep sense of peace and happiness settled over her. She wanted to stay like this forever, though something told her that wasn't possible.

"Where's Nina?" Dad asked.

"I-I'm not sure." Where *was* her sister? "Isn't she here?"

"I don't know. I'll go and look for her."

"No, stay with me a while."

"Okay." He stroked her hair. "My little red-head."

"I'm not really. Only a little, just enough for my classmates to tease me. Dad, what was Mom like?" It was a question she'd asked him a million times. She had a few misty memories of her mother but that was it.

He said what he always said. "She was kind, warm, loving, and smart. I always felt lucky to know her."

"I wish *I'd* known her."

"Me too. But it wasn't to be."

In the far distance, someone was shouting.

"What's that?" Miki asked.

But Dad didn't seem to hear. He was still, as if frozen.

"Dad? What's wrong? What's wrong with you?"

Her father was melting. His features were dissolving.

"Dad, don't go! Dad, Daddy, wait for me!" She reached out but he was gone. In his place was darkness, a starry sky, and the sigh of waves washing to shore.

"Where's he gone?!" Wilder yelled.

"He can't have got far by himself," said Niall.

"But we'll never find him in the dark." She added, more quietly, "Do you think he walked into the sea?"

"What're you chattering about?" Maddox asked groggily. "Some of us are trying to sleep."

Wilder answered, "Zapata's gone. Niall, you check the beach. I'll go inland. Maddox, you—"

"I'm not doing anything. I'm still in agony."

"I can help to look for him," Miki offered, sitting up. The dregs of her dream about her father clung on in her mind like the sweet after-taste of a dessert or the scent of a fading flower. She savored the sensation. Dad had visited her many times in her sleep, and each time she relished the memory, though it deepened her grief.

"Thanks," said Wilder. "Come with me. I don't want you searching alone. The Scythians might have found the bodies of the ones we killed and be looking for us."

"Look," Maddox said, "I don't want to sound callous, but if Zapata has gone off somewhere maybe it isn't such a bad thing. He's slowing us down and he knows it. If he wants to—"

"If anyone's slowing us down, it's *you*!" Wilder spat. "If you want to sacrifice yourself by wandering off, feel free."

Maddox gave her a black look but didn't reply.

While Niall headed up the beach, Miki walked with Wilder into the dunes. They had a tougher job than Niall. Zapata's footprints would be easy to spot in the sand on the cloudless night. As soon as she and Wilder stepped away from the beach a hilly expanse of dark clumps of vegetation and shadows confronted them. There was no sign of his passage and even at close range he would be hard to spot.

On the other hand, the man could barely walk. Niall was right. Zapata couldn't have gotten far. Perhaps he was hoping they would seize the opportunity to absolve their guilt about leaving him behind and not come after him.

Distant beams of light brightened the darkness.

"Huh?" said Wilder. "What's that?"

The light was coming from behind them, from the beach. It looked like three or four flashlights roaming the shore, as if looking for someone.

Shouts broke the quiet of the night. Miki didn't recognize the voices as belonging to Niall, Maddox, or Zapata.

"What the...?" Wilder muttered. "We should head back. Whoever those people are, they aren't Scythians, they're Concordians. We can explain about Zapata and ask them to help us search for him." As they pushed through the vegetation, she added, "This is fantastic. I don't know how they found us, but it's saved us a long, hard trek."

Miki was similarly confused but also happy. Their situation had reversed. They were no longer seekers but the sought. "Do you think someone on the *Sirocco* managed to comm the surface and told the people here about us?"

"That must be it! They told the Concordians we were coming to help them, so when we didn't arrive a search party was sent out.

Thank the stars. I was worried we weren't going to make it. Zapata can get medical help now too."

There were five figures on the beach, though behind the beams from the flashlights they carried they were little more than black shadows.

Wilder approached the nearest one. "Boy are we glad to see you. I'm—"

"There's another one!" the man yelled to his companions. He rushed at her and knocked her to the ground. In one swift movement he threw her on her front, put a knee on her back, and jerked her hands behind her.

Miki stared in horror.

Wilder screamed and fought, but her protests were muffled by the sand.

Miki was frozen. She wanted to help Wilder but the man was big and strong. She would never defeat him. And she couldn't shoot at him without risking hitting Wilder. Shock and bewilderment also made her hesitate. What was going on? Why were these Concordians capturing her companions? One thing was clear: she had to get away. If she didn't, they would catch her. Wilder's captor hadn't noticed her yet but he might any minute.

Slowly, she began to back up. She hit a spiny shrub and fell into it, gasping as the spines stuck in her skin.

The man looked up. "One more! Get over here, guys. Where are you?!"

Miki tried to get up but the more she moved the more she impaled herself on the spiky bush. She whimpered. Two of the strangers ran up and hauled her from her predicament. She shrieked as the spines tore at her. There was no sympathy from the men. As soon as they'd freed her they roughly bound her wrists and gagged her.

Where was Wilder? What had happened to Niall and Maddox?

One of the men pushed her toward the waves. Dread made her legs weak. Were they going to drown her? She stumbled, her knees slapping into the hard sand at the water's edge. Another man dragged her to her feet, and then shoved his shoulder into her stomach. He lifted her up and she dangled, helpless, her legs hanging down his front and her face lying against his back as he waded into the waves.

Water surged, closing over her head. She closed her mouth but the brine exploded up her nose and she coughed and squirmed. The water was gone. The man had grabbed her middle, pulled her up, and then threw her down. She tensed, expecting to fall into the ocean, but her back met something solid. He'd thrown her into a boat.

As the vessel rocked, she twisted her head to try to see what had happened to her companions. Three more bodies were piled on the bottom of the boat.

Someone shouted a command. An engine started up. The boat swerved, rose over a wave, and sped away from the shore.

18

"We're not spies!" Wilder yelled. "I've never met such a bunch of morons in my entire life! We've given you a million reasons why we can't possibly be working for the Scythians. Now let us go so we can help you fight them."

"Reasons?" asked the man. "You mean your cover story? Pathetic. Couldn't you come up with something better?"

He was swarthy—black-haired like all Concordians, but his skin was darker than usual. He must have spent time in the Suddene sun. He was stocky and broad-shouldered, mid-thirties. None of the men who had captured them had given their names, but he seemed to be their leader.

When she didn't answer, he got up and left.

Wilder didn't know what else to say to convince him she was telling the truth. Niall was concussed from the blow he'd sustained when the Concordians subdued him, Maddox seemed speechless with rage at their new predicament, and Miki was clearly simply terrified. They weren't going to be any help, yet if she didn't turn the situation around they could all be in a lot of danger. She didn't know what the Concordians did to people who sided with the enemy, but she knew it wouldn't be good.

If explaining their background and the reason they'd been in the desert wasn't going to work, she would have to think up a different tactic.

They'd brought them to Chimera. The excavation site for Concordia's fifth military silo had changed a lot from how she remembered it. When she'd come here after leaving the Immani ship, the cavernous space had been bare. Encampments of people sheltering from the biocide had dotted the ground but otherwise the area had merely been a hollowed-out chamber, cool and dimly lit by temporary lighting.

Now it was a village. Lines of low buildings formed streets, and streetlamps illuminated them. Sounds of bustling activity came from all around and the scent of humans struggling to stay clean filled the air. If it weren't for the dark roof arching high overhead, it might have been Sidhe all over again—Concordians driven underground once more by their age-old enemy.

Wilder wasn't sure what she'd expected when she'd suggested going to Chimera but it hadn't been this. She'd anticipated something more basic but, obviously, other minds had come up with her idea a long time ago. What better place to hide from the Scythians than on a continent where little grew and in a place beneath the ground, where aerial creatures couldn't venture? A number of Concordians must have fled here soon after the aliens arrived and they'd been here ever since, gradually improving their habitation, perhaps adding to their numbers with new people from Lyonesse over time.

Niall lifted his head and groaned.

She shuffled over to him on her butt. It was the most movement she could manage. Their captors had bound their ankles in addition to their wrists after dumping them at the dead end of a street. One of the four guards, standing with their backs to them, looked over his shoulder but then ignored her.

"How are you feeling?" Wilder asked. "Try not to move. It'll just make it worse."

He squinted up at her. "Wilder?"

"Yes, it's me."

He groaned again before murmuring, "Did you find Zapata?"

"No." Her heart heavy, she added, "He's still out there. When I've convinced these idiots we are who we say we are, I'll ask them to help us search for him. Unless he's done something stupid he should still be alive and not very far from the camp."

In a way it was fortunate that the pilot had escaped the Concordians' notice. The treatment her party had received had been rough and he was in no condition to endure it. Yet in another way things might have gone much better for all of them if Zapata had been captured too. His injury would have supported her story that their aircraft had crashed in the desert. Maddox only had bruising and a lot of complaints about the pain she was in, which their captors didn't seem to believe.

"What's going on?" Niall asked. "Why are they doing this?"

"They think we're spies, in cahoots with the Scythians. They say because we didn't have a boat that means we were dropped off, and if we were part of the rebel network we wouldn't be wandering the desert, we would know their location. We also wouldn't be armed. I guess there must be collaborators on Lyonesse."

He grimaced and slowly pushed himself upright with his bound hands.

"Maybe you should stay lying down," Wilder said.

He didn't reply until he was sitting. "I'm okay." He looked around him. "This is Chimera?"

She nodded. "It's changed, but this is it. No mistake."

"So we made it in the end."

The mild joke brought a smile to her lips. "Not exactly how I imagined."

"I heard their boat while I was looking for Zapata." He squeezed his eyes shut as a wave of pain seemed to hit before continuing, "I didn't recognize the noise. Thought it must be a Scythian engine—a new kind of aircraft—so I ran."

"That must have looked suspicious."

"Uh huh." He grimaced again. "I think I will lie down."

She wished she could help him as he turned to ease himself down to the ground.

The swarthy man returned. Jabbing a finger at her he said to the guards, "Bring the mouthy one."

Mouthy one?

A man cut the bindings around her ankles, grabbed her under her armpits, and yanked her to her feet. He gripped her biceps and forced her along the street in his commander's wake, taking her to a nearby habitation. She was led into a room and pushed onto a chair before her ankles were tied again.

The swarthy man was already waiting, sitting opposite her. He leaned forward and spread his knees, resting his elbows on them and clasping his hands. His gaze was keen and direct. "I'm going to be straight with you. You might have heard rumors about what we do with traitors. Maybe you've seen a body or two wash up on Lyonesse. Everything you've heard is probably true. When you die it'll be slow, messy, and agonizing, and to be honest my stomach turns whenever we do it, but people like you don't deserve any better and we need to set an example."

"I don't know who you think—"

He raised a hand. "Let me finish. I'm going to offer you a bargain. Give us useful information about the Scythians, and I promise I'll make it quick. Not only that, we'll let the girl live. Why you would bring someone so young along with you is beyond me, but then I never understood you guys anyway. We will keep her prisoner but she won't face execution. You have my word."

Wilder opened her mouth to speak but he raised a finger to silence her again. "Naturally, *I* will be the judge of whether the information you give about the Scythians is useful. We already know a lot. More than you think, I imagine. I'll give you five minutes to think about it." He rose to his feet.

"Please," Wilder pleaded, "listen to me. Everything I told you before is true. We're from the *Sirocco*. We've returned from our voyage to Earth and we want to help you fight the Scythians."

He sighed. "Not this again. You're wasting your own time with this nonsense. Five minutes. That's it." He moved toward the door. The guard opened it.

"Isn't there anything I can tell you that will convince you? There has to be something. My name is Wilder. I built the ship along with Niall. He's the man with us. *Please, wait!*"

He was gone.

19

Ever since the moment she'd been tossed into the boat, Miki had been operating in a fog. She'd barely registered being lifted out of the vessel and forced into the back of a vehicle, and nor could she recall much of the journey to this new place, though she remembered the sensation of traveling downward along a long tunnel. The voices of the people around her seemed muffled or as if she was hearing them from a great distance. Physical contact felt as though she was being touched through a thick blanket.

Her companions and she were in trouble. She knew that much. But she wasn't sure why, or why their captors hated them. For hate them they did. Of all the impressions she had of what was going on, she felt the hatred of the Concordians. It didn't make any sense. *She* was Concordian and so were Wilder, Niall, and Maddox. They were here to help their fellow colonists.

Why had everything gone so badly wrong?

And now Wilder had been taken away for some reason. Niall had passed out, and Maddox appeared to be suffering a silent rage.

At least things were becoming clearer now. The fog seemed to be dissipating. She shifted her position. Blinking, she took in her surroundings as if seeing them for the first time. She was sitting on smooth, bare, dusty rock. It had been carved out by machinery.

Narrow grooves covered the surface but they weren't sharp. They'd been softened by time and the passage of feet. This place had been created a long time ago.

The blank face of a building sat behind them, and on each side ran rows of more buildings, though these had windows and doors. Occasionally, people would wander down the street to peer at the prisoners or a head would poke out of a window to stare.

Why were she and the others on public show? Why didn't these people lock their prisoners away?

She became aware she was dreadfully thirsty. "Excuse me," she said timidly. "Could I have some water?"

The three guards looked uneasily over their shoulders and exchanged glances with each other. None replied.

She decided not to push it, though her throat was parched and her tongue thick in her mouth. Then one of the guards muttered something to another and walked away. A few moments later he returned with a cup of water and squatted down to give it to her.

Maddox announced, "I'll have that! I need it more than her. I'm injured. She's fine."

"We all need water," Miki explained to him. She was angry with Maddox, but it was true. "We were in the desert for two days. Niall especially needs it. Could we please have some more?"

The guard frowned, but he left again and returned with two more full cups. "Thank you," she called to the guard, who had helped them but he ignored her.

"I don't know why you're being so polite," Maddox snapped. "These assholes kidnapped us and they're treating us like shit. Ungrateful idiots! To think we wanted to help them out. We should have cut our losses and returned to Earth, or found somewhere else to live."

"It's just a misunderstanding. When Wilder explains why we're here I'm sure everything will work out fine."

"Huh! You sound like your dad. He was a naive fool too."

"Don't speak about my father like that! He was a good man." Tears of rage choked her. She wanted to slap the smug look off Maddox's face. "At least he didn't screw every woman on the ship." The rude language sounded strange as it left her lips but she meant every word. And Maddox had to know exactly who she was talking about. Maddox had adored Aubriot but the feeling hadn't been reciprocated. Aubriot had loved Cherry and everyone knew it.

"You little bitch!" Maddox hissed. "If I wasn't in agony from my ribs I'd teach you a lesson about talking back to adults that you would never forget."

One of the guards barked, "Quiet back there!"

Maddox glared.

"Cut it out," Niall muttered.

Wilder appeared in the doorway of a nearby house, her arm held tightly by a guard. He guided her over to them. Her expression was downcast. Her talk with the Concordians hadn't gone well.

"They aren't going to let us go?" Miki asked.

She shook her head. She seemed very upset.

"What's wrong? What's going to happen now? Did they tell you?"

"They...they..." Wilder gulped air and looked at Niall, who remained prone though his eyes were open.

"What's up?" he murmured.

"I-I couldn't convince them. They won't listen to me, won't even entertain the possibility we're from the *Sirocco*."

Miki asked, "Did you tell them about the crash site? If they found that they might believe us."

"I tried to explain about it before, but they only said of course Scythian spies arrived in a Scythian aircraft. This time around I wasn't even given a chance to talk. They just gave me an ultimatum."

"What was it?"

Wilder swallowed and her gaze traveled across her companions. She seemed unable to speak.

"Let me guess," Maddox said sarcastically. "They aren't inviting us to live with them happily ever after."

"They're gonna *kill* us?" Niall asked, turning onto his back.

Miki's heart seemed to stop. "What?!"

"They think we're collaborators, traitors," said Wilder. "To them, we're even worse than the Scythians because we've betrayed our own kind. But, Miki, they said they would spare you due to your age."

The fog that had enveloped her before returned, enclosing her in a thick, gray shroud. What Wilder had said was impossible. It couldn't be true. Her companions were going to be executed? And Nina was probably dead too, as well as everyone else aboard the *Sirocco*. The Concordians were going to kill the only people she had left, her only friends. They were going to die.

Someone was screaming.

It was her.

"SOMEONE SHUT THAT GIRL UP!" the Concordian leader yelled.

Miki was hysterical but what did he expect?

Wilder almost regretted revealing the truth to her, but it didn't really matter. She would know sooner or later that they'd been killed. She would react like this after their deaths too. Wilder only hoped she wouldn't see or discover *how* they'd died. The leader had threatened a torturous, drawn-out process. Perhaps he hoped to extract information about the Scythians while they were at the height of their agony. A tremor passed through her. The prospect felt unreal. The reversal of her expectations felt bizarre. This wasn't how she'd imagined her first encounter with the new Concordians would play out. Never, in all her imaginings of meeting the descendants of the people she'd left behind, had she anticipated this.

Miki screamed, writhed, and kicked, and Wilder felt helpless. Nothing she could say or do would calm the girl down or make her feel better. And she couldn't think of anything to tell the Concordians that would persuade them she was speaking the truth. When they listened they had an explanation for everything, and their explanations bolstered their suspicions. Now they'd stopped listening.

Grim-faced men approached.

They were going to do it so soon?

She was hauled to her feet and force-marched down the street. Where were Niall and Maddox? Poor Niall. He could barely walk. Someone else was screaming. Maddox.

The buildings passed on each side at a breathless pace. She

wrenched her head around. They were bringing Miki too?! "Leave her behind! Don't let her see. Please don't let her see!" She fought and kicked, lifting herself off the ground as the men's grips on her arms tightened painfully.

People emerged and clustered at the street edges, staring, jeering, cursing.

"This is a mistake!" Wilder yelled. "It's a stupid mistake! We're here to help you."

Where was the leader? He seemed to have disappeared. Wasn't he going to witness the result of his decision? He'd said it turned his stomach. What a miserable coward.

They'd brought them to the edge of the cavern, near the tunnel leading to the surface. It had been her first sight of Chimera just a few hours ago, when she'd believed the confusion could be ironed out. The lighting was dimmer here. Rocky walls towered into darkness. It was here she'd met Kes, Cherry, and Aubriot again after her long separation from the surface, living aboard the *Opportunity* with Quinn. The past seemed surreal, the future an empty blank, formless, meaningless.

She sagged, hope leaving her. She really was about to die.

What would the torture entail? How would they hurt her?

The only thing greater than her fear of the pain that lay ahead was her horror that Miki would see it. The poor girl had suffered enough. She would never get over what was about to take place in her presence.

The hands gripping her biceps thrust her downward so her knees struck the rock floor. She sucked air before exclaiming, "Please take the girl away! *Please take her away.*"

"You have one last chance."

She looked up. The leader had reappeared.

"Confess you're in league with the Scythians. Tell us all you know about them."

"We're not spies! I can't tell you what I don't know!"

He looked sorrowful. "I hate that you make me do this, but you've sided with our oppressors. You don't deserve any better. Don't worry. We will remove the girl before your execution." Miki's screams had ceased. She was slumped on the ground, slack-jawed as she regarded her surroundings. "And we won't torture you. That was only a threat to make you speak. The tales you've heard about what we do to prisoners aren't true. They're lies generated by the Scythians." He frowned down at her. "Does that change your mind? Will you tell us about them now?"

"You've got this all wrong," Wilder wept. "We're from the *Sirocco*. If you would just listen..."

He heaved a sigh. "Even at the point of death you remain loyal to humanity's enemy. You're disgusting." Looking at one of the guards, he gave a nod and stepped back.

The guard pulled a gun from a holster.

Wilder's insides lurched.

"Wait," the leader said. "Take the girl away."

"Noooo!" screamed Miki. "It was here! It was here! I remember now." She rocked backward and forward, mumbling and sobbing.

Her words triggered a wave of bewilderment among their captors.

"It was here!" Miki cried. "It was here Mommy died!"

Wilder gasped. "Oh, stars, she's right. Her mother died here during the biocide attack. I'd forgotten." *Poor Miki.* And she'd brought the girl here. What a fool she'd been.

"More bullshit," said the leader, but his tone was uncertain.

"No," Wilder protested. "It isn't bullshit. It's the truth. You think she's faking? Look at her."

Miki was having some kind of mental breakdown. Her hair hung over her face as she rocked and wept.

Her hair.

"Look at her hair," Wilder commanded. "Do it." She felt like shit making a spectacle of the girl while she was in the throes of grief and shock, but she had to save their lives. "Look at the red in her hair. She's Kes's daughter. Kes, who left on the *Sirocco*. You must have heard of him and Aubriot, the last of the Earth-born. Kes was known for his red hair. You *must* know about it." Her heart in her mouth, she turned her pleading gaze from the leader to each guard in turn, praying that at least one of them knew that tidbit of information about the Concordians who had departed the planet decades ago.

"Bring her into the light," the leader said.

Wilder tensed.

A sobbing Miki was gently lifted to her feet and guided into a pool of light spilling from a nearby lamp. The leader peered at the crown of her lowered head and softly touched her hair, parting the strands.

His shoulders dropped. He murmured a command to the men holding Miki and they led her away. To Wilder he said, "I will listen to your story."

20

Wilder couldn't stop the tremor in her hands. She'd come within a whisker of death. They all had. She'd known it was a possibility when she'd suggested the mission, but to be confronted with the reality, to have a gun literally pointed at her head, was a different thing entirely.

She wrapped her hands tighter around the mug of a warm beverage the leader had given her before properly listening to what she had to say.

They'd been taken to the lounge of a building near the center of the habitation. This place was far more comfortable than the bare room where the leader had announced his ultimatum, yet it was still sparse and the furniture was worn and shabby. Pictures adorned the walls, simple 2D artists' sketches, some colored with pencils. She recognized a view from a cliff at Oceanside and a town that could be Annwn, the capital of Lyonesse. The images brought a flood of associations into her mind, memories of her life growing up on Concordia. So much had happened since then. The memories felt dreamlike, unreal. Yet here she was, back on her home planet.

"I offer you my most sincere and deepest apologies," said the leader.

"Oh, thanks," said Maddox. "That makes everything okay then."

Niall and Miki had been taken to receive medical treatment, Niall for his concussion and Miki for her psychological state. Wilder would have to share the introduction to the new Concordians with Maddox only. The prospect was not inviting.

Their host winced. "You must understand, it's vital that our presence here remains a secret. We cannot afford to—"

"How long has it been since the *Sirocco* left?" Wilder interjected, dragging her gaze from the pictures.

"According to our records, sixty-three years."

Sixty-three years? Considering the amount of time the ship had spent in space after the jump drive failed, plus the time dilation effects, it added up. Yet a momentary sense of disorientation hit. She was thrown back to the moment she'd emerged from the Fila shuttlecraft after her trip to the Galactic Assembly, to find that Concordia had moved on five decades, the colonization had been a success, the colony had grown and developed, and nothing of her old life remained.

Maddox muttered darkly, "Everyone we left behind must be dead."

"And when did the Scythians arrive?" asked Wilder.

"Fifty-five years ago."

"Only eight years later?"

If the jump drive had worked correctly the first time, the *Sirocco*'s crew would have returned within months and begun the reseeding of the planet. They would have been caught up in the invasion. Could their presence have affected the outcome? It was doubtful.

"The colony was on the brink of disaster," said the leader. "We didn't stand a chance." He stood up and held out his hand. "I'm Meric."

Wilder shook with him. Maddox glared at his hand and then up into his face. Resignedly, he returned to his seat. "The colony gave up hope of your ship returning a long time ago. It was generally accepted that something disastrous had happened—the jump drive exploding, a Scythian attack—or that you'd simply decided to abandon the mission and remain on Earth."

"We would never have done that," Wilder protested. "We're Concordians. This is our home."

He shrugged. "Nevertheless, you didn't return and the colony moved on, or rather, struggled on. The last thing I expected to find out in the Suddene desert was crew from the fabled *Sirocco*. We regularly sweep the coastal areas to find escapees from Lyonesse. Occasionally we discover spies sent by the Scythians. We generally know who they are from their physical state and the equipment they carry. As you can imagine, humans are not allowed to carry weapons anywhere in Concordia. The fact that you were armed was a dead giveaway. That, and the fact you had no mode of transportation."

Wilder gasped and leapt to her feet. "Zapata! Our pilot. I'd forgotten about him. He's injured. We have to search for him."

"Please, sit down," said Meric. "Tell me more."

"Our pilot's leg was broken when our aircraft crashed. He walked with us to the coast but then he left our campsite when we were asleep. We think he didn't want to slow us down anymore."

Meric grimaced. "The desert is a harsh environment, and it's been hours since we picked you up. If this man was already injured..."

"I have to go and look for him," Wilder insisted. "You have to take me back to the beach where you found us."

"That's a bad idea. You won't last long out there in the heat. You aren't used to it, and how would you find your friend? I will send out a search team, men and women experienced at tracking in the wilderness. They will find him, but if I were you I wouldn't hold out hope for them finding him alive. Give me a minute." He rose and left the room.

Wilder sank into her seat. How could she have forgotten about Zapata?

WHILE HIS SEARCHERS went out looking for the lost pilot, Wilder asked Meric to bring her up to speed on what had been happening on Concordia while she'd been gone and the current situation. Maddox demanded to be taken somewhere she could lie down.

"I'm sorry," Medic said. "I should have offered you a place to rest earlier. You need time to recover from your ordeal."

"I'm *in pain*," she replied irritably. "Not that anyone cares."

Wilder explained, "We think Maddox might have broken some ribs in the crash."

Meric's eyebrows lifted. "In that case, I double my apology. You should be checked out. I'll find someone to take you to the medical center. We only have basic equipment and medications but perhaps they can do something for you."

After Maddox had left, Meric poured Wilder a top-up of her drink. "Where to begin? I hadn't been born when the *Sirocco* left. It's history to me, and difficult to believe you're *the* Wilder, the chief engineer, yet you're younger than me."

"That's time dilation for you. It throws everything out of whack. But I was also very young when we designed and built the ship, not much older than Miki."

"And does my memory serve me correctly when it tells me you were one of the first Concordians? You were born on the *Nova Fortuna*?"

"I don't know if you would describe it as *born* exactly. I was squeezed from a gestational sac, the same as the rest of the Gens."

And, as Cherry had said, she was the last of them, on Concordia at least.

"Huh!" He shook his head in wonder. "What a day I'm having. I receive a message that the Sweep Team picked up some spies and find myself faced with the distasteful task of executing them, only to end up sitting opposite a walking relic of the past."

Wilder's disturbed reaction to his description of her must have shown for he added, "No offense."

"You said the colony struggled on for eight years after we left. What happened?" She wasn't sure she wanted to know. She still harbored a lot of guilt over the malfunctioning of the jump drive. But her curiosity overcame her hesitancy.

"They were hard times by all accounts. I'm glad I didn't live through them. There were plagues of biting insects and insects that ate the crops—crops that were already meager and poor quality. A large fraction of the population died of simple starvation. Others died of malnutrition caused by an extremely limited diet. Only certain plants would grow, you see, and that's all there was to eat. Very few children were born, either because women couldn't carry babies to full term or they chose not to become pregnant, not wanting to subject their offspring to a hopeless, short life. Some colonists gave up and walked into the sea or hanged themselves. It must have been terrible."

Wilder wondered at what point the Concordians had given up hope the *Sirocco* would return. After six months? A year? Two years? She hung her head.

"What happened when the Scythians arrived?" she asked quietly.

"First, they attacked Oceanside and after that Annwn, blasting both from space. Then the bombardments suddenly ceased. No one could understand why the Scythians had spared us from complete destruction. It would have been easy for them to send down their spiders to kill anyone still alive, but they didn't. Things were quiet, and, once more, we began to rebuild. Crops were sown, roads and bridges were repaired, and new houses were constructed from the remains of the ones that had been destroyed."

He rose to his feet and walked to the window, which looked out on the street, where the people of Chimera walked past. "By that time, there were signs the ecology was beginning to recover. The numbers of insects in the annual plagues were not quite so vast, crop plants grew more strongly, and the vegetation in the landscape had become more varied. Prior to that, single species would dominate huge tracts of land. The sluglimpets returned."

"Ugh, really?"

He turned to her and smiled sadly. "Yes, of all the creatures to survive the biocide and regenerate, it had to be them." Returning his gaze to the street, he continued, "A few of the most optimistic Concordians began to hope the colony had reversed its decline and might regrow. Their comments and articles are in the archives. But it was a fool's hope. No rational person could have believed the Scythians were finished with us. Most colonists were waiting for them to return and sure enough, three and a half years after the bombardment they were back. Their builder craft landed in droves."

"Builder craft?" Wilder asked, though as the question left her lips she knew exactly what he meant.

"Specialized transports that construct their domes. They descended all over Lyonesse. More came each night. People would wake up to a Scythian ship in a neighboring field or sitting on the main road into town. At first, they only constructed the domes. Some people weren't even sure it was the Scythians doing it because we only saw their robots. But when they started the abductions—"

"The same as on Earth."

"What?"

"The same thing happened on Earth. The Scythians followed the same colonization process. Miki was abducted and lived inside a dome for a short while."

"Earth has been taken over by Scythians?!" Meric returned to his seat. "This is sad news. Why didn't you tell me earlier?"

"You didn't believe we'd been to Earth earlier, remember?"

He rubbed his chin. "So there's no escape." He appeared to be talking to himself.

"If you were thinking we could transport Concordia's population to Earth, it would have been difficult even if Earth was safe. The *Sirocco* isn't as big as you seem to think. I don't know how many people we're talking about, but—"

"No escape! Damn." He looked her in the eyes. "I confess that as soon as I accepted you'd been telling me the truth, I'd hoped perhaps you could help out the people here in Chimera. Concordians living on Lyonesse are a lost cause, I'm afraid."

"What are conditions like there? The Scythian colonization of Earth has only just begun. I don't know what things will look like decades from now if the Earthers don't manage to fight them off."

"Conditions? I suppose it depends what you mean. In some ways they're much better than pre-colonization. There's no starvation—as far as I'm personally aware. It's been years since I was there, and the information we receive is sparse and unreliable. But generally the human population seems healthier than it was when we were alone.

The Scythians understand how to replenish the depleted ecosystem and they have plants that grow well and that humans can also eat. But people are basically slaves. They only exist to serve the Scythians and if they fail in the task or stand up to them, or if a Scythian is having a bad day..." He drew a finger across his throat.

"The aliens keep adult men and women in separate living quarters and match them for breeding pairs, according to some criteria we don't fully understand. Babies are removed from mothers at birth and given to wet nurses and carers to bring up. Often, the infants are moved to another region, maybe to reduce the ability of their parents to find them. I never knew my mother or father. I have no idea who they are."

"Wow," said Wilder. "Me neither. That's how things were on the *Nova*."

"Really? I didn't know. So much information about the past has been lost, and after the Scythians arrived they confiscated all that remained. What we know now has been passed down orally. How strange that the Scythians and the Project's Founders treated the colonists the same way."

"Well, it wasn't exactly the same. I never had a mother, only an egg donor." Yet the similarity in the two processes *was* odd. The Founders' rationale had been they didn't want strong familial bonds to develop that might jeopardize the mission while the *Nova* was en route. Whereas the Scythians didn't want familial bonds to develop... The Founders had been as controlling as the aliens, though supposedly to fulfill a nobler cause. "What else is happening there?"

"Movement is extremely restricted and it's becoming more so. In the early days, when people began to escape to Chimera, it was hard but not impossible to break out and flee across the ocean. Nowadays it's virtually impossible. The Scythians figured out most of the ways their slaves were escaping. We haven't seen anyone except spies for years."

"So they know that humans are living here on Suddene?"

"They suspect it, but I doubt anyone has made it back to Lyonesse to confirm their suspicions."

"But they must know about Chimera. There's an ancient Scythian city here, right? Where they sited their planetary defense system when they left. They sent the compromised Guardian, Faina, to reactivate it." Cherry had told her Aubriot had destroyed the system after Faina led him to it.

"I'm not sure they do know about Chimera. The site was top secret even before the Scythians returned, right? And no domes have ever appeared on Suddene. The Scythians seemed to take the absence of human activity here as a sign the continent had been abandoned as the colony began to fail. They were right. No one lived here after the biocide attack. Port City and Chimera were abandoned. As far as we can tell, all the Scythians know is that the android managed to restart the planetary defense but then it ceased operation once more. Now, they have no reason to come here. Even if they did, they cannot access the control base themselves. It's buried beneath meters of sand. And they cannot trust humans to do it for them. It's far too dangerous."

They continued to discuss the situation on Concordia and what had happened on Earth. Meric was happy to hear about the Ark, replete with seeding material to re-start Concordia's biomes. But Wilder was dispirited. It seemed the efforts of the crew of the *Sirocco* had been useless. Humans on both planets faced an impossible task.

Several hours later, she was about to ask Meric where Chimera got its food and other resources when there was a knock at the door.

He opened it, and a man gave him a message she didn't catch. He thanked the man and closed the door. "Your pilot has been found. They're bringing him back. He's alive but in bad shape, dehydrated and suffering heatstroke. It's uncertain whether he'll live."

21

The sick bay was tiny. Just four beds squeezed into a small room. Niall was sleeping off his concussion in one and the other two were empty. Miki guessed space was at a premium in Chimera.

Chimera.

The place Mom died.

How could she not have known? Perhaps Dad hadn't mentioned the name. He'd told her it happened soon after Nina was born, that, due to the biocide attack, Mom had been forced to go somewhere remote, with minimal medical care. All the most vulnerable colonists had been flown to Suddene, where the progress of the biocide was slowest.

She'd thought she didn't remember Mom dying. She had fleeting, nebulous memories of times before that. She recalled Mom having a tea party with her and her dolls, and Mom waking her in the middle of the night to take her to another place. Dad wasn't there but Mom wouldn't explain why. She recalled flashes of brilliant light and sounds of thunder, and her Mom holding her tightly in the cellar of a strange house. That was her last memory. After that, Mom was gone, and it was just her, Dad, and baby Nina.

But the sight of the bare cavern walls, rising to darkness overhead, had brought it all back. Suddenly, she'd been a little girl again, waiting in a tent with a strange woman and her child while her mommy wailed and groaned next door. She'd known it was only baby Nina coming but she'd been scared nonetheless. Then the noises had stopped. The woman she was with went out and when she returned she'd seemed worried. Her voice had been too bright and cheerful, telling Miki she should sleep and tomorrow she would see her baby sister.

Miki had only wanted to see her Mommy, but she'd never seen her again. Someone had told her Mommy had gone far away. It wasn't until later Dad had explained she'd died.

It had happened here. Right here.

And she was back here again. Dad was dead too, and she didn't know if Nina was alive.

The doctor had given her something that made her feel groggy but the effects were wearing off. She was beginning to think straight again. She wished the new memory would go away yet it continued to play over and over again in her mind, along with the recollection of the moment Wilder had announced she and the others were going to be executed.

Things had nearly gone badly wrong. Things *had* gone wrong, ever since they'd left the *Sirocco*.

She sat up. She felt strangely empty and light, as if all her emotions had been drained out.

Where was Wilder? Why hadn't she come in to see her?

The door opened and a woman backed in, guiding a bed on wheels. A man was pushing the other end and another man lay upon it, who she recognized.

"You found Zapata?!"

"Not us," the woman replied. "We just fixed him up."

Miki leapt from her bed and crossed the room in hurried steps.

"Whoa," said the woman. "Back to bed, young lady. The doc didn't give you permission to get up."

A sheet covered the pilot to his chin. His face was thin and drawn, and his skin red from sunburn. He was deeply asleep, his mouth hanging open.

"Is he going to be okay?"

"We think so. He needs to rest, and he can't do that with you gawking at him. I thought I told you to go back to bed?"

Miki didn't think the pilot was in any state to notice her. The medic was only saying that to make her obey. But she did what she was told anyway and watched as they lifted Zapata onto a bed and covered him up before leaving.

Now there were two sleeping patients, and she had nothing to do. Did they really expect her to stay here indefinitely?

She lay on her back and stared at the ceiling. The empty feeling persisted. She felt like a sodden rag that had been thoroughly wrung out and hung up to dry.

Staying here any longer was impossible. She had to get out. She had to see things and hear things or she would go mad. Her ship's clothes sat in a little pile on the table next to her bed. She hastily changed out of the hospital pajamas. Her clothes seemed to have been washed. The grittiness of the invading desert sand was gone. The same couldn't be said for her boots. She turned them upside down and shook and hit them with the heel of her hand to shake free the remaining grains.

Taking care not to rattle the door knob, she opened the door and peeked out.

An empty corridor stretched from left to right. Sounds of voices and movement came from the left. She tiptoed along the right-side passageway until she reached the end. An open door led to the street. She had a momentary sense of guilt about leaving without permission, but she dismissed it.

Mom was dead. Dad was dead. Nina was probably dead too. The *Sirocco* was most likely lost. Earth had been invaded and so had Concordia. The future of humanity was grim.

What did anything really matter anymore?

She stepped outside.

Now she wasn't in a state of confusion and fear, she could take in her surroundings better. The last time she'd been in Chimera the only dwelling places had been tents. In the center of the cavern bright lamps had stood, the only source of light. The night Mommy died the lamps had been turned down low while people slept.

Was it nighttime or daytime outside? Lamps on poles stood every fifteen meters or so along the street joined by thick wires at their bases. The single-story houses seemed flimsy. Here and there a door or window was crooked or spaces gaped at their sides.

A man walked past, eyeing her curiously.

If she wasn't careful, someone would inquire at the medical center if she was supposed to be out and about. She walked briskly to the end of the street. Another crossed it, so she walked to the end of that one. More people passed. All of them stared. Everyone must know everyone else in Chimera.

A smell told her she was nearing latrines so she altered direction. She wasn't sure where she was going, only that she had to move. She had to act, to do something, to *feel* something. At a street corner she halted and looked up. Her gaze met only darkness. It seemed to encroach, to push down. Only the feeble light of the streetlamps kept it back.

She wanted to see daylight.

After growing up on the *Sirocco*, going planetside on Earth had been weird at first, but she'd grown to enjoy it. The apparently limitless space and open sky brought her joy. She longed to see it again.

Which way was the exit? In the maze of little streets it was impossible to tell. Instead, she looked for a wall and headed for it. When she reached the vertical surface she turned and followed it. The lines of houses ended abruptly at the edge of the cavern. There was no fence or other barrier to separate them.

It was darker here. She touched the wall as she walked alongside it. The rough rock had been worn smoother at shoulder height. No one seemed to come near the cavern boundaries, and she walked unnoticed by passersby.

Where was the exit? Would she have to circumnavigate the entire space?

The houses receded, leaving an open area. This was the place her companions and she had been brought, where she'd had her realization, the sudden familiarity smacking her in the face. It had to have been around here Mom's tent had been pitched, though she had no tangible memory of the site.

A wave of distress washed over her.

Yes, it must have been here.

A little farther on a hole yawned in the cavern wall. It had to be the exit, the opening of the tunnel that led to the surface. No one seemed to be about. She walked over, sauntering as if she was only here by accident. She guessed that leaving Chimera wasn't straightforward.

But no guards stood in the gap. The thick doors that barricaded it were open too. She slipped into the tunnel.

Walking to the top seemed to take forever. She trekked it in almost total darkness, groping along the wall for guidance. The air grew warmer and drier the higher she rose. Where the occasional light glowed overhead it revealed smooth tracks worn on the rough ground by the passage of vehicles. But then another light brightened her way —a light from up ahead.

She was nearly there, and it was daytime.

She hurried on.

"Stand back," a voice ordered. "Weapons at the ready. ETA thirty seconds."

The announcement brought her to a sudden halt.

Guards stood on each side of the tunnel and she'd nearly walked right into them. Bright, glaring sunshine had silhouetted the men and women, blending their figures with the general darkness, but at the command their shoulders had hunched and they lifted their rifles.

What was arriving in thirty seconds?

She edged closer.

A distant rumbling caught her attention. The people ahead of her collectively tensed, their postures tightening and feet adjusting their position.

Intrigue urged her on another few steps. She also longed for a glimpse of an open landscape, even though it would be dry and barren. Living underground made her feel like a worm in a hole, constantly fearing detection.

"Hey, who the hell are you?"

The commander had glanced back at the guards, perhaps checking their readiness, and spotted her.

She shrank into the shadows.

"Get out of here," the commander barked. "This is no place for a kid. Haven't you learned—" His head swiveled forward.

A dark shape blocked out the sun, and the tunnel resounded with the loud hum of an engine and the crackle of tires on concrete. A large truck was rolling in, nearly filling all available space with its bulk. Miki pressed her back to the wall. It rolled past her. A second truck passed, and then a third.

That seemed to be it.

The guards relaxed, and Miki judged it was a good time to slip away, but the commander yelled, "Who the hell *are* you?!"

She backed away as he bore down on her.

"Wait right th—"

"Scythians!"

The cry had come from the head of the tunnel. Guards were in the process of closing the doors, but they were half open. Through webbed sheeting, two shapes could be seen whirling in the upper atmosphere, their wide wings outspread.

"Shit! Seal the entrance." Cursing with worse words, the commander strode right past Miki as if forgetting her existence, and marched into the depths of the tunnel.

22

Meric's argument with the commander of Chimera's paramilitary had been building for half an hour. Wilder waited in an adjacent room with Miki as the two slogged it out. At first, their voices as they discussed Miki's transgression had barely penetrated the dividing door, but for the last few minutes the commander had been shouting, every sentence painfully clear.

"I don't give a shit who they are! They might have brought the Scythians right to our doorstep. And that idiot girl is a liability. She was a minute from wandering out into the open and giving us all away."

Meric's reply was soft, a murmured attempt at appeasement.

"Who cares whose daughter she is? You're seriously telling me you allowed Scythians spies to live because one of them has a bit of red in her hair? Are you insane?"

Again, the sound of Meric's response was audible but his words were not.

"They have no place here!" the commander yelled. "We don't know who they are or where they're from, and you're jeopardizing the safety of this community on a fanciful dream. The *Sirocco*'s crew died a long time ago and if they didn't they're whooping it up on Earth.

You'll be telling me next the guy in bed in sick bay is Ethan and their supposed pilot is Aubriot. They're all dead, Meric. Dead and gone. The sooner you accept that and get rid of our unwelcome visitors the better. If you don't, you should reconsider your fitness as Leader."

The door slammed open, and Wilder and Miki jumped in unison.

Casting each a baleful glare, the commander thumped past them and out the exterior door.

Meric appeared, his brow furrowed and rubbing his hands. "I guess you must have heard a lot of that?"

"We got the gist," Wilder replied.

"I'm sorry. Commander Orson is hot-tempered and speaks his mind, but he isn't rash. He'll calm down eventually."

"Do we have to leave?" Miki asked. "I didn't realize I was doing anything wrong when I walked up the tunnel. I only wanted to go outside for a little bit. I wasn't thinking straight."

"You picked a bad time, unfortunately. Usually, there would be guards at the inner doors. Chimera is guarded day and night at both ends of the tunnel in case of Scythian attack. No one living here would want to go out even if it were permitted. But the moment you chose for your excursion happened to be the scheduled arrival of a supply shipment. We're at our most vulnerable when we open up to allow the trucks in, so all guards were deployed at the surface."

Wilder asked, "Isn't it incredibly risky for Chimera to be supplied in that way? The Scythians would see the vehicles from the air."

"The entire route from the port is camouflaged, and the trucks only travel by day. The Scythians seem to have poor sight in bright sunlight, and the heat from the desert seems to confuse them."

"I'm sorry for what I did," said Miki. "If it would make things better, I'll leave. I could go on one of the empty supply trucks to—"

"You're not going anywhere," Wilder interrupted. She turned to Meric. "Right?"

"Right," he replied, but his tone lacked conviction.

The commander had threatened that Meric should 'consider his fitness as Leader' if he didn't make them leave. If Meric was no longer head of Chimera, he wouldn't be able to protect them from people who didn't want them here.

They had to show they were who they said they were if they wanted to remain. They had to demonstrate their worth, but in reality she wasn't sure they had any. What could they realistically do to expel the Scythians from Concordia? The second stage of their plan had been nebulous from the outset, and they'd even lost their only piece of equipment that might have helped them: the alien aircraft. Using that, they might have penetrated the heart of the Scythian presence on Concordia, perhaps taken high-ranking officials hostage. But the craft was smashed to smithereens, and they were just as weak and powerless as every other Concordian.

"Tell me more about the set up in Chimera." Perhaps there was a way to leverage the 'freedom' of the Chimerites to strike back at the aliens. "The base is supplied from Lyonesse?"

"We receive shipments every two or three months, never on the same day or at the same time. People slaving for the Scythians on Lyonesse smuggle food and other supplies out to us, and the only remaining cargo ship carries them over the ocean via an ever-changing route. The ship is camouflaged too, but that part of the operation is the riskiest."

"It's kind of the Concordians over there to support you."

"They love the idea that a portion of the human population isn't controlled by their overlords. Occasionally, they smuggle people over too, people at risk of being killed as agitators. We take in whoever they send, though we are over capacity."

"You told me you hadn't seen anyone except spies for years."

He looked somewhat abashed. "You must understand, I wasn't about to tell you all Chimera's secrets at once."

"But the situation here can't continue forever. How long has Chimera been occupied?"

"This will be the fourteenth year since the first escapee arrived."

Wilder whistled. "Fourteen years! That's a helluva long time to wait before fighting back."

Meric replied defensively, "Concordians here and on Lyonesse are fighting back every day. The mere presence of Chimera would be an abomination in the minds of the Scythians if they knew it existed, and the slaves on Lyonesse resist control in hundreds of ways. People working in the hatcheries kill Scythian young—"

"I did that," said Miki.

"What?"

"I worked in a Scythian hatchery on Earth. I tended their babies, though I didn't know that was what they were at the time. It would be hard to kill them while they were worms. I cut a worm in half once, but both halves lived."

"Uhh..." Meric seemed to lose his train of thought. "I'm not sure how they do it, but that's what I've heard. Other slaves spoil the crops, which is a big self-sacrifice. Humans eat the food too, so everyone goes hungry."

Wilder asked, "Is it true that adult Scythians are vegetarian?"

"That's what has been observed. Once they're past the youngling stage, where they eat each other, they consume plant food only. There have been no reports of Scythians eating animals. Not that animals would be easy to find on Concordia."

Except for the obvious.

"The two we killed in the desert looked different from the ones I saw on Concordia," said Wilder. "Their visors were darkened and so were their bodies. We didn't stick around long enough to find out if the skin coloring was natural or applied, but both observations have me worried."

"How so?"

"I think it's an indication that they're trying out ways to survive here without human help."

"So they're going to free all the people they're keeping as slaves?" Miki asked.

"No," Wilder replied heavily. "I really doubt it."

"Oh..." Miki looked down.

"This is bad news," said Meric. "I thought it was odd when you said they approached you during daylight. These new adaptations mean their behavior makes more sense now." He asked Miki, "You escaped a hatchery? How did you manage that?"

"With the help of a lot of the other prisoners. We dug our way out while some of the men tackled the guards."

"That was very brave. I've heard of escape attempts but most are unsuccessful. If people do manage to get away they're usually recaptured. There aren't many places to hide on Lyonesse. Then they're executed in front of their fellow slaves—as an example to the others, I presume."

"Meric." A woman had stuck her head in the exterior doorway. "The men in the clinic are awake and asking about their companions." She eyed Wilder and Miki.

"Maybe you should go and see them," Meric said, "while I approach Orson about you staying here a little longer. He might have cooled down a little. He's a reasonable man, only concerned about everyone's safety."

"Sure." Wilder got to her feet. "Come on, Miki. Let's go. Do you remember the way?"

Chimera wasn't so big it was easy to get lost in. Miki quickly figured out the direction in which the clinic lay. As they walked the narrow streets, they attracted the gazes of the Chimerites. Wilder had never been comfortable with scrutiny, and the hostility of the stares made her doubly uneasy. Attitudes toward them had changed since Miki's unfortunate escapade, though she was entirely innocent. But the people seemed to lack any compassion for the young girl. Perhaps they even doubted, as the commander did, that she was Kes's daughter.

Wilder put a protective arm around her. They needed an out, a way to disappear for a while, before their mere presence excited the suspicions and fears of their hosts to anger and violence. Yet traveling to Lyonesse on a returning supply truck seemed reckless, almost suicidal. The situation on the other continent had changed drastically since they'd left. It was now the heart of Scythian territory, and they didn't have a clue how to operate there undetected. How could they survive? What would they eat? Where could they live?

But perhaps there was somewhere else they could go...

"I didn't mean for all this to happen," said Miki. "I wish I'd never forced you to bring me on the mission. If I hadn't, I would be with Nina, wherever she is."

Wilder gave her a sideways hug. "You didn't force me or Captain

Vessey to include you. What you said was true. You do know more about the Scythians than anyone else. You heard what Meric said: people don't usually escape their domes alive. You could know things that turn out to be vital to defeating them."

"I really don't think I do. I think it was only by luck that I escaped. The Scythian colony on Earth was new, while they've been living on Concordia for decades. Everything is tight and organized here."

"Don't over-estimate them. Chimera survived all this time, right?" Miki didn't answer, and in the intervening pause Wilder's idea took shape. "There's another place the Scythians haven't been for a very long time, somewhere we might learn more about them—old secrets they might have forgotten. What do you say to going into their ancient city with me?"

"An ancient city? Where is it?"

"Right here at Chimera, or nearby. I'm not sure exactly. Cherry went there during the biocide attack, and Aubriot went in with a team afterward."

"I don't know. I'll probably slow you down or do something stupid."

Wilder halted and grabbed Miki's shoulders, turning the girl to face her. "You're not slow or stupid. You were a hero out in the desert, finding our supplies, carrying a huge backpack for kilometers in the heat. And you're still a kid! Stars, no one could have done any better. I wouldn't pick anyone else to come with me. Do you hear?"

Miki nodded.

"Good. That's settled. We'll tell Niall and Zapata, and then we'll go."

23

Niall insisted on coming too.

"No way." Wilder was perched on the edge of his bed. She reached out to take his hand, and he pulled it under the covers. She heaved a sigh and they held each other's gazes.

Miki didn't know where Maddox was—maybe in another room? —but Zapata was asleep. He looked better than he had when he'd been brought in. His skin was peeling but it had filled out and his eyes were less sunken.

Wilder was right. Niall certainly wasn't in any condition to be coming with them into the Scythian city. He looked better too, but he remained somewhat pale and drawn, and the dressing over the spot where he'd been hit was raised in a bump.

From the reactions of the Chimerites when they learned of the proposed mission, it was a dangerous place to be. Miki also understood the city was very big and there was no water down there. They would have to carry a lot with them, though Meric had also loaned them an old device that supposedly condensed water from the atmosphere. He hadn't been confident that it still worked effectively or how long it would last. And they couldn't hang around to test it. Orson was agitating hard for everyone from the *Sirocco* to be kicked out, Meric had said.

The inhabitants might be persuaded to show a little sympathy for the people still receiving medical treatment, but that wouldn't extend to Wilder or her—especially her. Somehow, the story of her trip up the tunnel had transformed into an attempt to rush out into the open and signal to the Scythians flying above. It was ridiculous, of course, but such was the nature of gossip within a small population living in close quarters under constant threat of discovery, said Meric. Stories became magnified beyond the simple truth and individuals were targeted and scapegoated. The Chimerites needed someone to blame for their predicament and someone to 'sacrifice' to prevent things going wrong. It had sounded as though he spent most of his days keeping a lid on his people's fears.

"You aren't better," Wilder continued, "and you know it. It's going to be tough going in there. What happens if you have a relapse and can't go any farther? What are Miki and I supposed to do then? We can't carry you far. Do you expect us to leave you behind?"

"Then wait until I am better," said Niall. "Give it 48 hours. The doc will write me a clean bill of health by then."

"We don't have 48 hours." Wilder turned to Miki. "Could you wait outside?"

Miki walked to the end of the clinic's corridor and leaned on the outer wall, kicking her heels against it. Passersby threw her dark looks. She went back into the clinic. Sound traveled easily here. Though the door to the room with the beds was closed, she could hear a whispered argument. Wilder and Niall were going at it. She hoped they made it up before Wilder left. It would be sad if Niall's last memory of her was the exchange of harsh words.

The door opened and Wilder came out, rubbing her eyes with the heels of her hands.

So much for that.

"Are you ready?" she asked. Their equipment was packed and waiting at the opening that led to the Scythian city.

"I'm ready."

"Then let's go."

"Are we going to say goodbye to Maddox?"

"What do *you* think?"

THEY COULDN'T REACH the city alone. The plain that surrounded it sat at the bottom of a drop that was too steep to walk down. They would have to be lowered to it, and then cross it to reach the city boundary.

"What's up there?" Miki asked, her neck craned as she tried to make out the edge of the upper expanse.

"A dome," replied Meric.

"Holy shit," said Wilder. "The biggest Scythian dome ever. They must have constructed it when oxygen levels rose so high the atmosphere became poisonous to them."

"That's where they got the idea for re-inhabiting Concordia and colonizing Earth," Miki said. "For them, it's old technology."

"You're right." Wilder gave her a smile. "Smart girl."

"Not really. I couldn't do half the things you do. I could never invent a-grav or—"

"There's more than one kind of smartness. Meric, can you lower us down now?"

"You got it." He walked to the cab of the excavating machine that had sat here next to the drop for who knew how long. The ropes from their harnesses had been wound around the machine's spiral-shaped point. Meric had managed to get the machine started but, considering its great age, Miki wasn't confident it would continue running. She had a vision of her and Wilder dangling in mid-air, halfway down the drop and out of reach of the side.

"Don't worry," said Wilder, appearing to perceive her uneasiness. "If this doesn't work we can get people from Chimera to lower us by hand and haul us up when we're done."

Or throw us into the abyss.

Wilder stepped off first. Her rope tightened. She beckoned to Miki. After some hesitation, she also took a step into darkness. Clinging onto Wilder, she felt her body sag into the restraints of her harness. *I really don't like this.*

There was a jerk, and the point of the excavator began to turn. Steadily, they dropped lower. The side of the cliff moved slowly past.

The ground presumably approached, though there was no sign of it. Pitch blackness sat beneath their feet.

Wilder said something.

"Huh?" Miki piped, her voice barely making it out of her throat.

"Goggles."

"Oh. Yeah." She pulled the night vision goggles that had been sitting forgotten on her head over her eyes. Instantly, the ground appeared, ghostly green. It seemed a very long way away. She gave a squeak and clutched Wilder.

"Best not to look down."

They had begun to spin the same time they're descent had started. All the while, the speed of their rotation had increased.

"Shit," Wilder muttered. She reached out to the side of the cliff but it was too far away.

The cliff appeared in Miki's view, and then the darkness—except now she had her goggle on it wasn't dark any longer. She had a glimpse of towering structures like angular mountain peaks, then they were gone, replaced by bare rock.

The city. It was surrounded by a high wall.

Rock.

Beyond the wall, the ground was strangely patterned.

Rock.

The city walls were patterned too. They looked like the hull of the Scythian aircraft.

Rock.

"I feel sick."

"I can't stop our momentum," said Wilder. "Try to hold on another minute. We're nearly there."

Their downward progress abruptly halted.

"Dammit," said Wilder.

Miki looked down. About ten meters remained between them and the ground.

"Meric!" Wilder called up.

When he replied his voice was faint. "Sorry, not sure what's wrong."

"Maybe we could jump the rest of the way?" Miki suggested.

"Are you kidding? One broken leg on the team is more than enough. Meric! Shut the entire system down and start her up again."

The quiet hum of the excavator engine ceased.

Silence.

They had continued to spin. If they didn't reach the ground soon, Miki was sure she would vomit.

Wilder muttered, "And to think Niall wanted to come with us! Can you imagine?"

The hum re-started and, with another jerk, so did their slow plunge into the unknown.

The last few meters passed surprisingly quickly and before she knew it, Miki's feet touched the ground. The ropes continued to spool out and pile onto their heads.

"We made it!" Wilder yelled up. "You can turn it off!"

Miki unfastened her harness and stepped out. "What do I do with this?" She gestured at the empty harness crumpled on the ground.

"Leave it right there. You're going to need it when we get back."

Miki looked at the harness doubtfully.

"You guys okay?" Meric called out.

"Yeah," Wilder replied. "Thanks for your help."

"Remember, if you comm me from outside the Scythian city I'll hear it, but once you're inside you're on your own. Good luck!"

"Thanks! You too. I hope Orson doesn't give you any more problems."

"Don't worry. I've got a handle on him."

The light from Meric's headlamp disappeared. The excavator's lights went out too. The plain and cliff face faintly glowed pale green.

"Cherry came here?" Miki asked.

"Aubriot too."

"What was my dad doing then?"

Wilder's expression turned sorrowful. "Miki, I haven't apologized yet for bringing you to Chimera. I'd completely forgotten your mom died here. If I'd remembered, I would never have agreed—"

Miki touched her arm. "I'd kind of forgotten too. I mean, I thought I couldn't remember it. It wasn't until I saw the place where it must have happened that the memory came back. Don't feel bad. I would rather remember than not. I don't have many memories of Mom."

"In that case, I won't feel so guilty. Are you ready?"

Miki tightened her backpack's straps. "Now I am."

"Then let's see what we can find."

They began the march to the Scythian city's walls.

Miki wondered if she would ever return. And if she couldn't, would she be sad?

24

Despite the many years they'd spent together on the *Sirocco*, Wilder could only remember Cherry talking about her trip to the Scythian city a handful of times, and she hadn't gone into detail. Aubriot had been an even worse source of information. She'd detested the man and only spoke to him when necessary. Had she known she would be coming here one day herself, she would have probed both of them deeply and even ignored her dislike of Aubriot to do it. Now he was dead and Cherry was many light years distant—assuming she was still alive.

Had she done the right thing in bringing Miki along? Her prospects seemed no safer in the city than they had remaining with the hostile Chimerites, and at least there Niall, Zapata, and—to a lesser extent—Maddox could be her defenders. She wasn't at all sure that here, in the metropolis the Scythians had abandoned millennia ago, she was equipped to protect Miki from danger.

One thing Cherry had said that had stuck in her mind was that the aliens, for some unknown reason, employed extremely soft, spongy materials in their constructions. In some places the material was sufficiently soft to allow passage through it with only a little pushing. The purpose for the odd property was unclear, and the discovery that the Scythians' main method of locomotion was aerial didn't shed any light.

Wilder scrutinized the crazy patterning of the city's boundary wall. "There should be a way through this."

"*Through* it?" Miki questioned. "I thought we were looking for a door."

"No. No doors. Cherry was very clear about that."

"I guess because they fly everywhere?"

"I guess so." She poked a swirl darker than the rest. It was soft but it also resisted her touch.

"I saw doors in the domes," Miki remarked.

"You did? Then maybe Cherry was wrong."

"They might have been there for us. For humans."

"Makes sense. This place was built before they even knew humans existed."

"*Oh!*" Miki's arm had disappeared into the wall up to her elbow. "I think I found the way in." She pulled out her arm and examined it.

"Does it hurt?"

"No, and that stuff doesn't cling. My arm's clean."

They regarded the spot she'd pushed through. It had sealed up smoothly.

Miki asked, "It isn't possible there's anything on the other side, right?"

Could the Scythians have entered the city from somewhere else? "Noooo…"

Miki threw Wilder a look, and then thrust herself into the soft area of wall.

"Hey! Wait! I should go first!"

But Miki couldn't hear. Her head had already vanished.

Shit.

The kid was being far too reckless.

She'd gone.

A second later, the wall bulged and then Miki's face appeared. "It's safe. There's nothing here except a huge maze. And it stinks."

"Don't do that again. Next time, *I* go first." Wilder forced her way through to the other side. It *did* stink. Miki's description of the structure that sat in front of them had been accurate. It was a maze, except they stood on top of it. Deep channels ran in all directions, cutting through the ground.

"What the heck is this?" Wilder asked. "Did you see anything like it in the domes?"

"No, but I only went to a few places—cells for prisoners, hatcheries, and the places where I was examined. I didn't see a lot else."

Wilder couldn't remember Cherry mentioning a maze, so she presumed it wasn't important or dangerous. They only needed to figure out a way across it. "This would be a lot easier if we could fly."

"Maybe that's the point." She stepped along the nearest path between two channels.

Already, the air was beginning to feel arid. Wilder's eyes felt itchy and sore and her skin seemed to have had all the moisture sucked out of it. She forestalled stopping for a drink of water as they navigated the maze, however. They needed to get used to the new conditions. They could be here for days. "Is there anything you remember about the Scythians that might be useful?" she asked, halting at the point of a channel.

"Like what kind of thing?"

"Like... Did you notice any weaknesses? We know they can't breathe our atmosphere and they prefer to go out at night. Did you notice anything else that might be a vulnerability, compared to what we can do, I mean?"

"They're stronger and bigger than us," Miki replied gravely. "And they have ready-made weapons at the edges of their wings, while we have to carry our knives and pulse rifles. But...they do have trouble getting around any place they can't fly. The two Scythians who questioned me seemed to be scientists. They were involved in gathering data about humans, and to move around, examine me, and input information into their system, they hung from a contraption attached to the ceiling. So their toes weren't encumbered, you see. I don't think the claws on their wings are particularly dexterous." She touched her cheek pensively.

"Did they..." Wilder hesitated. "Did they hurt you during your interrogation?"

"It was Nina they hurt to make me talk. They nearly suffocated her. But I fought with them before that, and one of them cut me."

"On your cheek?"

Miki nodded.

Wilder peered closer. Though she still wasn't used to the view through the night vision goggles, the definition was good. "I can't see a scar."

"The first one that examined me put something on the cut."

"It did? Why?"

"To stop me from bleeding, I suppose. It wouldn't want all that nasty human blood messing up its workplace."

Wilder smiled. "Whatever they used on you, it was good stuff."

Miki turned, surveying their surroundings. They were roughly half way across the maze. "I can't believe Cherry did this all alone. It's so lonely and dark, and if she fell, she only had one hand to save herself."

"She's a brave woman." Wilder studied the maze. The shortest route to the city became clear. "This way."

"Why did Cherry come here? Was she trying to find out stuff about the Scythians, like us?"

"She was following a Guardian. It had been picked up from the..." She swallowed. She didn't want to remind Miki about her sister's probable death. The *Sirocco* had most likely gone the same path as the *Mistral*. "The Scythians managed to get hold of one of them, and they programmed it to come here and reactivate their planetary defense system. Cherry suspected it was up to no good, so she followed it."

"Did she catch it?"

"Not until after it had done its job. That was why Aubriot had to go in and deactivate the system again."

"So we might find the system too?"

"We might, but Aubriot being Aubriot, he most likely put the entire thing permanently out of action. But there could be things to learn if we can find it."

"You don't know where it is?"

"Not a clue. The Guardian showed Aubriot the way, I think."

Miki seemed to take this news stoically, for no response came from her.

Wilder walked the final paces to the edge of the maze. "We made it!"

Miki joined her, saying somewhat dourly, "The first stage, anyway."

Wilder looked up. Walls of buildings on the city outskirts towered above them, forming a facade. There were no roads into this place. There were entrances, arched, doorless—and far out of reach.

Once upon a time, Scythians had flown to and from the portals, free of their breathing apparatus, while day and night Concordia's sky had curved overhead. What color would it have been while rich in CO_2 and low in oxygen? Then the atmosphere had altered, building in poisonous gases, until finally the decision had been made to enclose the metropolis in a gigantic dome to keep the citizens safe. What a feat of engineering it had been. Eventually, Concordia had become unliveable and the Scythians had built their starships and flown away, off to colonize new worlds.

"Here's a way in," Miki announced, up to her armpit in a wall.

"Stop doing that! I told you, I go first. You don't know what's on the other side."

But Miki was already forcing herself into the Scythian city.

Muttering curses, Wilder followed.

25

Wilder could not imagine how Cherry had managed to travel through this place alone. It was hard enough for two entirely able-bodied people working together. The spongy barriers had seemed to exist only on the outskirts. Once they were past them, all the interior walls were solid and they were forced to use the same openings the Scythians had, only without the benefit of flight. The aliens had also had the option of simply flying higher and out of the ceiling-less rooms.

Fortunately, she'd had sufficient knowledge of what lay ahead to know they had to bring knotted lines and grapples as well as plenty of water. But the weight of the precious fluid made climbing hard. She might have been able to haul herself hand over hand up a rope— mostly due to her lightness rather than upper body strength—but with a pack on her back it was impossible.

Miki was the stronger of the two of them despite being younger. After throwing up a grapple and testing the security of the rope, she would climb up first. Then Wilder would attach a pack to another line and Miki would haul it up. After she lifted the second backpack, Wilder would climb up. Then they would lower themselves into the next room, cross it to the exit, and begin the process again.

Some portals were close to the floor and they could simply throw their packs through and then follow them. If there was a choice of exits they would pick the lowest one. The climbing was their most arduous task, and going out of their way to reach their destination was a small price to pay for an easier ascent.

Strange debris filled several of the rooms they passed, flakes of a dull, dusty substance that gave no indication of what it might once have been. The first time Miki had descended into the debris she'd disappeared over her head and Wilder had quickly jumped in after her, fearing she might not be able to breathe. They'd misjudged the depth of the material, estimating it by comparing it with the placement of the floor in the room they'd just left.

Scrabbling around for Miki in the clouds of dusty wafers, she'd quickly located her and scooped the stuff from in front of her face. Again she'd thought of Cherry, who was about Miki's height, and hadn't had anyone to find her or help her.

On and on they went, deeper into the still, silent city, until Wilder was utterly exhausted. Lying on the floor of another anonymous Scythian room, she was too tired to speak, too tired to think. She'd briefly checked the pathfinder to make sure they hadn't deviated far from their intended course toward the center of the city. Then, she'd taken a deep drink of water, heedless of the necessity of conserving it. She was beyond parched. Her tongue was thick and her head pounded. Any sweat her body produced had been instantly absorbed by the bone-dry air.

"We're stopping here for the night?" Miki asked.

"Can you go any farther?"

"I could manage a little more."

"I can't."

Miki allowed her pack to fall to the floor and dropped down next to it. She took out her water bottle and shook it before taking a careful swig.

"I don't know how you have so much energy," said Wilder. "You've done the majority of the work, lifting up the packs."

"I'm younger than you."

"Are you calling me an old lady?"

Miki chuckled. "I'm going to take off my goggles and see what this place looks like without them."

"I wouldn't if I w—"

She pushed them to the top of her head, checked around her, and swiftly pulled them over her eyes once more.

"Pitch black?" Wilder asked.

"Uh huh," Miki replied tremulously. She tapped the goggles. "How do these work?"

"Echolocation."

"They use echoes?"

"They're constantly sending out sound waves too high pitched for us to hear. When the waves bounce back, the goggles interpret them to create a picture of our surroundings."

"So the picture isn't real?"

"It's as real as the picture your brain creates from the signals it receives from your eyes. More real, in fact. Your brain fills in a lot of what you think you're seeing. The goggles also process the information they receive, just a tiny bit slower."

A pause.

"What happens if they break or run out of power?"

"They won't," Wilder replied, though a shiver coursed through her at the scenario Miki's speculation had painted.

"You know so many things. You're so clever. I wish I was as smart as you."

"Knowledge and intelligence aren't the same, and there are many ways of being clever. Let's eat and get some sleep. We have a long way to go tomorrow."

Checking the water condenser—some had accumulated but it wasn't much, so the condenser was either faulty or the small amount really was all that could be pulled from the arid atmosphere—she reflected that she didn't *feel* clever. She never had. Outside of engineering endeavors she was constantly confused, all at sea about people, about how they thought and felt. Too many times she'd assumed everyone was the same as her only to be caught out again and again.

'Clever' would have been figuring out how to deal with Niall's attitude, and she was hopeless with that. Dragan had tried to give her a clue but his insight hadn't helped. How could she be compassionate toward someone who repeatedly rejected her attempts to show affection? She suspected the problem wasn't with her at all, that Niall was entirely the one to blame for their disastrous relationship. If that were the case, there wasn't anything she could do about it. With a heavy heart, she wished they hadn't parted on bad terms.

As they settled down to sleep, Miki said, "Should I take off my goggles?"

"You'll be more comfortable without them, but put your hand on them so they aren't too hard to find when you wake up."

Wilder took hers off too, and then lay awake, staring into the dark, until long after the sounds of Miki's breathing had become deep and regular.

AT HER FIRST movement as she woke, her arms protested violently. Her legs and stomach muscles were loud with their complaints too. It took her a few moments to remember where she was and why her surroundings were wholly dark. She patted the floor. Her bulky goggles appeared under her hand and as she sat up she put them on.

Miki was gone.

Wilder scanned the bare space. Like all the other rooms in the city it was featureless, its original purpose obscured by the passage of ages.

There was her backpack. The fast beat of Wilder's pulse eased a little.

A grapple gripped in inner ledge of an opening.

Dammit.

"Miki! Miki!"

"Wilder?" Her voice sounded distant. "You're awake? I'll be there in a minute."

Wilder snatched up her water bottle and sucked. Her mouth had felt like it had been scoured by desert sand. She was tempted to squeeze out a scant handful of liquid to wipe her face, but they couldn't afford to waste even a drop. The moisture would disappear within seconds anyway.

Sounds of effort came from the direction of the opening. She walked to it and peered up. "Don't disappear like that. You nearly gave me a heart attack."

Miki didn't answer as she climbed. When she reached the ledge, she peeked over it and said, "You were sound asleep. I didn't want to wake you. I thought I would explore."

"We're all alone in here! What if something happened to you?"

"But it didn't, did it? Besides, I found something cool. Are you ready to go?"

"Ready? I need to eat, and so do you."

Miki climbed down.

Wilder was beginning to find the girl's gung ho behavior alarming and concerning. Since her unauthorized visit to Earth with her sister, Miki had been quieter than normal, as if her experiences had chastened her, but then she'd demanded to come along on the mission to Concordia. And although she'd been subdued in Chimera, her demeanor had done an about-face again after entering the Scythian city.

Wilder stole glances at her as they ate. Something was going on with Miki but she couldn't figure out what. She berated herself for her lack of people skills. If only Kes were here, he might understand what was up with his daughter. Then again, if Kes were here she probably wouldn't behave like this. "Miki, I don't know how to put this gently so I'm just going to come right out and say it: you need to take it easy. Even if we weren't inside the ruins of our enemy's city, this would be a dangerous place to be. If you break a leg, how would I get you out? I would have to go for help and you would be waiting here alone in the dark for who knows how long. And how do you think the Chimerites would take it if some of them had to risk their lives for you? Assuming they would. They don't like us as it is."

"Ugh, okaaaay." Miki drawled like the archetypal surly teenager.

If the situation weren't so serious Wilder might have laughed. "Miki, I'm not kidding around. Do you hear me?"

"I hear you, *Leader Wilder*."

"Good." A memory flashed into her mind. She was at Cherry's house when Cherry had been General of the colony. She'd been confined there 'for her own safety'. She saw herself climbing out the kitchen window and inwardly groaned. If the colony was ever at peace again she would never have children.

Never.

"What was the cool thing you found?"

"Eat up, and I'll show you."

Miki refused to be drawn on the subject over the time it took to finish eating and pack up. As Wilder hauled herself up the rope to exit the room, her muscles screamed. Her hands were raw. How would she ever manage another day like this? How much farther would they go? They'd discovered nothing useful about the Scythians or anything even remotely interesting so far.

She lowered herself down the other side. It felt no easier going down than it had going up. A room similar to all the others confronted her. Miki was already on the other side, tossing up the grapple. Wilder dragged their backpacks across the intervening space while Miki ascended.

When she reached the opening, she leaned down to say conspiratorially, "I think Aubriot's team might have been here."

Wilder squinted up. "That's the big secret?"

Miki chuckled. "Bet you can't guess how I know."

"I bet I can't. And you're not going to tell me, right? You're going to make me climb up there and see for myself."

"Tie on the first backpack," Miki said, grinning.

Wilder frowned as she squatted and grabbed her pack. Miki's mood had improved but she seemed to have gone too far in the opposite direction.

After both packs were hauled up, Wilder climbed after them. As her head rose over the ledge and she got a view of what lay beyond, she sucked in air sharply, which caused her to cough. There was little else she could do except cling on while waiting for the uncontrollable fit to pass.

When she finally caught her breath, Miki was watching her with concern. "Sorry, I should have told you so it wasn't a surprise."

A long passage stretched from left to right, the walls rising high on each side, dotted with openings. As in the rest of the city, the passage had no ceiling and the dome arched high overhead. It was some kind of Scythian thoroughfare, a direct route—for once—leading deep into the city. At one time, it must have been thick with Scythians, flying to and fro.

Yet that was not the most remarkable thing about it. The most astonishing feature, the one that had made Wilder gasp was around two meters up from ground level.

Words had been scratched on the wall next to an arrow pointing left.

THIS WAY, LOSERS.

26

The relief at simply walking rather than endlessly scaling and descending ropes was immeasurable. Even more important, the discovery of the passageway meant they would make faster progress. The time they were spending in the city had become a concern. Their water supply was rapidly dwindling despite their conservative consumption, and the condenser's output was pathetic.

She hurried along with Miki down the passageway. After a hundred or so meters it split, forking to their right and left. Aubriot had helpfully scratched an arrow to indicate the correct direction so they took it without hesitation. Rather than wandering vaguely toward the center of the city they were finally going somewhere.

They were heading for the control room of the Scythian's planetary defenses, no doubt. It seemed as good a destination as any to Wilder. Aubriot might have scuppered the controls but she might learn something from them nevertheless.

"How did Aubriot know which way to go?" Miki asked. "Did he have a map?"

"He had a Guardian guiding him. Then I guess he scratched directions on the way out, after he'd found the control room, in case anyone wanted to follow in his footsteps." It was typical of the obnoxious man to want to leave evidence of his presence to people who might come after, yet it was fortunate for them he had. Otherwise, they might have wandered uselessly until it was time to return, empty-handed, to Chimera.

The new 'road' stretched into the distance, but they hadn't gone far before they encountered another arrow, this time pointing upward. Aubriot had helpfully scratched another instruction: *UP AGAIN, WANNABES.*

Above, the widest, tallest, and highest portal they'd seen yet, opened in the expanse of wall. Climbing up to it would have been easy for the dead Earthman. He'd been powerfully built. For Wilder, the prospect was daunting. She developed somewhat of a technique over the previous day, employing the traction of flexible soles of her boots on the walls while hauling herself hand over hand, but she was most definitely unsuited to the task. The discovery of straight passages through the city had given her a ray of hope that the regular climbs were over.

"You can do it," said Miki, apparently reading her crestfallen expression.

"Maybe, but can you throw a grapple up there?"

It took Miki three tries but she managed it. She also managed the climb without pausing, though, agile as she was, even she was panting by the time she reached the top. She immediately turned and dropped a second rope to pull up the backpacks.

Then it was Wilder's turn. As she climbed, mentally forcing away the protestations of her exhausted body, she reminded herself that Cherry had done this with only one arm. Or perhaps she hadn't made it this far. Aubriot had completed the task for her, or something like that.

Miki's encouraging face grew slowly closer. Wilder concentrated on moving just one hand, then just one leg. The other hand. The other leg. On and on. She did not look down. She dared not.

Damn the Scythians and their wings.

Why, of all the possible enemies of humanity, did we have to have one that could fly?

The ledge was within reach.

She swung a sweaty hand at it—and missed.

Miki squeaked.

Her body slapped into the wall. She was dangling by one arm, her entire body weight pulling on one hand. She was not a heavy person. Why did she seem to weigh so much?

Her arm felt as though it was being wrenched from its socket. The ground seemed very far below.

"Give me your other hand!" Miki exclaimed, leaning precariously far out from the ledge. "Give it to me!"

She tried. She threw her free hand upward, but Miki couldn't reach it.

She'd been too hasty. She should have climbed a little higher before going for the ledge.

"Move back," she commanded, "or you'll fall."

Miki shuffled marginally backward. At the same time, Wilder grabbed the rope with her second hand and put the toes of her right boot against the wall. She hung there for several moments, catching her breath. It was time to live by her own advice. *Take it easy*.

Just one hand. Just one leg.

Miki moved closer, ready to help her.

"Stay away. I don't want to pull you down. I can do it myself."

Another hand. Another leg.

The ledge was within easy reach. She climbed onto it.

"I knew you could do it," said Miki.

Wilder waited for her panting to subside before replying, "You're a good big sister."

Instantly, Miki's features clouded and she looked like she might cry.

"Shit, I'm so sorry." Wilder reached out to touch her shoulder.

"It's okay." Miki sniffed and turned, saying, "Look!"

Beyond the large portal was the biggest space they'd ever seen inside the city. Fifty or more meters square, it was adorned with long, thick poles. Many had fallen and crumbled, but some remained in their original settings, protruding from the vertical sides. At one time, even thicker poles must have stood at intervals across the floor, smaller counterparts sticking out of them.

"Oh!" Miki exclaimed, and clapped a hand over her mouth. Giggling, she added, "They're perches."

She was right. In Concordia's deep past, this had been a gathering place for hundreds of Scythians, perhaps some kind of council or parliament. Wilder estimated they were near the center of the city, so it made sense—from a human perspective.

Aubriot had not left instructions for the next part of the journey. It was obvious. Directly opposite stood a wide opening that ran from floor to the top of the wall.

Her immediate reaction on seeing it was delight. "Thank the stars we don't have to climb in there."

They did, however, have to descend from their current position.

WILDER DRAGGED herself across the remaining distance to the opening, walking around any obstacles too large to step over. Her backpack felt like a lead weight, even though they'd drunk most of its original contents. If she hadn't been deathly curious about what lay before them, she might have called a halt so she could rest a while.

The ghostly vision of her night goggles revealed sectional spaces separated by waist-high barriers. Something was odd. She looked up.

Ceilings!

They were rutted, criss-crossed by grooves, and fractured. Some had entirely collapsed, but they were unmistakable.

"Is this like what you saw inside the domes?" she asked.

Miki drew her gaze from the horizontal surfaces overhead. "The ones in the domes were made from a flexible material. Not like these."

"They must be the original type and the Scythians invented a more versatile version later."

They followed the scratched directions.

Thanks, Aubriot.

In this place the aliens must have walked, easily surmounting the low divisions between rooms. Broken-off pedestals marked the spots controls may have sat. One area was open to the dome. An exit point? In another large section, shards of poles littered the floor.

Scrawled across the floor in front of one short barrier no different from the rest was the word *BULLSEYE*.

"What's bullseye?" Miki asked.

"No idea, but I think it means we've reached the control room."

They stepped over the wall.

Judging from the room's appearance, she was right. A massive pole stuck up from the floor, thrust deep within a square hole. She stepped closer. Beneath the floor was a mess of destroyed wiring and boards. They were not rusted or decayed, only crushed and broken by the operation of the pole. It was a miracle they'd survived so long. The chamber must have been sealed when the Scythians departed.

"Are these the defense system controls?" Miki asked.

Wilder nodded thoughtfully. "The compromised Guardian must have opened this up, fixed whatever had failed, and restarted the system. It fired once, just before Aubriot arrived. Then he put it out of action." She winced. The Scythian planetary defenses had destroyed the *Opportunity*. If she hadn't already transferred to the Immani vessel she wouldn't be here now.

"Where are the armaments?" asked Miki. "I thought they would be nearby."

"We never found them. We had plenty else to do rebuilding after the attacks. They're probably somewhere on Suddene or perhaps under the ocean."

Miki knelt down and leaned over the hole. "Can you learn anything from *that*?"

Wilder didn't answer. As she'd expected, Aubriot had done a number on the Scythians' system. That man had never done anything by halves. He hadn't only put the system out of action, he'd annihilated it beyond rejigging or soldering it back to functionality. There would be no reverse engineering it.

She sank to the floor next to Miki.

"Is it bad?"

Resting her elbow on her knee and her forehead in the palm of her hand, she replied, "I don't know why I ever thought it would do any good to come here. We've trekked through half the city, climbed and descended hundreds of meters in total using those damned ropes, slept in pitch darkness, been parched with thirst... And for what? We're no better off than when we left Chimera. We haven't learned a single thing about the Scythians that we didn't already know."

Silence stretched out in that silent place.

"What do we do now?" asked Miki.

Wilder was too sunk in depression to answer. How could they force the Scythians to leave Concordia when the aliens had the upper hand—or wing—in every way? Humanity was on its knees and there was nothing to be done about it. And now the Scythians seemed to be moving to phase two of re-establishing their presence on the planet, removing the need for humans slaves entirely.

"Wilder?"

She groaned and sunk her head into her hands. "I don't know."

After a short while she heard Miki get to her feet and walk away.

Still, she didn't move. Should they go farther into the city? There seemed little point, and already she doubted they had sufficient water to make it back to Chimera while enduring extreme thirst. Worse, even with enough water she wasn't sure she could make it. She was bone-weary. If she held her hands in front of her they trembled. With a day or two to recover she might be okay, but they didn't have an extra day's water.

It was a horrible predicament. Although she'd thought of a potential solution she hesitated to voice it. She doubted Miki would either agree or have the fortitude to see it through.

"Urghhh!" Miki exclaimed. "What's this?"

Wilder looked up.

Miki was stooping. When she straightened up she was holding an object at arm's length by the tips of her fingers. The object was ovoid, partially burned and...had tufts sticking out of it. Miki had gripped the thin strands.

"Bring it here."

"I'd rather put it down again. It's disgusting."

"Miki..." An idea was forming but she couldn't figure out the ramifications. It might be something amazing or nothing at all. "I think I know what it is."

Miki walked over, holding the thing in front of her as if fearing contamination. "I think it has an *eye*?!"

"No kidding." So she was right.

Miki dropped the thing in her lap. It landed with a thump, its weight belying its size.

Looking up at Wilder with a frozen, one-eyed gaze was a Guardian's head.

27

Wilder said it was the head of a Guardian, the one that had led Aubriot to the control room. *A head*? Miki looked more closely. There were the remains of its hair, the partial mouth, and the eye she'd noticed a moment ago. Wilder was right. It was a head. The thing had been smashed up then burned, or burned then smashed up.

She shuddered. Did Guardians feel pain? No one had ever mentioned it. She'd seen one on Earth, called Strongquist. If she hadn't been told he was an android she would never have guessed. He hadn't only appeared to be completely human, he'd also seemed nice.

Wilder was turning the horrible object over in her hands.

"What's it doing here?"

"I don't know. Cherry never mentioned what had happened to the Guardian that showed Aubriot the way through the city. I'd assumed it had been destroyed, by her order. She hated the Guardians."

"Uhh, it *is* destroyed, isn't it? That's only its head."

"Guardians aren't animals. Decapitating them wouldn't necessarily put them out of action. Though this one is certainly not working."

"Did the power run out?"

"Maybe, or the head doesn't have its own supply, so when it was separated from the body..."

Miki scanned the room. "I can't see the body anywhere."

Wilder smiled. "This thing was *sawn* off. It would take more time than we have to fix the damage and rejoin it to the body, and I don't have the tools anyway."

"How long *do* we have?"

"I'm not sure, but we can't stay here much longer. We don't have a lot of water left."

"Sooo...this is it? This is our big find in the Scythian city?"

"This..." Wilder put the head down, balancing it on its neck "...is it."

The head toppled to the side and rolled to a stop.

"You know," Miki said, "of all the things we might have found, I never imagined it would be that."

"You're telling me."

"Can we do anything with it?"

"It's a long shot, but maybe. Let's get out of here. We aren't going to find anything else in this hellhole."

"I preferred the desert."

"Me too." Wilder opened her pack and picked up the head.

"I'll carry it."

Wilder hesitated but then passed it over.

It was a sign of her weakened state. Ordinarily, Wilder would have refused to allow her to take the greater burden. She was that kind of person, and she'd been a kind of proxy Mom for a while. But her face before she woke up this morning had shown lines of exhaustion, and she'd moved more slowly and with greater effort all day. Wilder had little muscle or fat on her. Physically, she was unsuited to feats of endurance, and she was quite old. She had to be in her mid-thirties.

Miki stowed the head and shouldered her pack. She took a drink of water before they set off for home. Or rather, not home, but Chimera, where they were generally disliked.

THEY FOLLOWED Aubriot's directions in reverse order, returning to the main thoroughfare. Instead of climbing up to the opening where they'd entered it, they continued along it to its end. Aubriot had thought up several more taunts for the later generations he'd imagined might follow him. *SUCKERS, HAS-BEENS*—Wilder pointed out that they couldn't be both *WANNABES* **and** *HAS-BEENS*—and *ALSO-RANS* were the politer insults, if there was any such thing. Then the arrows directing them along the passageway ceased.

At first, they thought it was only that Aubriot had run out of put-downs or had grown bored with the exercise. The passageway continued onward, straight as an arrow, so they followed it. Their goggles only revealed open space up ahead, and though the route might be a longer way to return to Chimera, it was infinitely easier.

Miki was happy for Wilder more than she was for herself. She hadn't been sure she would ever leave the city and she'd made her peace with the prospect. But Wilder had people to live for. She had some kind of complicated thing going on with Niall. And if anyone was going to free Concordia of the Scythians it was her. But if they had to return the same way they'd come, she wasn't sure Wilder could do it.

They'd been walking in silence for a while. Even talking dried out your throat here. They'd kept the same, medium pace but Wilder softly panted. As Miki was about to suggest they stop for a drink, she reached behind her for her water bottle, taking her gaze from the road ahead.

"Miki!" Wilder grabbed her arm and pulled her so sharply backward she stumbled and fell on her backside.

"Why did you do that?!"

"Look!"

Wilder was no longer looking ahead but downward. Straight down. "Don't come too close."

Miki crawled forward.

The passageway abruptly ended. The walls continued the same as before, but the floor disappeared into empty space. On each side the walls descended deeper than they rose to the dome above. She couldn't see their end.

She wasn't sure how they'd come so close to tumbling to their deaths. Perhaps they'd been too lost in their thoughts to pay attention, or maybe the walls created an optical illusion from afar. The vision from their goggles might also have confused them.

This was not the way out. No wonder Aubriot's scratchings didn't direct people here.

"We must have missed something," Wilder said. "We have to retrace our steps."

They turned back.

A hundred meters or so along the path they hit an arrow they'd missed. It pointed upward.

SOZ NUMPTIES

Wilder tilted her head to gaze at the opening above, her dismay almost palpable.

"It's okay," Miki said. "You can do it."

Wilder gave her a sorrowful look and nodded. "You first."

28

Wilder woke. The first thing she did was check for Miki. This time, the girl was sitting right beside her, cross-legged and frowning.

"What's wrong?" The words came out as a croak.

"Have some water." Miki held up her water bottle to her lips.

She turned her head. "I don't need it."

"You do." Miki added accusingly, "You've been drinking less water than me, haven't you. All yesterday, as we were coming back from the control room, you didn't drink anything. It took me a while to realize. I thought about it overnight, and I don't remember seeing you drink once. Not even after we stopped for the night."

"I can manage until—"

"You can't. You're worse off than me. Now drink."

Chastened, she took a sip. The liquid felt like nectar in her mouth and throat. It was all she could do to stop herself from gulping it all down. "Did the condenser make much?"

Miki picked it up and shook it. There was perhaps fifty mil in it. "This thing's a piece of shit."

"We only have a day's march. If we can just make it back to the exit to Chimera, we'll be okay."

"A day's *climbing*," Miki corrected.

The fact settled heavily in the pit of Wilder's stomach. "Yeah, climbing."

Aubriot's route was some way off the one they'd taken on their way in. Theoretically, considering his had been created according to the advice of the Guardian, who had insider knowledge from the Scythians, it should be the most direct. Yet, if it were the most direct, it was not the easiest. The aliens would have flown it, and the android would not have felt fatigued by all the ascents and descents. If anything, their new way out had proven harder than their entry route.

The aches and pains she'd felt on previous days were nothing compared to how she felt now. Even her head throbbed. They were probably only a day's journey from Chimera, but it felt like the other side of the galaxy.

She had to do it.

She sat up and instantly lifted a hand to her head, as if pressing it might take the pain away.

"Drink some more," Miki urged.

"No, you need—"

"Drink."

She took another welcome sip but couldn't help eyeing the container. There was perhaps a liter in it. In other circumstances this wouldn't have been a problem, but her experience of the city was that it sucked moisture like a hull breach sucked air.

"Let's go." Miki rose to her feet. "The sooner we're out of this nightmare the better. And we have a prize to bring back." She lifted her pack, which contained the Guardian's head.

What an odd find it had been. It might be a treasure trove of information if they could get it working and delve the secrets of its electronic mind. But first they had to get it back to Chimera.

She also stood up, though shakily.

Miki threw a grapple at the nearest opening high on the wall and hauled herself up the rope.

Another day within the Scythian city had begun.

THREE HOURS LATER, Wilder was done. Her hands shook and refused to grip. Her arms, legs, and stomach were balls of fire. Her mouth was as dry as the ancient dusty flakes littering the city.

Her water was almost gone. Back in the desert, Niall had said if your water supplies were low it was still better to drink when you needed it. Otherwise dehydration would make you confused and cloud your judgment. But what were you supposed to do when your water ran out?

Miki stood at the base of a wall, watching her and waiting. "Just one more, Wilder. You can do it."

She'd said *Just one more* before the last five ascents.

"I can't." Wilder walked to the edge of the room and slumped to the floor. It was hard to talk when your mouth had zero moisture. "I'm sorry, but I really can't. You go on ahead. Take the pathfinder in case you miss one of Aubriot's arrows. I'll wait here."

"I'm not going without you."

"Unless you can fit me in one of the backpacks, you don't have a choice."

"But by the time I get to Chimera and send someone to find you, you could die of thirst."

"If you don't leave now, *you'll* die of thirst. I'll be fine as long as I don't have to climb that damned rope one more time. If I'm not exercising I won't sweat as much." She had actually stopped sweating as far as she could tell.

It took more arguing than they had time for, but eventually she persuaded a very reluctant Miki to leave.

She pressed the condenser into Wilder's hands, "Promise me you'll still be alive when I get back," she choked. "Promise me."

"I promise."

Wilder rested the back of her head against the wall as she watched Miki climb the rope. She was so brave for someone so young. And it hurt like hell to force her to navigate the remainder of the Scythian city alone. Miki had lost her mother, her father, and maybe her sister too.

Turning onto her side to rest, Wilder vowed that she would not die and be the last of Miki's friends to desert her. She would keep her promise. She would remain alive if it killed her. She smiled grimly before slipping into exhausted unconsciousness.

When she woke, everything was dark.

Her dreadful thirst hit her and she remembered where she was.

Reaching out, she patted the floor for her goggles, She patted a wide circle, getting onto her hands and knees and crawling around.

Shit!

Where could they have gone?

There was nothing and no one else here. Hopefully, Miki would be reaching the city's outskirts by now. She might even have made it to Chimera and a rescue team was on its way. Miki would definitely not have snuck back and taken her goggles while she was asleep.

They had to be here somewhere. She crawled until she hit a wall, wincing at the pain from her blistered, raw hands. Then she crawled along it until she came up against a corner. She would search the room methodically, end to end and side to side. It was possible she might have moved in her sleep, disturbed by her predicament, and pushed the goggles far from her.

Rationality niggled at the back of her mind.

You couldn't have moved them that *far. You should have been able to find them easily.*

Desperation forced her to ignore the logical conclusions, and she began her search. Crawling painfully up and down the room, she swept it with groping hands. Keeping to a straight line was impossible now she couldn't see anything, and she arrived at the opposing walls at odd angles. Nevertheless, she completed the task fairly confident she'd covered all the floor space. The chances of missing her goggles were slim.

They simply weren't here.

She crouched into the opposite corner from where she'd started. Her thirst was a nail being hammered into her head. It was sandpaper scouring her throat. And now, somehow, her goggles were gone too.

She sank her face into her hands—and felt her goggles!

She'd been wearing them all this time. Dehydration was muddling her mind.

She slipped the goggles off, shook them, and tapped them. Feeling out the lenses by touch, she peered through them.

Darkness.

They were broken or had run out of power, as Miki had feared they might. How old were they? Maybe they dated back to the time before the departure of the *Sirocco* or even the biocide attack. Manufacturing in the colony had been devastated back then and had probably never recovered before the Scythians returned.

Even sitting up was too tiring. She lay on her back and stared up sightlessly.

"Wait! Just a couple of days." Niall had said.

"I told you, we can't."

"Can't or don't want to? You're just playing the hero again. It's always been the same, right back to when you invented the a-grav. You had to be the center of attention."

"That's not true. You know it isn't. Why are you doing this? Why are you always so mean to me?"

Niall's anger fell away. "I don't know. I'm sorry."

"Sorry isn't enough. I'm sick of your hostility and I'm sick of you. I try to be nice to you over and over again, and over and over again you push me away. I'm not trying anymore. We're done."

She had left him then, not looking back as she stalked away from his hospital bed. She hadn't seen his expression, hadn't taken a last look at him. He'd offered the opportunity to at least part on good terms and she'd scorned it, flung it back at him, just as he'd thrown her gestures of affection back at her. Only Niall had good reasons for being the way he was. What excuses did she have?

She lay in the dark silence for what seemed to be hours, though she had no way to track time. With no other living thing for kilometers around, she felt utterly alone.

Then the hallucinations began. There was the drip of water somewhere far distant. Impossible. Colors swam in her vision. *Things* touched her. Creatures scrabbled across the floor. Sluglimpets were coming to get her. They always attacked at night, and here the night was endless.

29

When Miki reached the comm station at the base of the cliff on the edge of Chimera, she couldn't speak. She opened a channel but couldn't say a word. At the other end, Meric said, "Hello? Hello? Who's this?"

There seemed to be nothing to tell him who was comming him.

"Is that you, Wilder? Are you back?"

"No, it's Miki," she said, but no words came out. It was as if the dust in the city had clogged her vocal cords. "It's me, Miki," she said voicelessly.

In frustration, she tapped the device.

"Is someone there?"

Yes!

She tapped again, forcefully. Then she picked up two rocks and smashed them together. Anything to make a noise.

"Huh, odd," Meric muttered to himself. Then the comm cut out.

She opened the channel again. *Meric, listen to me! I made it back, but Wilder needs your help.*

He took a minute to answer. "Wilder, if that's you, I'm on my way. If this is a prank, whoever you are, you're in serious trouble for wasting the Leader's time."

Miki sank to her knees.

A few minutes later, the beam from a flashlight shone down. She looked up, squinting, and waved.

"Only one of you?" Meric called. "Who is it? Where's the other one?"

How to explain without the use of her voice? All Miki could do was step into the harness and fasten it as a signal she wanted to be pulled up.

The hum of the excavator's engine started, and it was like the most wonderful music she'd ever heard. Now if they could only reach Wilder in time, everything would be okay. She drew level with the upper surface. Meric halted the excavator's tunneling spike, climbed down from the cab, and reached out for her. Swinging her to safety, he asked, "Miki? Why have you come back alone? Is Wilder injured?"

She gestured at her throat and shook her head.

"You hurt your throat and that's why you can't speak?"

She mouthed the word *water*.

"Ah, of course. I was forgetting how dry it is in there. Come with me. Can you walk?"

Niall had left the medical center. As she was brought in she looked for him, but his bed was empty. So was Zapata's. The first thing she'd said after Meric had given her water was that Wilder was still alive and she had to go back and bring her out. But he'd told her he would send in a rescue team, and that she was in no fit state to be going anywhere.

So here she was. The medic had inserted a tube into her arm to give her fluids. He was examining her hands when Niall burst in, wild-eyed.

"Where is she, Miki? Where's Wilder?"

"I'm sorry. She made me leave. I didn't want to abandon her, but she couldn't go any farther."

"I understand. I know you wouldn't leave her alone if you could help it. But do you know where she is?"

"I gave Meric the pathfinder. I marked the position I lef—"

He was gone.

The medic gave her something to help her sleep. As she was drifting off, she imagined Wilder all alone in the Scythian city. It was a horrible place, the most awful place she'd ever been. Even the interior of one of their domes was preferable. At least there you had the company of others. You had food and water, light and noise. Journeying through the ancient metropolis was like being in hell, the punishment being the requirement to climb and descend ropes, no matter how tired or thirsty you were. She could not have conceived a better place to put people sentenced for terrible crimes.

What would she do if Wilder hadn't survived? How could she live with herself knowing she'd left her there to die alone? She'd abandoned Nina, and now she'd abandoned Wilder too. How was she supposed to go on, those actions weighing her down the rest of her life?

She awoke, and the first thing she did was to check the nearby beds. They were all empty. Wilder had not been brought back yet, or she had and she was...

She swallowed and tears rolled from her eyes onto her pillow.

How long had she slept? If it was only a few hours it was too soon for the rescue team to have returned. She wasn't sure how long it had taken her to complete the remainder of the journey to the city's edge on her own but it had been a long time. And then she'd had to navigate the maze.

But if she'd been asleep a long time perhaps the team was already back. She listened. When she'd been in the medical center before it had been possible to roughly tell the time of day by the noises from the street. It had been the quiet time when she'd returned, when most Chimerites were asleep. The outside remained quiet. She must have only slept a short while.

Her hands were swaddled in dressings. Gingerly, she pushed herself up with her elbows until she was partially sitting up. How to find out if there was any news? She pressed the button next to her bed with the tip of her least-sore finger.

Several minutes later no one had arrived. She pressed it again with the same result.

"Hello!" she called out. "Is anyone there?"

Again, there was no answer. She would have to get out of bed and find someone. She pushed down her covers and swung her legs out. They, too, had dressings on them, at her knees and feet where she'd gripped the rope. Moving had made her woozy, so she waited for the dizziness to subside. When she felt a little better, she eased herself off the bed and balanced precariously on her bare feet.

Maybe this wasn't such a good idea.

"Hello! Can someone help me?"

Where were all the medics?

A sudden horror struck her. Had the Scythians discovered Chimera? Was there currently a battle being fought for the site? Was that why the clinic's staff was absent?

"*Hello*?"

A flurry of noise and movement came from directly outside the room. She walked, wobbling, to the door and pulled it open.

The passageway was full of medics. Niall ran in, carrying Wilder in his arms. Her head lolled and her eyes were closed. Her skin was deathly pale. She looked more dreadfully thin than ever. Miki lifted her hand to her mouth.

He spotted her standing in the doorway. "She's alive, Miki. She's still alive."

30

The supply trucks were ready to return to Lyonesse. They would be traveling in the second one, in the center of the convoy. There were no creature comforts in the back of the vehicle, not even a cushion. However, they would be given food and water for the journey, Meric had reassured them. His expression had been sad when he'd announced his 'decision'. It was clear it was not his decision at all. He'd bowed to pressure from Orson and the general opinion the commander had whipped up.

"It's not so bad," said Zapata, patting Miki's shoulder. "It doesn't make any sense for us to stay in Chimera. What good can we do here, skulking with the other cowards in their hideaway?"

The sharp intakes of breath and the glowering of Orson as they waited to board the truck showed his comment had hit home, as no doubt he'd intended.

The commander stepped forward. "There are no cowards here, only loyal Concordians. You should count yourselves lucky you're getting out alive. If I had my way this truck would be carrying out your corpses to be dumped at sea, like the rest of the spies." He swiveled to Meric, who also stood with them, waiting for the supplies to arrive. "You realize we could be playing right into the hands of the

Scythians? If these people are who I think they are, we're sending them right back to their masters with all the information they came here for—the fact Chimera exists, how many people are living here, how we're supplied—everything except our damned location, and that's only because my men blindfolded them before bringing them in. You even let them go into the Scythian city to do who knows what."

"They're not from Lyonesse," Meric replied patiently. "They're from—"

"Yeah, you told me. A starship that flew out of the past. If they're from the *Sirocco* where is it? How did they get here? Did they float down from orbit?"

"That's all been explained to my satisfaction, as well as details about the ship, their journey, and Earth no one else could know."

"Information you're unable to verify, that could easily be made up."

"Robert, if you would just listen, there's still time to call this off."

Orson glared at Miki and the others. "And there's still time to put an end to the doubt once and for all, and avoid risking the lives of everyone in Chimera based on outlandish lies."

People arrived carrying the backpacks, now full.

"I think we'd better get on the truck," said Niall quietly.

Miki silently agreed. Things might turn nasty. Deadly, in fact, if Orson got his way.

Niall took the backpacks and slung them into the truck. Niall held out a hand to help Miki up. When she was inside, she pushed the backpacks to the front while the others climbed in. Wilder's weakness from her ordeal still showed, and Maddox winced as she made the effort. Her ribs were still healing. Getting Zapata aboard was even more of an exercise. His broken leg remained encased in a tough cast and he had to use a crutch to walk.

Meric moved to the end of the truck and peered in. "I'm sorry about this. If there were any other way…"

"It's fine," Niall replied tightly. "We appreciate everything you've done."

"Tensions are high, you see, after Scythians were spotted flying directly above us. People are scared, and when they're scared it makes them less hospitable."

"Don't apologize," said Wilder. "Zapata was right. Not about you being cowards, I mean. But that we need to go to Lyonesse if we're going to do any good in the fight."

Meric seemed to accept her point. "Your weapons will be returned to you when you arrive at your destination."

"Where exactly are we going?" Niall asked.

Meric glanced at Orson. "I can't tell you, but it's within inhabited regions."

Wilder said, "There has to be a Resistance organization operating over there, who supply Chimera. Are you sending us to them?"

"I'm afraid not."

"Compromising Chimera's security isn't enough for you, huh?" Orson barked. "You think we'll let you infiltrate the Resistance too?"

"Leave it!" Meric warned. He nodded to the three men who had brought their packs. "Guards are coming with you, and you'll be blindfolded for the duration of the journey."

"Fantastic," said Maddox. "I guess now's a bad time to tell everyone I get motion sickness?" As the men climbed into the back of the truck, she added, "Hope you guys don't mind vomit on your boots."

BLINDFOLDED, sitting in a corner of the truck, Miki tried to figure out what to do next. She was to blame for them being evicted from Chimera and sent to Lyonesse, which was infested with Scythians. If she hadn't stupidly wandered to the top of the exit tunnel just as the supplies were arriving, if she hadn't allowed herself to be spotted by the commander, the Chimerites might have allowed them to stay. She'd put her friends' lives in danger, and she didn't know how to make it up to them.

The truck ride was smooth as it traveled upward. Wilder and Niall were talking but too quietly for her to hear. They were probably discussing the Guardian's head. They still seemed to hold out hope they could get it working, and that it would reveal useful information about the Scythians. But Niall had fiddled with it for a couple of days already, and Wilder had worked with him as soon as she was well enough to sit up. Nothing they'd tried had activated it, and they'd complained they didn't have the equipment to access its drive. So where was their optimism coming from? It had to be because they were desperate. They were ready to believe in anything that might mean the mission wasn't how it was—an absolute disaster.

Faint words were exchanged outside the truck. A rumbling started up and the vehicle's movement evened out. She could sit straight and didn't have to press her hand on the floor to remain upright. They had to be out of the tunnel and on the surface.

As the journey progressed and she tried to think up the best thing for her to do when they arrived in Lyonesse, the truck's interior grew warm. Despite the camouflage netting, Suddene's hot sun was reaching them, beating down. She grew warm, too, and lay on her side.

Maddox demanded water. At first, the guards refused, one of them announcing there would be a stop for water and food before the sea crossing. But Maddox argued, and whined, and argued some more. Eventually, they gave in.

"Do you want some, Miki?" Zapata asked, nudging her foot.

"No, I'm good."

Maddox did throw up, as she'd warned. They didn't stop the truck for her when she said she felt sick, but led her to the end and made her vomit in the road. That did *not* improve her temper, but Miki was way beyond caring. She zoned the woman out and concentrated on her own problems.

Some time later, the truck slowed to a stop and the engine was turned off. They were made to get out, still blindfolded, their wrists were bound, and they were marched a short distance. Miki could hear waves. They were forced into the water. She was in up to her hips, the waves splashing up to her shoulders, before their wrists were untied and they had to climb into a small boat.

"This is fucking ridiculous!" Maddox exclaimed. "Are you hoping

we'll drown? Is that the idea? So you won't have the deaths of innocent Concordians on your conscience?"

She was ignored.

The trip to the larger boat took a few minutes. Ropes were tied
under their arms, and they were hauled aboard and deposited on the
deck.

"Surely we don't need to wear blindfolds now?" Maddox
complained. "What are we going to see? A whole lot of water?"

A voice growled, "The first one of you who takes off their blind-
fold goes over the side. Got it?"

No one answered.

They were given water and food as the ship got underway. The
voyage didn't register heavily on Miki. She noticed Niall, Wilder, and
Zapata talking softly, and Maddox threw up again. She felt nauseated
too but managed to hold it in.

Hours later, the steps of their arrival on the vessel were reversed,
and they were deposited on a beach. Their wrists were rebound and
they were forced up the sand. Miki's feet hit something different. A
shock of recognition passed through her. She was walking on a
rubbery groundcover plant. The sensation felt deeply familiar. She
must have walked on it many times as a small child, though she didn't
remember it. The plant was probably destroyed by the biocide. But
now, decades later, it was back.

A hand grasped her shoulder and pushed her to her knees.

"Wait here," a voice said.

Footsteps tramped away. There came the sound of bodies pushing
through vegetation, then silence.

After several minutes, Zapata asked, "Are they gone?"

"I don't think they're coming back," said Wilder. "They want us to
delay freeing ourselves until they're out of sight." There was the
sound of movement. "They're gone."

Taking off their blindfolds was the easy part. Their wrists were
secured behind their backs, and untying the knots proved much
harder. They had to work by feel alone, sitting back to back. As soon
as Niall was free, however, he quickly untied everyone else.

They were sitting on the groundcover Miki faintly remembered, surrounded by spiny shrubs. They were not far from the ocean—the sound of the waves hitting the shore was clear. Having no desire to alert the Chimerites to their unbound state, they remained where they were for a while longer, giving their captors plenty of time to leave.

While they waited, Niall and Wilder searched the surrounding scrub, keeping low, but came up empty-handed. When they were confident the Chimerites must be gone, they searched more widely. They were in a sandy cove, high cliffs on each side. The water was empty. The larger vessel must have anchored out of view.

At the place where the beach met the vegetation lay five pulse guns.

Niall stooped, picked one up, and checked it. "Fully charged."

"We have supplies too," said Wilder. "Things could be worse."

"Speak for yourself," Maddox said. "My ribs are killing me."

Niall stowed his weapon. "Meric said we would be dropped in an inhabited region. We need to find people who can introduce us to the Resistance. Then we can start to turn things in the colony's favor."

"Have you lost your mind?" Maddox asked. "Concordia has had it. The best we can do is not be killed or taken as slaves by Scythians. This mission was doomed from the start."

"Thanks," said Wilder. "We can always rely on you to cheer us up."

"I'm just saying it how it is. There's no point in sugar-coating it."

"And how does that help? If you can't think of anything positive to say, keep your mouth shut."

"Who made you Leader?"

"Shut up!" Niall ordered. "Both of you. We aren't going to get anywhere if we're constantly at each other's throats. Let's walk inland and see if we can figure out where we are."

Miki didn't recognize this place but she didn't expect to. Her memories of Concordia were hazy at best. It didn't really matter where they were anyway. Her mind was made up about what she had to do.

31

Wilder climbed with Niall to an area of high ground while the others waited in a hollow at the bottom. They'd marched a kilometer or so inland along a thin, overgrown trail between low hills. Though Meric had assured them they would be dropped in an inhabited region, they hadn't come across any human dwellings or Scythian domes. That wasn't so surprising. Concordia had always been sparsely populated compared to Earth, even during its most peaceful and productive period. Vast tracts of wilderness on Lyonesse had barely been explored, let alone settled.

They seemed to be in an area of the coastline north of Oceanside. The southern region was fairly arid, but here the few types of vegetation that had recovered from the biocide grew thick and lush. A type of short-stemmed, supple, tough groundcover plant that Wilder remembered from her days at Sidhe flourished, and the spiny shrubs they'd encountered near the beach proliferated over most of the terrain. The latter's presence made progress difficult, snagging on clothes, backpacks, and skin as they were forced to push past it.

It was horrible stuff, yet its presence and vitality lifted her heart. Life was returning to her country despite all the onslaughts it had suffered. Hope remained, no matter what pessimists like Maddox thought.

Niall stooped and put a hand on her shoulder. She followed his suggestion and crouched low as they moved higher. They were nearing the top of the rise, where the shrubs grew more sparsely and provided little cover. The wind blew stronger. As they drew closer to the top the shrubs disappeared, leaving only dirt, rocks, and patches of thin groundcover. They crouched lower until they were crawling on their bellies.

A gentler sun than Suddene's was high in the sky, peeking out between scudding clouds, but this would not stop the Scythians from patrolling, as they'd discovered. For the moment, the skies were clear.

They were moving along flat ground, and the land beyond slowly came into view. At first, Wilder thought they were looking at the shore and they'd turned back on themselves, but then she spotted a thin line marking a farther shore.

A vast estuary spread out before them, dotted with sand banks and water of varying colors according to its depth. In some places it was deep blue, where it had cut a channel through the bed and the river ran fast. In others it was pale and festooned with green seaweed.

She checked to her right. A mountain range rose high, its peaks dusted with snow. Before reaching the range the water narrowed to a wide river. "I know where we are. This is the mouth of the Vimur."

Ethan had famously first encountered the Fila on the other side of the range, caught and trapped by them in an underwater chamber while they investigated this strange new species that seemed to have suddenly appeared on Concordia.

"You're right," Niall said. "Has to be. But...shit. Look over there."

A little farther inland, on the nearside banks of the estuary, stood three Scythian domes, equidistant from each other. The tops were closed and no aliens appeared to be circling, but this was clearly hostile territory. Then again, as they understood it, so was most of Lyonesse.

"I'd hoped they hadn't come this far north," said Wilder.

"They've been here a long time. They will be wherever people are and, from memory, this place had been settled a while before the biocide attack."

Wilder thought back to the Concordia she remembered from before the Scythians returned. "You're right. There was the beginnings of a tourist industry. People came here to swim, sail boats, and play with the Fila. It was easier in the shallow water."

Near the domes was a patchwork of fields. As they'd seen in the images recorded from the *Sirocco*, crops were being grown, presumably for human and alien consumption. Concordians would be the farmers, though none were visible.

"I can see buildings," Niall said. He pointed.

They were in the typical Concordian style, a throwback to the prefab colonization kits, low, simple, functional.

"The Scythians allow their slaves to live outside?" It seemed lax and overly trusting.

"They probably don't want them cluttering up their domes."

"I wonder if there are any Resistance members living among them."

"Only one way to find out," said Niall. "We can either try to approach those people or head down south. What do you think?"

"We should put it to the others, but I can't see any point in going south. It's more populated down there, and more people means more Scythians. Besides, we'll use up our supplies for no purpose. We need to find the Resistance. We stand as good a chance finding them here as anywhere else. Maybe a greater chance. This must be one of the areas that sends food to Chimera, or else how would the ship's captain know about the cove where he dropped us off?"

"All good arguments. Let's see what the others say."

"THAT'S A DUMB IDEA," said Maddox. "Those people are Scythian slaves. They aren't going to risk talking to us."

A muscle in her jaw twitching, Wilder turned to Zapata. "What do you think?"

"We don't have a choice. We have to make contact with the people living around here. How else are we going to survive when our supplies run out?"

"Easy," Maddox said. "We go north, build our own place, live off what we can find and grow."

"What would be the point of that?" Wilder asked.

"Not dying, which I happen to think is a very good point."

"That won't work," said Niall. "Aside from the fact that we came here to do a job, a job we can't do unless we interact with Concordians, the Scythians regularly patrol, looking for human activity. Sooner or later they'll spot us and we'll either be killed or made slaves, the same as everyone else."

"Not if we're careful."

"That's such bullshit," Wilder spat. "You think the rest of the people living here weren't careful? You think they didn't try to get away to safer areas and hide?"

"Maybe, for some of them, it worked. We just don't know about them."

Wilder groaned and sank her head into her hands.

"My first point still stands," said Niall. "We came here to do a job."

"An impossible job," Maddox countered. "It amazes me that two such supposedly intelligent people haven't figured that out yet. It's time to call it quits and make the best we can of a bad situation. The Scythians won, and that's that."

Wilder turned to Miki. "What do *you* think?"

She shrugged. "I'm happy to do whatever you guys think is best."

Maddox asked, "No devastating insights about Scythians to reveal that might help us with our decision?"

"Stars, that was mean," said Wilder.

"And uncalled-for," Niall added.

Maddox widened her eyes. "What? That's why she's here, isn't it? To give us the benefit of her detailed understanding of Scythian behavior. I mean, she *demanded* to come along." She turned to Miki. "How's that working out for you?"

Wilder slapped her so hard her head jerked around. She drew back her hand for a second slap but Niall grabbed her wrist. "Cut it out. And Maddox..."

The woman was clutching her face and glaring at Wilder.

"...any more picking on Miki, or anyone else for that matter, and you're off the mission. You can find out how well your plan of traveling north works when you're alone."

Maddox's shoulders slumped. "Sorry. My ribs are hurting me."

Wilder didn't think that was sufficient excuse, but she said nothing.

Zapata cleared his throat. "We need to make an effort to not fight among ourselves."

"Agreed," Niall said. "The majority view is we approach the people tending the fields near the estuary, so that's what we'll do. There's no point in waiting for dark because, if anything, it'll be easier for the Scythians to spot us, and we're fairly rested, so I say there's no time like the present."

It was agreed that Zapata would stay with the backpacks. Not only would he slow them down, if Scythians spotted them he wouldn't stand a chance of running away. Maddox insisted on staying behind too, citing her injured ribs.

Wilder rolled her eyes but didn't object. She was sure the woman's reluctance to take part was driven more by fear than pain, but, in truth, she didn't want her around anyway.

The trail they'd followed through the low hills continued in the rough direction of the estuary. As they stepped along it the hills became taller but then lower again and lower still, until they were walking through open country. They stooped low.

Wilder felt naked and defenseless as they crept across the flat landscape. The memory of long, scaly, Scythian toes gripping her like a vice around her middle as she was carried aloft grew vivid. The alien stench was strong in her nostrils, and the wind in the upper atmosphere seemed to stir her hair. The sky was empty, however, and no sign of activity appeared at the three Scythian domes looming in the distance.

The scene remained serene. It was a pleasant day, and though the variety of plants in the landscape was extremely limited, it might have been any other peaceful day on Lyonesse before the Scythians returned. She recalled the heli flight she'd taken with Kes to examine the crashed vessel in which the Guardian returned to Concordia. Sadness welled up.

They reached the edge of the farmed land.

"Do you recognize that crop?" Niall asked.

A purple-green plant trailed over the ground, spreading out from a central crown, leaves like fingers, long and limp.

Wilder replied, "It must be one of the plants Meric said the Scythians introduced to feed themselves and humans."

Niall's nose wrinkled. "Looks disgusting."

Miki gave a soft "*Oh!*" followed by "There are people."

She was looking in the direction of the estuary.

There *were* people, six or seven, wading thigh-deep through the water. At the distance it wasn't possible to tell what they were doing.

"We're looking for Concordians," said Wilder. "They're as good as any others."

Keeping low, they cut across the field.

The estuary was farther away than it appeared. The flatness of the landscape was confusing. As they worked their way closer, Wilder kept a close eye on the domes. What should they do if a Scythian patrol emerged? If they were discovered, could they pretend they were farmers? Did the aliens keep a tally of the humans working for them?

Despite their efforts at avoiding detection, as they approached within ten meters of the men and women working in the estuary they were noticed. The people stopped work and turned to watch them. They wore wide-brimmed, woven hats and loose tops, tied at the waist with twine. They also wore shorts, wet from contact with the water. On their backs were net bags.

Their stances grew stiffer. Presumably they realized these people creeping toward them were strangers. A woman, hunched with age, flapped a hand toward Wilder and the others, gesturing at them to go away.

"They don't want to see us?" Miki asked.

"I think they might be frightened," said Wilder. "Let's try to talk to them anyway. We have to talk to *someone*."

When she saw her gesture hadn't worked, the older woman shook her head emphatically and began to sidle toward the bank. A couple of her companions glanced nervously at the domes.

"They really don't want to meet us," said Niall, slowing down. "Maybe it's dangerous for them to talk to people they don't know."

Wilder halted. "We only want to talk to you. We aren't from around here."

Following the older woman's lead, the men and women walked to the edge of the water. Their net bags streamed water as they left it. Fronds of seaweed hung from the gaps.

"We don't mean you any harm," Niall called out.

"Then go away!" the woman yelled back. She and her companions hastily waded the final steps to shore and then set off at a brisk walk, their bags bumping their thighs.

"Scythians!" Miki hollered.

Four aliens had exited a dome.

"Shit!" Niall exclaimed. "Get down!"

Wilder had already dropped, pulling Miki with her. They lay flat under the foliage.

"Do you think they saw us?" Miki whispered.

"Hard to tell. It might be a coincidence they came out or they might have spotted us crossing the field." She asked Niall, who was on the other side of the row, "Can you see them?"

He peered out. "Can't see a thing."

Wilder waited, hardly daring to breathe. Just when she was beginning to think the Scythians weren't looking for them an impact sounded behind her, along with the crash of disturbed foliage. One of the aliens had landed.

She cursed. Niall met her gaze across the gap. If she'd remained still before, now she was utterly frozen, partly to avoid attracting the Scythians' attention, partly out of pure fear.

Niall was mouthing something at her.

What? she mouthed back.

His lips puckered up as if to peck someone on the cheek, opened a little, and then widened while his teeth drew together. *W... A or O... T.*

Water

As understanding must have dawned on her face, he looked purposefully toward the estuary.

He thought they should go into the water?

But the aliens would see them.

Of course. He was right.

While this exchange had been going on, a second and a third impact had sounded in the field. The vegetation rustled as the Scythians walked through it, clearly searching. If they fired on them they might take out one or two, but there were four. And there were probably hundreds altogether in the three domes.

"Miki," she whispered, "if it looks like we're going to be found, run into the estuary."

"What? Why?"

"They can't follow us there. They can't move in water, only in the air or on land."

"Then they'll just shoot us."

"If they're using the same weapons as the Scythians on Earth, the rounds won't penetrate deeply. The water will slow them down fast. You need to swim deep and only come up for air when you absolutely must."

Miki looked at her with disbelief.

Could she even swim? She'd grown up on a starship.

"Just stick with me."

A heavy footstep hit the ground terrifyingly close by. Between the stalks of the crop plants, a scaly leg with long, prehensile toes could be seen. A horrible odor wafted down. Wilder slowly turned her head. Directly above them was the biggest Scythian she'd ever seen. A rifle slung across its midriff, it peered from side to side, its head encased in a tinted globe.

Then it directed its attention downward. The wings folded inward and with two of its claws it reached for the vegetation over their heads.

Wilder's lungs filled with air. "Run!"

She bolted.

She flew into the water and was up to her waist and about to dive before she noticed Miki was not with her.

There was a splash. Niall disappeared under the surface.

Where was Miki?!

She checked over her shoulder.

Three Scythians stood in the field. Another batted its wings above, aiming its weapon at her.

Miki faced one of the aliens, her arms up, as if offering herself as a sacrifice.

Wilder hesitated, horror and incomprehension echoing through her bones.

The three in the field focused on Miki.

The zing of a bullet passed her ear accompanied by the tiny plop of it hitting the water.

She turned away and dove down to the bed.

                                  32

By the time they made it back to Zapata and Maddox, the enormity of what had happened finally hit. Until then, Wilder had swum, sipped breaths, crawled from the water with Niall farther downstream, and returned to the hiding spot with a foggy confusion. All the while, the image of Miki holding up her arms to the aliens, as if begging to be taken, had stuck at the front of her mind.

Had she given herself up because she couldn't swim?

Had she thought the situation was hopeless and that they would all be captured regardless of what they did?

Had she done it as a distraction to allow her friends to get away?

Why? Why? Why?

Collapsing to the ground, she buried her face in her hands.

"Where's Miki?" Zapata asked. "Is she on her way?"

"She isn't coming," Niall replied, his tone hard. "The Scythians have her."

"You let them take her?" Maddox asked accusingly. "Oh well, no big loss."

Wilder's head snapped up. "Shut up! Shut your goddamned face!"

"She went with them willingly," said Niall.

Maddox scoffed, "Why the hell would she do that? Are you sure you're telling us the truth?"

Wilder launched herself at the woman, elbow pulled back. Niall grabbed her and wrestled with her. Her body went limp and she began to weep. She'd failed Miki. She didn't know how it had happened or what she'd done wrong, but she'd failed her. She should have known the girl had something going on. She should have been able to read the signs.

"She'll be alive still," Zapata said. "I'm sure of it. They will put her to work like they did on Earth. They don't seem to be in the habit of killing people, only turning them into slaves."

Wilder sniffed. "We don't know that. Even if she is alive, we can't rip the lid off a dome like we did before. How will we get her out? The Scythians treat their slaves badly, starving them half to death." She recalled what Meric had told her about the aliens pairing humans up for breeding. Her stomach churned.

"I'm just saying, we shouldn't give up. Miki got *herself* out before. She might do it again."

"Things were different on Earth. People were resisting the colonization. Here, they seem to have given up."

Niall said, "Losing Miki is a big shock. We need to calm down and think things through. There is a Resistance here. If we can contact them they might be able to help us free her."

"How can we contact them if no one will talk to us? You saw how those people at the estuary behaved when they saw us. They don't want anything to do with outsiders."

"People at the estuary?" Zapata echoed.

Niall filled him in.

"So the Scythians allow humans to work outside the domes unsupervised? That's a good sign."

"Is it?" asked Maddox. "All it says to me is Concordians are so under their control they don't even bother watching them."

"I swear," Wilder said, "if you don't—"

"I'm allowed an opinion!"

"Keep your opinions to yourself for now," said Niall. "If we want to hear what you think, we'll ask you."

Maddox folded her arms and looked away.

"You should try the buildings near the fields," said Zapata. "*We* should try them. I'll go with you this time."

"With your leg like that?" asked Niall.

"Especially with my leg like this."

THEY WENT AT TWILIGHT. As they'd watched and waited, people had come out to harvest the strange, leafy crop from a field. Then, when they collected the bundles from the ends of the rows and carried them in, they slipped among them. It wasn't until the farmhands drew closer together they were noticed in the half light. Zapata was the first to draw attention, hopping along on his crutch.

An uneasy stir passed through the men and women but they seemed too scared to say anything. Scythians had begun to leave their domes, flapping lazily up into the dimming sky. If they scanned their slaves for newcomers, they weren't able to spot them, for Wilder, Niall, and Zapata made it to the barn where the leaves were being taken.

Once they were under cover, a lanky man spun to face them. "You're the newcomers! Get out of here before you get us all in trouble."

"We need help," said Zapata. "I've hurt my leg."

"Why should we care? The Scythians will do worse than hurt our legs if they find out we're harboring foreigners."

"Foreigner?" Wilder asked. "We're from Lyonesse like you."

"You aren't from these parts, and if you were traveling legally you wouldn't be sneaking around. I'm sorry. We can't help you."

"Surely you wouldn't turn away a fellow human being in need?" asked Zapata. "If you could just give us shelter for one night so we can rest? Then in the morning we'll be on our way."

"Maybe one night won't hurt," said a woman. "They could sleep here. If the Scythians find them we can say we didn't know about them."

"They won't believe us," the lanky man retorted, "and even if they do believe us they'll punish us anyway."

"We had a spot inspection the other day," someone else said. "They won't be back for a while."

The lanky man strode to a stack of harvested plants and dumped his bundle on the top. "Have it your way. I don't want any part of it." He marched out of the barn.

"Don't pay any attention to him," said the woman. "His son lives in a dome. Makes him extra cautious."

"Thanks for your hospitality," Niall said. "We understand we're asking a lot. I'm—"

"No names, please. It's safer that way. Make yourselves comfortable. There's a bit of space at the back you can bed down in. I'll come by later with water and food, though we can't spare much."

"You're very kind," said Wilder, feeling guilty at the offer of food when they had plenty in the backpacks they'd left with Maddox. Maybe they would find a way to give them some. They had brought only one thing with them aside from Zapata's crutch, and it wasn't supplies.

"It's no trouble. As you said, it would be wrong to turn away a fellow human being in need. We're all in this together, right?"

"Right."

As the woman and the other workers left, Wilder relaxed. Step one had been accomplished. From now on, all her efforts would be focused on getting Miki back. Defeating the Scythians could come later.

Zapata hop-stepped around the bundles of drying plants and Wilder and Niall followed. As the woman had said, a small area of bare ground lay between the plants and the barn wall.

"What about Maddox?" asked Niall. "Should I go back and get her?"

"Screw Maddox," said Wilder. "She can fend for herself for once and see how she likes it."

Niall also didn't seem to feel any sense of urgency about collecting their remaining mission member, and neither did Zapata.

The pilot eased himself to the ground, one hand on the planks of the wall for support. "They seem to think we're vagrants."

"Or escapees from another Scythian-controlled territory," said Niall. "I got the feeling we aren't the first they've seen."

"I suppose it must be a thing," Wilder said, joining Zapata on the ground. "There must be a few Concordians wandering about, keeping out of sight of the Scythians, but unable to gather in sufficient numbers to fight back. They won't have weapons either. The first thing the aliens would have done is confiscate and destroy any they found."

"Can you pass me the head?" asked Niall.

"You want to give it another go?" She reached into the bag and drew out the grisly artifact.

A figure stepped around the stacked plants, and Wilder shoved the Guardian's head behind her back.

"I brought you this," said the woman who had spoken to them earlier, holding a jug of water and a small cloth sack. "It isn't much."

Wilder was tempted to say they weren't hungry but it would appear suspicious. For the time being, it seemed better to go along with the woman's assumptions about them.

Niall accepted the jug and sack. "Would you stay a while? We only arrived today and we'd like to learn about this place."

Alarm appeared in her features. "Uhh… Maybe later. If I can slip away."

She was gone.

After waiting a moment in case of further interruptions, Wilder passed the head to Niall in exchange for the food and water. She took a drink from the jug and gave it to Zapata. Then she widened the drawstrings holding the neck of the sack. The scent of the ocean wafted up. Inside were dried strands of seaweed, the same weed they'd seen the people in the estuary gathering, presumably.

After handing some to Zapata, she chewed the salty leaf. It expanded in her mouth, quickly absorbing her saliva and turning into a gooey, chewy mess. It tasted familiar. Perhaps she'd eaten it once long ago, before the world had turned to shit.

Niall didn't eat or drink. He was busy examining, prodding, and poking the Guardian's head. Ever since they'd had it, Niall and she had been trying to activate it. During the days she'd spent recovering at Chimera, he had attempted various methods of supplying it with power while also avoiding the risk of overloading or short-circuiting it.

If the problem was a lack of energy, they hadn't solved it, and if it had power and there was another way of starting it up they hadn't found it yet. Wilder had speculated that, as neither she nor Miki had seen the Guardian's body, it must have been only its head that Aubriot had taken into the city, which meant it had operated on its own. What it *had* done, it *could* do, hypothetically. Moreover, either the head had run out of juice after Aubriot had left it behind—the idea of the intelligent AI spending decades alone down there, unable to even move, sent shivers down her spine—or he'd turned it off. And if there was a way of turning it off, there had to be a way of turning it on.

They'd looked the thing over a hundred times, trying to find the 'switch'. But the head was a burned, smashed mess. If there had been an on/off button it was no longer recognizable. And if there had never been a button, both she and Niall were flummoxed as to what else could be used to activate it.

She watched him, chewing the seaweed, as he tried again all the things they'd tried before. It was dumb but she understood his frustration. The vegetable matter in her mouth didn't seem to be getting any smaller. She forced the bolus down and held out her hand. "Let me try."

Heaving a sigh, he lifted the head to pass it over.

Whatever he touched as he did so, it must have been the magic spot.

The Guardian's eye blinked to life.

33

A woman screamed.

The person who had brought them food and water had returned unnoticed. She was staring at the head, her hands clutched to her face, her mouth an O of horror.

"It's fine," said Wilder. "It's only…"

The woman had darted away.

"Shit," Niall said. "What do you think she'll do?"

"What do *you* think? Everyone within five klicks must have heard her."

"We'd better get out of here," Zapata said, struggling to his feet. "There's no telling what people will do when they're frightened."

Wilder shoved the awakened head into her bag. They left the sack of seaweed and the jug and hurried to the door of the barn, but they were already too late. Seven or eight farmers blocked the entrance and more were running over, eager to see what the commotion was about.

The man who had objected to their presence stood at the front of the throng gripping a short knife, probably used for harvesting. His companions held similar 'weapons'. One held a long-tined fork aloft, another had a thick stick with wide strips of smooth material hanging from it.

"I knew there was something not right about you lot," said the lanky man. "Where's that thing you're carrying? Hand it over."

After spending days trying to activate the head, Wilder was damned if she was going to give it away. She clutched the bag tightly. "Let us out and we'll leave peacefully. We won't bother you anymore."

"You're not going anywhere. Someone's getting the message to the Scythians right now. They'll be here soon enough."

In the corner of her eye, Wilder saw Niall's arm slowly moving toward the back of his pants. "If you've already betrayed us, why do you want what we have? Won't the Scythians take it anyway?"

"So you don't hurt anyone with it before they get here," the man sneered.

Zapata said, "Please, let us go. We don't mean you any harm and we never did. We're all Concordians. We should help each other, not fight among ourselves. All that does is make the Scythians' work easier for them."

"They won this planet a long time ago. The fight is over, and we know our place." The lanky man's knife-wielding arm dropped a notch. "Fine. If you refuse to give it to us, we can wait for the Scythians to arrive and take over."

"We know our place?" asked Wilder. "What kind of defeatist talk is that? People died to make this planet ours. They toiled and fought and sacrificed their lives for Concordia. You know your place? You should be ashamed."

The man's face paled. He lifted his knife and took a step closer to her. "There's no shame in honest work. As long as we stick to the rules the Scythians treat us well. All we have to do is not step out of line."

Fury rose up in her. She'd been playing along, keeping the argument going, to distract from what Niall was doing, but this man's sentiment sparked rage. "Spoken like a good slave!" She turned her attention to his companions. "Look at you! If I hadn't seen it with my own eyes I would never have believed that Concordians had sunk so low. You're no better than animals, beasts of burden, working for masters who don't give a shit whether you live or die. What kind of legacy is that to leave your children? What kind of gratitude are you showing to your ancestors? Generations of people lived out their lives aboard a starship, colonists endured bombardments and floods and attacks, and every time, after each disaster they started again from scratch and rebuilt. Again and again. And all for what? So their pathetic, disgusting descendants could bow down to Scythians and 'know their place'."

Niall's gun whipped up. The farmers' rapt attention broke and their stares shifted to the weapon.

"Move aside," he said, stepping forward. "I don't want to hurt anyone but I will if I have to."

"I knew they were Resistance," the lanky man muttered.

Wilder took out her gun too.

The man drew back along with the rest, creating a gap. Zapata stepped through it. Niall went next and Wilder walked out last, turning to aim at the onlookers.

While the altercation had been going on more people had arrived. A loose group of thirty or forty hung around the entrance to the barn. Uncomfortable tingles ran through her. For now, the guns were keeping the farmers back, but with so many against so few the tables could turn quickly. All it would take would be for one brave person to break ranks and risk being shot, and the battle would be over.

Yet no one did. Perhaps they thought it was easier to leave the work to the Scythians, or perhaps they were too cowed, too used to being ordered around, and to step out of line and do something different from everyone else was scary and strange.

Wilder and the others walked away from the barn unimpeded and unchallenged. She scanned the dusk sky, the first stars glimmering. Whatever method the farmers had for contacting the Scythians it was not speedy. The small settlement sat only a kilometer or so from the nearest dome. One of the aliens could cross the space in half a minute, but no winged shapes blotted out the stars.

A fast runner had to be on his way to a dome. As soon as the alert was given the aliens would be on their way, and there was no cover anywhere nearby. With their infrared vision the Scythians would spot them easily.

They were at the end of the last building, the farmers watching them, silent and still.

Niall hissed, "Run!"

She sped into the dark field, gun in hand, Guardian's head in a bag bouncing against her hip. They had no plan, no agreed place to rendezvous, no strategy for what to do if one or more of them were captured by the Scythians. Hell, at this rate, they were all highly likely to be captured, especially Zapata, who could barely walk, let alone run.

So much for making contact with Concordians. She didn't think she'd ever felt so disappointed so disheartened, or so embarrassed for her people. She'd meant every word she'd said to them. All her efforts, all of Cherry's, Kes's, Ethan's, Cariad's, and every other person who had arrived on the *Nova Fortuna* had been an utter waste. What was the point of saving such miserable cowards? Maybe Maddox's idea had some merit. The prospect of giving up on freeing Concordia from Scythian control was appealing. Why keep on fighting when the people you were fighting for weren't worth the effort?

"Stop!"

Someone was behind her, running after her. He'd shouted something else but she didn't catch it, her blood pounding and her gasps for air loud in her ears.

So one of the farmers did have some balls after all, even if it was only to capture her for the Scythians.

She sped up.

Her lungs labored as she raced across the field, leaping the clumps of plants that only became visible when she was nearly upon them.

"Stop! Wait!"

She didn't have breath to answer. If she had, she would have given the type of reply Aubriot had been in the habit of giving.

Footsteps thudded behind her, getting closer. "Stop, dammit! I—"

Arms wrapped around her thighs and she and her pursuer smacked into the ground. She kicked and struggled, swinging for the man's head.

"I'm trying to—"

A punch connected. Bone and flesh met her knuckles with a crunch while pain exploded in her hand.

"Arghh!" He moved on top of her, crushing her with his weight and pinning her wrists to her sides. "I'm trying to help you, you stupid..." He panted, catching his breath, and repeated more quietly and urgently, "I'm trying to help you."

"Help take me to the Scythians!" She lunged upward, teeth bared.

"No! Come with me now. They'll be here in less than a minute." He released her and rose to his feet. "Follow me, or don't. Your choice. I'm done risking my life for you." He loped off across the field.

She checked the domes. Black humps against a blacker sky, their tops were fuzzy and active. Scythians were pouring out of them. The alarm had been given and they were on their way.

The man was already becoming indistinct in the darkness. She couldn't see Niall or Zapata.

She ran after him.

He was moving fast. She had to force her aching legs to move fast enough to keep him in sight. She had no chance of catching up to him.

Then he vanished.

She slowed. Where had he disappeared to? One second he was there, the next he'd gone, as if he'd melted into the night. Her run slowed further to a jog. The scene was surreal. The landscape was empty save for the wide fields, the glints of the distant estuary, and the alien shapes speeding toward her. Had she imagined the encounter? But her chest ached from where she'd hit the ground.

Something snagged her ankles, grasped her tightly, and dragged her down. She was falling. She smashed into something spongy, softening her impact. Starlight above abruptly cut out at the sound of a trap closing. Another type of light flared, and there was the man who had chased her.

He held out a hand to help her to her feet. "I'm glad you made the right choice."

She dusted herself down. "You're with the Resistance, right?"

34

"Please either remove me from this bag or de-activate me."

Wilder almost leapt out of her skin. In the rush to escape from the angry farmers and her subsequent hauling beneath the ground by the Resistance man, she'd forgotten the Guardian's head had 'woken up.'

Her savior also jumped and stared at the cloth bag slung over her shoulder, the origin of the voice. She'd only just stood up from her cushioned landing and shaken hands with him. He was in his twenties and he appeared to know something about her, otherwise why was he risking his life to protect this stranger from the Scythians? But she doubted he expected her to have a talking bag.

"I, er, I'd better take it out," she said apologetically. "It's scary-looking, but there's nothing to be afraid of."

He frowned. "It would take a lot more than a comm speaker to —*Whoa!*" He stumbled backward.

She'd lifted out the Guardian's head. It happened to have its face toward him, partial mouth, single, roving eye and all.

"What the...?" he breathed.

"My name is Faina," the android said. "My bearer is correct. You have nothing to fear from me. Please attempt to overcome your natural repugnance at my appearance. Who is holding me?"

Wilder turned the head to face her.

Faina studied her features. "You have aged, but I believe you are Wilder, one of the original colonists. Remarkable. What year is this and where am I?"

"You're on Lyonesse, near the mouth of the Vimur, and the year is…" She looked at the man questioningly. She'd actually forgotten the exact year.

When he told Faina the answer, the android said, "Interesting. I didn't expect to be re-activated. Did you reactivate me, Wilder? And for what reason? Why have you brought me to Lyonesse? The last thing I remember is Aubriot shutting me down in the Scythian city on Suddene."

"That's a lot of questions. Maybe we should go somewhere we can sit down and talk about it." She didn't want to answer in front of this man she didn't know. He might be Resistance and he might have saved her from capture by the Scythians, but as she'd learned in Chimera, not all Concordians were friendly or sympathetic to her cause.

The man opened an arm wide, inviting her to pass into a low passage.

"Can I put you back in the bag?" Wilder asked Faina.

"No."

The passageway was so low she had to stoop. It had been dug from the subsoil and propped with beams. It didn't look at all safe. The Resistance man lit the way with his flashlight.

As they went along, Faina said, "I would like to take this opportunity to make it clear that, though I may not be organic, my mind was derived from a wide and numerous range of human minds. I think and, I believe, I experience my surroundings and the passing of time as a human does. When my head was severed from my body I lost my ability to de-activate myself. Thus there is a risk that, were I to be lost or left somewhere and forgotten, I would remain awake but alone and unable to move until my power ran out, which would be a very long time. This would be torturous to me. So I ask that you take especial care to avoid this happening. If there is a chance I may be separated from you or another bearer, please pre-emptively de-activate me."

"I understand," Wilder replied, "and I'll do it."

The android had made her point clearly and without a hint of self-pity despite the horrific scenario she'd conjured.

While Faina had been speaking, the man had cast alarmed glances over his shoulder.

"But," Wilder added, "I don't know how to shut you down. I don't know how we activated you in the first place. We'd been trying for days."

"I can describe the spot to you when we reach a resting place."

The man straightened up. They'd reached a circular chamber, floor, walls, and ceiling made from concrete. Out of the shadows, Niall and Zapata rose to greet her.

"Guys! I was worried about you." She hugged Zapata tightly, Niall a little less so.

"You've got the head?" Niall asked. "Thank the stars for that. I was worried you might have dropped it."

"My *name* is Faina," said the Guardian.

"Weirdest thing I ever saw." The man shook hands with Niall and Zapata. "I'm Steven. I take it my friends brought you here?"

"We've been through the introductions," Niall replied. "The others went to check on Scythian activity."

"Please, take a seat. I'm sorry it took us so long to find you. Meric sent word you would be arriving in Lyonesse, but you didn't appear at the location he named. Did you meet Orson?" After noting their nods, he explained, "We think he told the captain of the vessel that brought you over to drop you in a different place. You're lucky he didn't drop you over the side. I guess he didn't have the stomach for the cold-blooded murder of fellow Concordians."

Wilder had placed Faina's head next to her on the low wooden bench, leaning the back of it against the wall to keep it upright.

"Sounds like we had a near miss," said Zapata. "A fourth member of our party is waiting for us in the nearby hills. Could someone find her and bring her here?"

"Later," said Steven, "when things have died down a bit. It's too dangerous right now. As long as she stays where she is she should be safe. The Scythians don't maneuver too well in woodland."

"What is this place?" Wilder asked.

"It's an old grain store, re-purposed not long after the Scythians arrived." He gave a wink.

"So we're near the farm buildings?"

"Not far away. Most of the farmers don't know we're here. A few are Resistance, like us. They told us you'd turned up, but we couldn't approach you before the traitors informed on you."

"Traitors is a strong word," Zapata said mildly.

"What else would you call them?" Steven's jaw muscles clenched. "If we could just all band together and stand up for ourselves, we might make life so difficult for the Scythians they would leave us alone. But half the population is too scared and the other half is too plain lazy. As long as they have enough food in their bellies to keep them from starving they're content. Some of them even seem happy with the status quo, saying things like *This is how it's meant to be* and *The Scythians are better than us. That's just how it is. No point in denying it. And it* is *their planet, after all*. It makes me so angry, I want to knock their heads together. So what if it was originally someone else's planet? It was empty when we got here. How were we to know it had once been the home of another intelligent species? That was a long time ago, and they can't live here without our help. It makes more sense for them to bugger off and leave us to it. We're the ones who can develop this place to its full potential, not them. They had their chance." His rant dried up and he looked at them sheepishly. "Sorry, I get carried away sometimes."

"Honestly," Wilder said, "it's a relief to talk to someone who has a fire in their belly. All I seem to have heard since we arrived is excuses. And you're friendlier than most too. Half the people we've met have wanted to kill us."

"So you really are from the *Sirocco*? It's just a little hard to take in. I learned about your ship when I was a kid and only half believed it. Stupid question, right? Considering you have a talking head."

"Faina isn't from our ship. She's one of the Guardians who arrived on the *Mistral*. I found her in the Scythian city near Chimera."

"This gets more fantastical by the minute. Maybe it's a sign things are going to change around here. Maybe we'll finally have the uprising we've been working toward for so many years."

"Tell us about the Resistance," said Niall. "How many of you are there? How far does the network spread?"

"I can't answer you, I'm afraid. None of us can. It's too risky for any one member to know too much information. If the Scythians catch us, they try to extract as many details as they can before execution. We've only been able to survive this long by limiting our knowledge of our own organization. I know the people in this sector, and one person here is in touch with the nearest branch, and so on."

"It doesn't matter," Wilder said. "We've made contact with you at last, and we have a new source of intel on the Scythians." She gestured toward Faina. "We can begin to put the wheels in motion. It's long past time that Concordians fought back."

35

Preparations began.

As the days passed, their knowledge of the Concordian Resistance grew exponentially. The restricted access to information of ordinary members of the group was not applied to the newcomers from the *Sirocco*. First, they were taken overland by routes the Scythians only sporadically patrolled to visit the hubs of Resistance activity. They were introduced to its governing council, a group of seven men and women, the main decision-makers and organizers of acts of resistance.

They learned of the history of the group. In the beginning, despite the weakened state of the colony, the Concordians had fought the Scythians viciously and desperately, throwing everything they had at the invaders, risking their lives again and again. Many died. The death toll and destruction had been devastating. The aliens had all the advantages: technology, numbers, firepower, and maneuverability, whereas the colonists had already been on their knees before their attackers even arrived.

Finally, the new Leader—the person in charge when the *Sirocco* departed, Barker, had been killed during the initial invasion—was faced with the choice of allowing the hopeless war to continue, ensuring the deaths of yet more thousands, or to surrender and save the remaining lives. He had decided that enslavement and the hope of one day turning the tables and breaking free was a better alternative to continued slaughter.

There were plenty who did not agree, and they were the genesis of the Resistance. Cells formed across the land, hideouts were built and supply lines created. Some members were never enslaved, others managed to escape the domes, the towns now patrolled by Scythians, and the fields.

In the beginning Concordia had been in a state of flux, but the aliens steadily tightened their control, inflicting savage punishments on dissenters. Over the years things settled down. The domes proliferated and, ironically, the human population increased too. Now the colonists had a steady food source from the plants the aliens had introduced, and the destroyed ecosystem began to re-establish a modicum of balance, life became easier.

Meanwhile, the Resistance disrupted this new 'normal' when it could, but it faced a difficult problem. Scythians generally lived in close proximity to humans. Large numbers of Concordians inhabited their domes and the surrounding areas. Towns like Annwn and Oceanside were shadows of their former busy states, but, though people still lived there, so did the aliens. They'd taken over the largest buildings still standing after the war, sealed off the main sections for their own living quarters and arranged for live-in servants. No matter where the aliens were, any attack was guaranteed to result in human deaths and casualties.

The movement had been hamstrung from the start but it had done what it could, targeting patrols, blowing up domes under construction, organizing breakouts, and committing other acts to subvert Scythian domination. Chimera had been established. It was in fact only one of three safe sites the Resistance had created. The members had done much over the years to work against their overlords, but they had not even approached the goal of returning Concordia to human ownership.

The arrival of the group from the *Sirocco* was supposed to change all that.

They'd been stationed in the cave complex near Oceanside. The honeycombed cliffs had once been the site of another rebellion. In a schism during the first months of the colony Gens had created their own settlement here, free from Woken control. But an act of sabotage had flooded the system with millions of cubic meters of water. Scores of people had died, very nearly including Cherry, as she'd told Wilder once. Now the caves were dry once more, though as far as she was aware they had never been re-occupied before the Resistance moved in.

The appropriateness of the choice of abode wasn't lost on her.

The Resistance had dug, tunneled, and blasted connections between the various caves within the soft limestone of the cliff. Traversing the cliff face didn't only pose the danger of losing one's grip and tumbling into the ocean, it also risked the observation of a passing Scythian patrol. Wilder's small space was at the end of one of the narrow passages, which meant no traffic passed her door. Not that she had an actual door, only a curtain on a rail.

One day, roughly a month after meeting the Resistance, she was in her room when someone beyond the curtain said, "Knock, knock." It was the standard method of announcing your arrival and saved hurting your knuckles on the bare rock.

"Hi, Niall."

He pulled back the curtain and poked his head in. "Got a minute?"

"For you? I don't know. I'll have to think about it."

He smiled and stepped in. "I was wondering if you'd got any further with the head."

"My *name* is Faina."

The android was facing out to sea. Wilder had put her in her usual place on the cave floor near the cliff-side opening. Not *too* close, in case a strong gust of wind should blow her from her perch. Though the Guardian might survive submersion they would likely never find her again.

"We've been going through some things," Wilder replied. "I don't think we came up with anything new."

The problem with plumbing Faina's memory of her time with the Scythians was that they'd tampered with her, inserting new pathways and removing others, in order to re-program her. Some of the damage had been undone but not all of it. She could not, for example, talk about the aliens' planetary defense system or what she'd done to fix its controls. Her ability to run diagnostics on herself had also been compromised. She couldn't tell whether what she recalled was real or fictional, uploaded by the Scythians in case their machinations were discovered.

She'd told of a vast starship, apparently larger than any Scythian ship Wilder had ever seen, where the alien technicians had worked on her. It had taken years to travel to it, according to her memory, and she didn't recall going to any of the aliens' planets. This last item of information had been a disappointment. If the Resistance knew of something vital to Scythian survival, something not easily created, like CO_2, or easily obtained, it could have been the key to eliminating their presence from Concordia. But Faina hadn't come up with anything like that.

Much of what else she could tell them they already knew. The aliens' main method of locomotion would have been a revelation once upon a time. Now, humanity was as familiar with Scythians as Faina had become, of not more so. Nevertheless, this hadn't stopped Wilder from continuing to question the android in the hopes of prompting the recollection of something useful.

"Shame," said Niall, sitting next to Wilder on the only place to sit, her low cot.

"Any updates on the plans?"

"That was what I came to talk to you about. They've set a date. One week from today, Operation Rebirth begins."

"So soon? Are they ready?"

"They obviously think they are. From our perspective it's a little hard to tell, but I guess they know what they're doing. They've been anticipating this moment for decades, remember. All they needed was a push to set things in motion, and that's what our arrival provided."

Wilder's impression had been the same. The *Sirocco*'s return did seem to have galvanized the Resistance into action. The ship had to be a reminder of the good old days, when Concordia still belonged to humans despite the Scythians' many attacks.

Yet she harbored doubts, which apparently showed on her face.

Niall put an arm around her. "You're not sure about this, are you?"

She looked from his arm to his eyes.

He didn't remove the limb.

"Are you?" she asked. "Do you get the impression they're ready?"

"Well, Chimera has confirmed. They'll be crossing the ocean in groups over the next few days and moving into position."

The Resistance was in contact with its Suddene branch via an undersea cable.

She repeated, "Do you think they're ready?"

"I think they've been ready in a certain way for a long time. Whether they're adequately prepared and equipped is another question."

As newcomers and with restricted movement it had been hard for them to assess the true scope of Concordia's Resistance. The leaders had given them information in dribs and drabs, and they were privy to much more intelligence than rank and file members, but they hadn't spent years at the top as the leaders had. They didn't know everything by a long stretch.

Wilder's gut told her the planned uprising was at best a hopeful rather than confident endeavor. At worst, it was a desperate final gasp for freedom for those who would die before they accepted alien rule. "What worries me is the Scythian space fleet. Assume everything goes according to plan and the Resistance manages to kill or imprison most of the enemy and free the slaves. What then? We know there's at least one fully operational military starship in orbit. And it's been weeks since the *Sirocco* attacked the others. They could have repaired them by now, or more could have arrived. So what if the Resistance wins the day on the surface? The Scythian reprisal will be fast and devastating. I take it there's still no sign of our ship?"

"You know I would have told you."

No Concordians appeared to have even noticed the battles the *Sirocco* had fought in the sky. They didn't have access to satellite data, telescopes or anything else that would have told them what was happening in the heavens. If any flashes or streaks had been spotted they must had been dismissed as shooting stars. The lack of evidence must have been the reason the Chimerites to be suspicious of their tale, at least in part.

On the other hand, no wreckage from a starship had been found, which gave her hope the *Sirocco* hadn't been destroyed. It was a tenuous hope, however. Oceans covered two-thirds of Concordia's surface. It was more likely than not the ship would have fallen into the sea or the uninhabited deserts of Suddene.

She heaved a heavy sigh. "I feel like we've been living a dream ever since we got back to Concordia, a hopeless delusion that this planet could ever be truly ours again. We would have been better off turning around and heading straight back to Earth. We would have stood a better chance of survival there."

"We've been over this. Everyone from the *Sirocco* has. Concordia's our home."

"For how much longer?" She didn't mean before the Scythians took over the planet entirely. She was wondering how much time Niall and she had to live. "Hey, Zapata mentioned it was you who got me out of the Scythian city. Why didn't you say?"

"There didn't seem much point, but why would you think it was anyone else? You know I would risk my life for you in a heartbeat."

She didn't answer. She *did* know that. She didn't even have to think about it. "Well, thanks."

"You don't have to thank me. You would do the same for me."

He was right.

"Uhh..." said Faina.

Wilder started. She'd forgotten about the android. "Yes?"

"Could you please deactivate me? This view is pleasant but it grows boring eventually. You can wake me first thing tomorrow."

Wilder got up to press the tiny nubbin on Faina's neck that was her 'switch'.

"How is Zapata?" Niall asked as she returned to the cot.

"He's doing great. He's started walking without his crutch. I heard Maddox is still complaining about her ribs though." She avoided the woman as much as humanly possible.

"Any news about Miki?"

"I haven't heard anything. You?"

He shook his head. The Resistance had put out feelers to locate the fifth mission member but no word had come back. It was presumed that, if she was alive, she was inside one of the three domes on the banks of the Vimur estuary. The human population in that area was especially under the Scythians' sway. Intel on the aliens' activities was hard to come by.

Wilder looked out to sea. The sun was going down and, despite Faina's complaint, the scene was breathtakingly beautiful. The lowering rays were kissing the tops of the waves, gilding them red-gold. But Wilder's mind flew far away, to the depths of the Scythian city. She was beyond exhausted. Her palms were open, bleeding blisters, each movement was excruciating, and her throat had closed up with dehydration. A young girl was saying softly, *Just one more. You can do it.*

She rested her head on Niall's shoulder and they didn't speak. After a while he left to attend to Resistance business.

Later, when the cave complex was quiet and the stars were bright over the dark ocean, she heard another, quieter, "Knock, knock."

She opened the curtain to let him in.

Niall didn't leave until morning.

36

As Miki had hoped and predicted, the Scythians didn't kill her. They put her in a cell with a bunch of other people. She wasn't dropped in from the ceiling as before This cell had a door. She settled into a corner, regarding her new companions uneasily. Their expressions weren't friendly or welcoming. They seemed suspicious, and no one spoke.

This place was different from the domes she'd been inside on Earth. There were beds—of a kind. Rows of stuffed cloth mattresses crossed the floor, walking space between them. There were no chairs or tables or other furniture, only the beds, but the prisoners were allowed possessions. A small pile of belongings sat on each mattress: clothes, combs, small oblong objects that might be bars of soap, dishes and spoons.

"Who are *you*?"

A slight, bony woman with a high forehead and prominent cheek-bones had spoken. She glared but Miki couldn't tell if she was fearful or angry.

"My name's Miki."

"And where are you from, *Miki*?" The woman stepped closer.

Miki suddenly realized all the fifteen or so people in the cell were women. They ranged from teenagers like her to gray-haired women even older than Wilder. There were no children.

"I'm from…" She hesitated. Most of the Chimerites hadn't believed she was from the *Sirocco*. If she told these women the truth, would they suspect she was lying? They already seemed to dislike her, even though she hadn't done anything to offend them.

"Did you forget?" The bony woman asked sarcastically.

"I'm from down south. Annwn."

This appeared to mollify her questioner. "Another runaway. They always get them in the end. You can have that bed." She jerked her chin at an empty mattress. "Just to be clear. We operate by strict rules here. Everything's divided equally. No one gets any more or any less than their fair share."

"I would never—"

"Yeah, everyone says that. Until the hunger starts to bite. We have ways of dealing with thieves and people who push their luck. You've been warned."

Miki rose to her feet and walked to the empty mattress. There were no sheets or other bedding. The cloth was dirty and greasy from the bed's previous occupants. She wrinkled her nose. The floor looked more appealing as a sleeping place.

A girl little younger than her appeared at her side and said quietly, "It doesn't look nice, does it? But you'd better use it or Margie won't like it. She'll say you think you're better than everyone else, and then no one will talk to you."

Miki weighed up the prospect of being ostracized against sleeping in someone else's dirt. It was a hard call to make. "What's your name?"

"Dana."

"Thanks for the tip, Dana."

"Can I sit down?"

"Sure."

Miki perched on her new place of rest. Perhaps it wouldn't be too bad as long as she kept her clothes on.

"My family are from Annwn, too," Dana said.

Uh oh.

"You might know them."

"Probably not. You know what it's like living under the Scythians. I hardly got to see anyone before I escaped."

"You escaped? That's awesome."

Miki wondered how else people got away from the aliens.

"How did you do it?"

"I...er..."

Margie had walked closer and was making no secret of the fact she was eavesdropping.

Miki proceeded to relate the tale of the break out she'd taken part in. The story fit the situation perfectly, providing things were the same on Concordia as they'd been on Earth. In truth, she had no idea, but it was either that or make something up, which was even riskier.

Dana's eyes grew rounder as she talked, and Miki was reminded of Nina. Her sense of the resemblance increased until she was forced to stop and swallow, hard. Dana, most likely mistaking her emotion as relating to the escape, touched her arm and murmured, "You were very brave."

Miki concluded her narration, stating, "After we got out, we split up. I don't know what happened to the others, but I came north. I hoped I might find somewhere the Scythians didn't control and live there, but they caught me by the estuary. And here I am."

Margie said, "I never heard of any successful escapes around Annwn, but that isn't so surprising. We don't hear most of what goes on, and most of what we do hear is bullshit. But I believe you. Sorry for being harsh earlier. The Scythians put spies in the cells sometimes, to listen for dissenting remarks or plans to get out. We can't be too careful."

"I get it."

A dull thump resounded from the door. Dana ran to open it. A man stood outside holding a large metal container. Dana took the container, thanking him before he closed the door. It didn't seem to be kept locked. Margie supervised the portioning out of the food. Miki took her bowl and ate the scant contents—a porridge similar to the stuff she'd scraped in handfuls from the floor of her cell on Earth.

Naturally, the Scythians here had their systems all worked out by now. They kept the humans inside the domes under control by a number of methods. Near-starvation was one. It was hard to stage a breakout when you were weak and tired. Persuading the humans to police each other was another. The spies the aliens planted in the cells were probably rewarded with extra food or special privileges. And the sheer force of habit and lack of expectation for anything better from life seemed a powerful factor too. The women here appeared to have accepted their fate. Dana had been excited by the story of an escape from Annwn, but her reaction had been as if she'd been watching an engaging vid drama, a fiction, not something that could ever happen to her.

"How come there are only women here?" Miki asked her new acquaintance as they put their dirty bowls into the now-empty container.

Dana gave her a quizzical look. Apparently realizing the question was serious, she flushed. "Because…you know."

"I don't."

"Weren't the men and women segregated in the domes in Annwn?"

Miki became suddenly aware of Margie hovering close by. "Uhh, yes they were. I just never understood why."

"It's so they…so the Scythians can choose…who has a baby with who." Dana had turned deep red.

"Oh, yeah. That makes sense. I was stupid not to figure it out."

Dana looked at her as if she didn't quite believe her. "They haven't selected any pairs for a few years here. Maybe they're phasing out the breeding program."

"Why would they do that?"

Dana shrugged.

A second thump came from the door. The man had returned to collect the food utensils. He handed Dana clean bowls and spoons in exchange for the dirty ones. No words were spoken. Perhaps it was forbidden.

The man pointed at her. "You. Come with me."

Her cell companions fell silent and watched as she walked to the doorway. "Where am I going?"

The man didn't answer, only grabbed her biceps to guide her. His other arm was wrapped around the empty container.

She felt like another consumable to be delivered. "Please, where are you taking me?"

"Shut up, or you'll get us both in trouble."

They stopped at a wall. The man positioned her so she stood exactly upon two spots marked on the floor

"Don't move. Not a centimeter. Understand?"

She nodded, and the man left.

Minutes passed, and still she waited. High above curved the upper shell of the dome. Scythians flew over wearing breathing apparatus.

They were wearing breathing apparatus *inside*!

This entire section had an oxygen-rich atmosphere suitable for humans.

Something grabbed her waist from behind and she screamed with shock. Whatever it was, it was pulling her backward, into the wall.

It was pulling her *through* the wall.

She slid into the soft, porous material and out the other side, exactly as she had in the Scythian city. The thing gripping her waist was a set of alien's toes. She turned and held her breath as the creature's stench hit. It towered over her, peering down.

Releasing its grip, it said, "Lie down. Do not resist or you will be restrained."

The voice she heard had been synthetic. There was a flatness to its tone that told her a computer had generated it. The creature's mouth had moved but the sound of its vocalization hadn't escaped the globe enclosing its head.

She recognized the circular platform she was supposed to lie on as the same as the ones they used on Earth. Steeling herself for what was to come, she did as she'd been instructed. A needle and syringe on a metal arm rose up from the side, pierced her arm and drew a sample of blood. As quickly as it had arrived, the equipment disappeared.

The Scythian scientist—if that was what it was—had tippy toed in its harness over to a console and was ignoring her as it consulted the screen.

Would she be allowed to return to the cell now, or were there more examinations to take place?

Beep. Beep. Beep.

She couldn't tell where the noise was coming from. It wasn't loud like an alarm but it was insistent. It also got the scientist's attention. It leaned closer to its console, and then its head swiveled to face her, the vertical-slitted eyes staring fixedly into hers.

"You are not from Concordia. You are from Earth."

37

They had put her to work cleaning the skin of Scythians suffering from some kind of fungal infection. The humans called it Sticky Mold. What the aliens called it Miki had no idea. They didn't refer to it as she worked, though sometimes they spoke to her about other things. For this job she had to wear a respirator as she had when she'd worked in the hatchery on Earth. The device contained a comm or translator. She wasn't sure which. She only knew that when the aliens spoke she could hear what they said, in English, in the same flat-toned computer voice she'd heard in the examining room.

Dana cleaned the aliens' skins too, and she had been tasked with training Miki. She'd shown her which side of the crescent-shaped tool to use, how to draw it gently over the creatures' bodies and the webbing on their wings, and where to put the black, tacky scum she'd gathered. Then she had to apply a soothing balm, rubbing it gently into the cleaned areas. Perhaps the ointment helped to protect against further infections. Again, she did not know.

The most important thing was that she was inside a dome again, which was the best place to be if you wanted to learn about Scythians and their weaknesses. The only downside was that Wilder would be furious with her for the risk she was taking, but she had to do it for everyone's sake, and if she'd mentioned her plan to anyone they would have stopped her.

There were actually two downsides. Working with Dana reminded her of Nina. Their names were even similar. Though Dana was older than her sister she was just as sweet and gentle, and she'd taught her how to perform her duties inside the dome, the same as Nina had on Earth.

A new client arrived, waddling into the room. Dana and the other girl were already busy whereas Miki's seat was empty. She drew back, bowing her head respectfully as the creature lowered itself to the chair and reclined, stretching out its wings.

She began work at the tip of its right wing. You had to start at the edges and work inward. Apparently, dragging the implement over large areas of mold was painful to them. This one was quite badly affected. Its skin was almost entirely a dark, dusky gray, even its face. She would have to use a smaller instrument for that. She really disliked cleaning around their weird eyes and lipless mouths. Otherwise, it wasn't too bad. The respirator cut out most of the smell, and it was better than dealing with vicious Scythian larvae.

As she bent down to drag her tool over the lip of the receptacle to clean it of mold, her client said, "You are the Earthling?"

She paused momentarily before completing her task and returning to the wing. A small patch of bronze skin had been revealed in the gray. "No, sir. I'm Concordian." She called them all Sir and none had corrected her. No one she'd spoken to could tell whether Scythians were divided into two sexes like humans.

"You maintain your lie even now?"

When the scientist had challenged her about her origins she'd pretended she had no idea what it was talking about. If she'd revealed she was from the *Sirocco* all hell might have broken loose. What they might do if they knew she was from the ship that had been to Earth, and that had fired on the vessels they had defending the planet? They might interrogate her or even torture her for more information. She knew the aliens had to be desperate for the jump drive.

"I'm not lying, sir. I'm from Annwn." It was the truth. She *was*

Concordian and she *was* from Annwn. That was where her mom had given birth to her.

"And yet no humans have been reported missing from that area, and your genetic code clearly demonstrates your close affiliation with the earliest phase of human colonization of this planet."

"I'm afraid I don't understand about genetics. All I can tell you is I was born here and my mother and father are dead, so I can't ask them about my heritage."

The statement she didn't understand about genetics wasn't strictly true. Dad had taught her and Nina quite a lot, and when the scientist had told her she must be from Earth, she'd realized he must have analyzed her DNA from her blood sample. She'd wondered if she'd been mistaken when she'd assumed the scientist on Earth had known she was Concordian from the language she spoke. Perhaps it only had a record of Concordian genetic patterns, and hers had matched.

Her client stretched its wing wider, increasing the tension in the webbing so she might clean it better. "It is beyond doubt that at least one of your parents belonged to the original stock of settlers from Earth. The only other possibility is that an Earthling came here and mated with a Concordian the year before you were born, but we know that to be impossible. No Earth ship came here then."

Though the creature had concluded she was lying, it didn't seem angry or even perturbed, though what those emotions might look or sound like she wasn't sure. She decided to take her chance. After a nervous swallow, she said, "Can I ask you something, sir?"

"Your request is granted. Perhaps I will not answer, but you can ask."

"Are you..." It had to be the best question she could think of. She might not be allowed a second one. "Why are you making records of our genetic codes?"

"To maintain healthy stock. Humans must be capable of performing all the tasks we require of them. Unfortunately, your colony is somewhat inbred. It lacks diversity, which is likely to result in the emergence of congenital diseases and the colony's eventual collapse. We are trying to mitigate against these effects by careful selection of mating partners. Nevertheless, our best geneticists predict we will only forestall the failure by a few generations." The creature turned its head to stare at her. "Does that answer your question?"

"Yes, sir. Thank you, sir. You seem to know a lot about humans."

"We have been studying your kind for many years. The research findings on a new semi-intelligent species have been illuminating."

She started scraping the underside of its wing.

"Please apply the balm before you do that."

It had to be sore from the infection and wanted some relief. She put down her tool and dipped her fingertips into the ointment before gently massaging it into the wing's upper side. "May I ask another question?"

The creature's mouth had gone slack at her soothing touch. "You may."

"What is this disease that afflicts Scythians so badly? You are an advanced species, far superior to us." A little buttering up wouldn't go amiss. "It seems strange that you don't have a cure for it."

"We're working on a preventative and a treatment. Concordia is the first planet where we've encountered it. The infection may be something humans introduced, or it may be due to the altered climate. We prefer drier conditions than exist on this continent, but we cannot live on..." the word came through the translator unchanged, and for the first time she properly heard a Scythian voice. It was liquid and guttural. "The climate there is perfect for us but humans would find it unendurable, and we require slaves for many purposes."

She recalled the arid atmosphere inside the Scythian city, which made her think of Wilder. How were she, Niall, Zapata, and Maddox getting on? She was glad that Niall and Wilder didn't seem to be in the dome. As far as she could tell, they'd managed to escape.

"Sir, I know it is very impolite of me, but may I ask your name?"

"You cannot pronounce my name, Earthling."

"Is my service pleasing to you?"

The Scythian regarded her intently. "It is unlike a human to care about the quality of their performance."

"Your infection seems to hurt you. I would like to suggest at your next treatment you ask specifically for me, and I will do my best to ease your pain."

The creature held her gaze for long seconds. She stared back, frankly and confidently.

"I will bear your suggestion in mind."

"Thank you, sir. Shall I start on the underside of your wing now?"

It lifted the appendage to allow her access. Secretly, she smiled to herself. She was gaining the creature's trust.

38

His name was Klghurrshhh. That was the closest Miki could get to the correct pronunciation. It was way off. She couldn't reproduce that weird hissing sound the Scythians made. The closest she could get was *Shhh* like hushing a baby to sleep. The alien seemed to like the fact she tried, however, and when he came for his scraping and balm he always asked for her. She was sure he timed it so she was on duty when he came in. She thought of Klghurrshhh as a *he* but, even after all these weeks, she still didn't know anything about Scythian gender. It was just easier to think of him that way.

She was so used to seeing him that she recognized him immediately when he entered the treatment room. She'd begun to distinguish between the other aliens too. When you saw them all the time, you began to spot differences between their faces and the subtle patterning of their skin. They were different in size too, the same as humans. The girls who did the treatments had joke names based on the aliens' bodies. One was Pot Belly, another was String, and they called a Scythian with particularly undefined facial features Gloop. Naturally, their giggles were saved for when no aliens were around. The Scythians had learned the signs of human insubordination and punished it severely.

One time, an alien with very short, bandy legs waddled into the room, and a girl from another cell had burst into semi-hysterical laughter she was unable to stifle. The creature had sliced her cheek open with its claw and she was not allowed to leave or even to try to stem the flow of blood until her workday was over. Miki and the other girls had cleaned the floor in somber silence.

The incident had left a strong impression, and she was extra careful to be polite and respectful at all times, but especially with Klghurrshhh. Her relationship with him was fragile. Scythians had no respect for humans. It was clear they believed them to be only one step higher on the evolutionary scale than dumb animals. A single wrong word, look, or movement could shatter the bridge she was building, and then she would have to start all over again with another alien.

At every opportunity, she would probe Klghurrshhh for information, but she had to be extremely subtle. He was smart. It wouldn't take much for him to realize what she was doing. It was possible he'd already guessed but he was turning a blind eye to it. Maybe he enjoyed the special attention she gave to his treatment and he was indulging her in kind. Maybe he thought it amusing that a human being might imagine they could manipulate a Scythian. Regardless, she was sure she was learning useful things, information her friends from the *Sirocco* or humans on Concordia could exploit to defeat the aliens.

One tidbit she'd learned was that some Scythians didn't mind the fungal infection too much because it helped to protect them from the sun's rays on day patrols. There was something about the structure of the hairlike fibers that when they embedded in the aliens' skin, it prevented sunburn.

"Is it helpful to *you*, Klghurrshhh?" she had shyly asked.

"Not particularly."

"Is that because you...your job isn't to go on patrols?"

"I am a nursery supervisor. I avoid leaving the dome if I can help it. Exposure to the external atmosphere makes my condition worse."

"Oh, I'm so sorry. I hope the scientists come up with a medication soon."

"Either that or I'll apply for a transfer off this dank, putrid planet."

That a Scythian could refer to Concordia as putrid when they stank to high heaven themselves was laughable.

Naturally, Miki did not laugh. Neither did she delve into the opening Klghurrshhh had created with his mention of alien movements offplanet. It might be vital information, but going after it at the first mention would be too suspicious. She forced herself to not respond to the remark, while also filing it away to bring up another day, as if it was something she vaguely remembered.

"I used to work in a nursery," she said.

"You did, Miki?"

Her heart skipped a beat. He'd used her name! He'd asked her it only once, weeks ago, and when she'd told him he'd mocked its simplicity. Not reacting had been hard. Dad had told her once that Mom had picked her and Nina's names. Her name was all she had left of her mother—about all she had left of anything. But she'd managed to keep the anger out of her expression.

After that, he'd never mentioned her name again and she'd assumed he'd forgotten it.

"I was in the... I don't know what to call it. The starter room? I took the little w—" She gulped. Would he be offended if she called the first stage Scythians worms? "The littlest ones out of the soil and put them in the nutrient solution. Then, when they grew bigger I would put them in the cages with the...the others." The savagery of the attacks the young aliens inflicted on each other was indelible in her mind.

"The early stages of our growth cycle are excellent at weeding out the slow and weak. Only the strongest and most intelligent survive. The human system is far inferior. You nurture every baby regardless of its qualities or deficiencies. It is no surprise your species has barely achieved space travel or that we defeated you so easily."

"You're right, Klghurrshhh." She tightened her grip on the scraping tool as she drew it over the alien's skin, a line of gray-black sludge building up on the edge. "You're so right."

39

It had been a hard trek for Wilder and Niall to return to the mouth of the Vimur in time for the launch of Operation Rebirth, but that was where the Resistance had felt their talents would be best put to use. The area was judged to be one of the Scythians' most secure strongholds, due to the human population's extreme obedience and docility. The Resistance couldn't count on them for their support. They might even turn against the fighters and defend the aliens. Their reaction when everything kicked off was an unknown factor in the battle plan, so Wilder and Niall were to bolster the local branch's numbers and fighting ability.

Wilder had tried to explain that neither she nor Niall were skilled in combat, but her efforts had been to no avail. They'd acquired a mythical status somewhat similar to that of the *Sirocco*. They'd stepped out of history, arrived to put right all the wrongs inflicted on Concordia. They were here to replenish the planet with new species from the old world and to free its people. Both beliefs were true in a sense, but Wilder had anticipated a more advisory role like the Makers on Earth. She was not a fighter and neither was Niall.

Yet she was glad to be back at the estuary. If Miki was alive she was in one of the domes. Even if Operation Rebirth failed and they didn't manage to persuade the Scythians to give up their colonization, if she could just free Miki, that would be enough. Perhaps they could find a secluded place to live as Maddox had suggested. However, she wouldn't be telling Maddox about it.

Steven greeted them warmly when they'd reached the old underground grain store, shaking their hands. "I never thought I would see you back here again. You guys certainly lit a fire under us."

"That was our intention, I guess," Niall replied. "What's the plan for tomorrow?"

"You need to be in position by 2 a.m. That's the time most patrols are taking place so the domes are at their emptiest. You're leading the attack on Dome Three, the one nearest the mountains."

"Leading?" Wilder asked. "We've never even been in a dome before."

"They're all the same inside. I'll show you a model. You'll blow open the shell where it faces the river. That's smack in the middle of the area pressurized with CO_2 and unlikely to contain many humans. Scythians will pour out and you pick them off as they come. Give it a couple of minutes for the gas to escape, then you go in."

"Do we have breathing masks?" asked Wilder.

"You shouldn't need them."

She looked doubtfully at Niall. They wouldn't be able to tell if they were breathing an atmosphere rich in carbon dioxide, and it would kill them fast. The gas was odorless and colorless. It was also heavier than regular air. The domes were tall. It might take longer than a couple of minutes for the CO_2 to dissipate.

"The Scythians will call the patrols back immediately," Steven went on, "but we will be waiting to take them out as they arrive. Once you're inside, your goal is to kill every alien on sight. We don't have anywhere to put prisoners and they're dangerous even when unarmed. When the fighting dies down you can get the people out. They don't know you're coming. We couldn't risk warning them in case a traitor informed on us. You'll be able to tell where the people are by the doors in the walls."

He smiled. "That's the short version. We can go into more detail over dinner. Then you'll have a few hours to sleep before you leave for the domes."

Wilder didn't think she would be sleeping at all tonight, despite her tiredness from her week-long trek. Niall seemed to have reservations too. But this was what they'd come here for, and once they were out in the field they would be able to call the shots. If they needed to amend the plan of the local Resistance they would.

Before they ate they took a look at the model of the Scythian dome. Then as they ate they talked business, preparing for the big attack. When it came time to sleep she was feeling a little more optimistic. She'd also talked to the other team leaders and given them a description of Miki, emphasizing her most memorable characteristic: the red in her hair.

She lay next to Niall in a room near the grain store. This place had been dug out of the ground and the floor was hard, stony subsoil. It was deeply uncomfortable. Even if she hadn't been about to risk her life she would have struggled to sleep, and the snores of other Resistance fighters in the room with them didn't help.

Niall was trying but, though his eyes were closed, she could tell he was awake. She leaned close and kissed his cheek. His eyes opened.

"If things get dicey tomorrow," she whispered. "What am I talking about? *When* things get dicey tomorrow, and assuming we both survive, don't be mean to me, okay?"

Her request clearly troubled him. "I'll try. I might need to stay away from you for a while."

"I can live with that."

Later, to her surprise, she found herself being shaken awake. She had managed to fall asleep after all. She blinked at Steven, who was standing over her. "Time to get up?" she asked. Everyone else in the room remained asleep, including Niall.

He didn't answer, only beckoned.

She tiptoed out, following him into the low passageway. He led her away from the sleeping men and women.

"What's going on?" She was growing more puzzled by the second.

"Something very weird. A capsule has been found on the shore of the estuary."

"Capsule?"

"I don't know how else to describe it. It's like a coffin, only a bit longer and wider and it's oblong, not rectangular."

"Right."

He looked at her expectantly.

"I have no idea what you're talking about."

"Well, that's even stranger. I thought you would know what it is because it has your name on it."

"*My name?*"

"There aren't any other Wilders around here."

She stared at him.

"Do you want to go and see it?"

"Do I have time?"

"We have two hours before we have to leave for the domes. It's about a half hour walk to the place. I can take you there if you like."

She was never going to get back to sleep, not with the puzzle of a mysterious object with her name on it whirling around her mind. "Let's go."

AS THEY WALKED through the darkness, she had an inkling of what the thing might be. It reminded her of something she'd heard about, though that had been very long ago. She'd never seen the item in question so she couldn't make a comparison. The description sounded the same but everything else about her guess was impossible. Yet what other explanation could there be? Was Steven pulling a prank on her? That was even less likely.

Then she saw it. Even from afar and in the dark, the sight made her stomach flip.

"Do you know recognize it now?" asked Steven in a hushed whisper. They crouched in tall weeds at the edge of the sand.

"I think I do, but it can't be." The implication of what she was seeing had rocked her. It had her name on it, and that meant only one thing.

"There don't seem to be any Scythians around. You could take a closer look. I'll keep lookout."

"Steven, if that thing is what I think it is, I'll need to leave for a while, and I'll need your help to do it. Is that okay with you?"

"Huh?"

"Just trust me."

"Will you be back in time for Operation Rebirth?"

"I don't know."

"I guess you've got to do what you've got to do, but I'd appreciate it if you could explain. I'll have to tell the others something."

"Come with me to the water's edge."

It was a Fila capsule. There was no mistake. The transparent cover was open, revealing a single seat. There were no controls. The passenger didn't pilot it. She hadn't seen the ones Ethan and Cherry had traveled in during the early days of the colony, but she knew a little about them.

Her name was on the side like the name of a ship, the word written in a long, flowing script like Fila tentacles. She had no doubt what it all meant—her name and the appearance of the capsule on the estuary shore. It was an invitation.

"I have to get inside. When the lid closes, push me out into the water. That's all you need to do. You can go back to the hideout. I remember the way."

"P-push you out into the water? But there's no sail or engine or... What the hell is that thing?"

She was already climbing inside. "Just do as I say, please." A sense of urgency had hit. Perhaps there was time to call off Operation Rebirth. Perhaps there was another solution.

As soon as she lay down in the reclined seat, the cover automatically swung over and sealed. Steven gazed through the barrier, wide-eyed.

Push me, she mouthed. *Hurry.*

He disappeared from view. The capsule jerked as it broke free from its position and then the sand ground underneath it moved closer to the water. The movement became liquid, the capsule lifted as a low wave caught it, and then she was floating free, bobbing on the surface. Wilder craned her neck but she couldn't see Steven. She hoped he'd left and wasn't hanging around out in the open, his surprise making him forgetful of the threat of Scythians discovering him.

40

She was being carried out to sea, as far as she could tell. From her reclined, submerged position she couldn't see hardly anything. The water above was dark save for glints of light that might be starlight penetrating the surface. She'd felt the capsule turn so her feet faced the ocean, but she hadn't noticed anything else except acceleration.

Of course she was being taken to the ocean. That was where Ethan and Cherry had gone, down to the metropolis on the ocean floor.

The Fila were back! It had to be good news for Concordians. They'd helped them so much in the past, introducing them to the Galactic Assembly and helping them in the Scythian wars. They must have returned to lend humanity a hand once more. She only hoped her meeting with the aquatic aliens would be over in time for her to report to the Resistance before Operation Rebirth launched. A lot of bloodshed could be prevented.

The capsule sank deeper. The glints disappeared and darkness entirely enclosed her. She began to grow cold and very aware of the fact she was in an extremely confined space, surrounded by water. How deep was she? How great was the pressure? Her breathing sped up and cold sweat bathed her. Years living aboard the *Sirocco* had helped her overcome her claustrophobia somewhat, but now it returned in a wave of panic. Her hands clenched as she resisted the urge to bang uselessly on the hull overhead and scream.

She had to find a distraction. She thought of Niall. Was he awake yet? Had Steven explained where she had gone? What were Zapata and Maddox doing? Was Maddox still complaining about her ribs?

She closed her eyes and imagined she was somewhere else. She was back in her treehouse outside Sidhe with her childhood friends. What an amazing time that had been, so full of excitement and hope. How young she'd been. How innocent. The threat of the Scythians' return had hung over everyone's heads, but to her it had been a vague possibility for the future. Her focus had been on the here and now. The future had been...

It was no good. Her treehouse melted into nothingness. Her eyes snapped open. She was in utter darkness and the chill of the ocean depths was invading her bones. She was trapped in a fragile bubble, a thin layer of material separating her from pressure that would pulverize her body before she had time to breathe in a lungful of water and begin to drown.

Lights appeared. For a second she thought the capsule must have risen to the surface and she could see starlight again. Had the Fila decided to not meet her?

But the lights were colored and moving, undulating gently. And the colors were changing, coruscating, pulsing. A Fila was approaching. She was transfixed. Cherry had described the sight but words didn't encompass it.

"Wilder?"

"Yes!" she exclaimed. She was no longer alone.

The Fila moved so close it was directly outside the capsule. It had been years since she'd seen one, and even now she couldn't see it properly, only the lights it emitted.

"I didn't know the Fila had returned to Concordia. How long have you been here?" Why was there only one? She'd imagined she was going to meet many of them.

"It's so good to see you again."

A pulsing tentacle touched the hull directly over her head.

"It's good to...? Quinn! Is that you?!"

"I thought you might have died, Wilder. Humans live such a short time."

Her throat swelled and she blinked back tears. Reaching up, she touched the inner hull opposite the tentacle. They had never made physical contact in all the time they'd known each other. "It's good to see you too. I thought I would never see you again. What are you doing here? Are you living here alone?"

"There are many Fila on Concordia. You're traveling to our city now, but I wanted to meet you on the way. I have missed you greatly."

"How did you know I was back? I got the shock of my life when I saw my name on this thing."

"We monitor the human communications between Lyonesse and Suddene. We have a policy of never interfering in land affairs, but when I heard your name had been mentioned I was concerned for your safety, and I wanted to see you again. I persuaded our authorities to organize this meeting."

"You have a policy of never interfering in land affairs? What do you mean? Quinn, how long have the Fila been living on Concordia?" she repeated more urgently.

"We returned not long after your ship departed. The biocide had worked itself through the oceans and faded out. The water was safe once more. But we made a decision to not become involved with humans again."

"I see," she said quietly. It was no surprise. Entangling themselves with humanity's problems had cost tens of thousands of Fila lives, wiped out by the biocide. "So you knew about the Scythian invasion? You were here then?"

"We were. The Scythians are aware of our presence but they tolerate us, providing we remain neutral. They have no use for the oceans."

In response to her silence he went on, "Planets that are habitable for my kind are rare in the galaxy, Wilder. Perhaps it seems disloyal, but..."

She swallowed. Her dreams of the Fila coming to the colony's rescue were crashing around her ears. "I understand."

"The communications implied you made it to Earth, but you've been gone a very long time."

"We did make it there eventually." She explained about the jump drive failing. "Scythians are invading Earth too. They learned its location from the Guardian they salvaged from the wreck of the *Mistral*."

"I am sorry to hear that. Humans may have to accept enslavement for the time being if they are to survive."

"Do you know about Operation Rebirth?"

"We do. That was another reason I wanted to talk to you. I advise you not to take part. It is almost certain to fail and you might be killed."

"The same idea had occurred to me, but what choice do I have? The Resistance are determined to do something. Humans don't submit to slavery easily. At least, most of us don't. When it comes down to it, we would rather die."

"But all humans die eventually. I don't understand why they don't value their lives more. Surely it's better to live as long as possible, even if your life is spent under another's control?"

"We don't see it like that. We only get one, short life. We want to make it the best we can. Otherwise, what's the point?"

Quinn's tentacles moved over the surface of the capsule as he considered her answer.

They would probably never fully understand the other's viewpoint. Fila lived forever. Only accident or disease killed them, hence their unending quest to find new planets to inhabit. Maybe it made sense that a Fila would think a less-than-perfect life was better than dying.

An idea struck and hope surged in her again. "Quinn, could the Fila contact the Galactic Assembly for us? We must still be members. They have a duty to come to our aid when we're attacked by hostile forces."

"The Galactic Assembly is already aware of the situation on Concordia."

"Huh? Then why haven't they done anything?"

"They have re-classified the Scythians' actions from an unprovoked assault to a territory dispute. The Scythians proved their ownership of the planet to the Assembly's satisfaction when they applied to join. Their application process is ongoing."

"What the...?" Air left Wilder's lungs in a great *whoosh*. She couldn't have been more flabbergasted or more disappointed. Humanity's allies had deserted it. They were alone in the galaxy, doomed to choose between thralldom and death. "What about what's happening on Earth? That *is* an unprovoked assault."

"Not entirely unprovoked, considering that humans colonized Concordia without permission from the Scythians, but there may be a case to answer. I will ensure your point is made to the Assembly, but as I understand it, Earth is outside its jurisdiction."

"Nooo! No more, Quinn. I can't stand it."

"I am very sorry, Wilder. You know I want to help you. I am trying to help you now."

"What you've told me—is that what your authorities were going to tell me at the meeting?"

"I believe so. They were also going to ask you to avoid revealing to the Scythians that we've been in contact."

"I won't tell them. Stars, that's the last thing on my mind. But if that's all they have to say, I'd prefer to skip it and go back to the Vimur. The Resistance attack will start soon. If I can get this new information to them it might change things. They could call off the operation."

"I will have to—"

"I don't have time for bureaucracy. Please take me back."

She felt the capsule's progress slow. It stopped, and then reversed.

"I may get into trouble for this, but it was worth it to see you again."

Wilder rubbed the heels of her hands into her eyes, and for some time she couldn't speak. The hopelessness of the situation on the surface had plagued her for months. This brief encounter had removed it momentarily, only to dump her deeper in it than ever before. Finally, she managed to say softly, "I wish we could have met at a better time. Will I see you again?"

"I don't know how that will be possible. Human and Fila networks are no longer connected, and we can't risk depositing more capsules on beaches just for you to pay me a visit. The Scythians will notice."

"So this is our last meeting?"

"I believe so."

Specks of light appeared in the dark water, separate from Quinn's luminescence.

"I'm glad I got this chance anyway."

"Me too."

Water drained from the capsule's surface and it bumped as it hit sand.

"Take care, Wilder."

The lid opened.

"I'll miss you, Quinn."

But she didn't think he heard. His tentacles were already trailing out of sight.

She stood up, and the capsule rocked. It wasn't quite out of the water. She was forced to wade to shore.

What time was it? How long had her journey taken?

She looked up the estuary to where the Scythian domes stood, softly glowing silver. The night was still and peaceful.

An explosion split the air, startling her as the shockwave passed through her skull. It was quickly followed by another, and then a third.

Operation Rebirth had begun.

41

Miki was in the process of finishing up when Klghurrshhh walked in. She was at the end of her shift, so Dana stepped forward to offer him a seat.

"It's fine," Miki said. "I have time for one more."

She hadn't seen him for a couple of weeks. The fungal infection had regrown over his entire body. It would take her an hour at least to clean it all off and rub ointment into his skin, but it didn't matter. The rapport she'd been building with him was worth the effort. Though he was only a nursery supervisor, not an important official, she still might learn something useful from him. There might, for instance, be a key part of the aliens' growth cycle that humans could disrupt or another weakness that could be exploited.

He was beginning to lose his reserve around her. She'd played her part as the subservient, admiring human well, and now she was sure he completely believed it. Why be careful about what you said when the 'thing' you were talking to was in awe of you?

"You must be uncomfortable, sir. Please sit down and allow me to help you."

He lowered himself into the seat and spread his wings.

"Have you just finished work, sir?"

"Never mind what I've been doing. Be silent and do your job."

She was so taken aback she almost dropped her scraper. But she managed to compose herself.

"You're far too familiar with me, Earthling," Klghurrshhh complained. "It's time to put a stop to it. Do you understand?"

"Yes, sir."

He muttered something else her translator didn't pick up. Then he said, "They'd damned well better not try it."

She was dying to ask him *who* had damned well better not try *what* but she didn't dare. From his tone and the rigidity of his wings it was easy to tell he was angry about something.

"It's time I left this miserable planet and its ungrateful humans," he went on. "Do you know that if it weren't for us you would all be dead? Every single one of you would be dead by now. And how do you repay us? Uprisings! Rebellions! Attacks! It's outrageous. We should wipe you out, give up the re-colonization, and leave. Concordia is a museum, a monument to our past, and that's how it should stay. Do you hear me?"

"Yes, sir," she timidly replied.

"After all we've done. All the trouble we've gone to in order to keep your miserable species alive..."

Clearly, he'd heard something to set him off on his rant. She could only guess at what it was. Something to do with humans fighting back.

She started on the underside of his wing, taking care to keep her head low and avoid making eye contact. She was also especially gentle. He seemed to begin to calm down, his wing relaxing under her hands.

"Perhaps it's nothing," he murmured. "Only a rumor. There are so many going arou—"

An explosion shattered the quiet. Miki was thrown across the room and into the wall, passing right through it into the wide passageway outside. She hit the farther wall and bounced off it before landing heavily. Too shocked to take in what was happening, she stared stupidly at her scraper, still in her hand.

She dropped it.

Klghurrshhh's suspicions had been correct. Concordians were

attacking the dome. She realized she'd heard two more explosions, quieter than the first. All three domes were being attacked. She leapt to her feet. She had to help free the other humans.

Air wafted downward, carrying with it an unmistakable odor her respirator could not entirely eliminate. She froze and looked up. Klghurrshhh was flying above her. He'd survived the blast. He must have either penetrated the wall or flown over it.

She ran, but his toes descended on her shoulders and dug in like pincers. In another second she was aloft. Where was he taking her? Chaos reigned below. Aliens sprawled everywhere, some still, some moving, their wings broken, limbs missing, guts trailing.

A great hole had opened in the side of the dome. Debris was piled around it. Through the hole she could glimpse people. They were firing at Scythians who remained alive, but none had entered yet. What were they waiting for?

Klghurrshhh flapped higher. The dome swarmed with flying aliens. Some flew haphazardly. Klghurrshhh narrowly avoided one on a collision course. Others were heading in the same direction as him.

She saw the human quarters. A few adventurous people were poking their heads out of doors. Scythians wearing breathing apparatus fired at them. A few fell and were dragged inside by their cellmates. The doors slammed shut.

Where was Klghurrshhh taking her?

His flight was growing ragged. He dipped, as if he was struggling to remain airborne. Of course! The carbon dioxide was leaving the dome through the blast hole. He rallied, then dipped again. He was dropping steadily now, his wings outstretched so he glided rather than flew. His grip on her grew slack too. If she fell from this height she might break her legs.

The flying aliens converged on a large chamber, but most were not making it. They plummeted, their wings and eyes closed, impacting heavily with the ground. But one reached it, and she understood why Klghurrshhh wanted to go there. The Scythian who had landed slit the ceiling open with a claw and slipped through. It was like the ceilings in the domes on Earth, covered in a translucent material that contained the atmosphere. It would reseal automatically after it was cut.

Klghurrshhh hit the very edge of the room. Apparently with his last gasp, he drew a claw through the ceiling. His grasp of her was weak. She pushed his feet away and jumped for the edge. She might hurt herself leaping to the ground from this height but maybe not too much.

Toes fastened around her ankle and her captor dragged her into the room. They toppled to the ground together.

Only he and the other Scythian had made it to safety—albeit a temporary one. The attack was going on around them. A Scythian fell to the ceiling and hung there, making the material sag. It was not dead from asphyxiation but from a pulse round to its head. Shots from the aliens' guns rang out. The human attackers might have imagined they would kill a lot of Scythians by depriving them of CO_2, but the ones in the human zones wore respirators. The battle promised to be bloody.

Klghurrshhh's hold on her had broken as they fell. He lay on his back, wings spread out, chest heaving. Miki crawled away from him and straight over to the nearest wall. She pushed on it. It did not yield to her touch.

"No escape from this room, Earthling." He was regaining his strength.

She shrank into a corner.

"Your Resistance won't win. That's guaranteed. But in the meantime, if any humans happen to make it this far, you are my personal guarantee." He climbed to his feet and tottered closer. "We carry our own weapons, you see." He lifted his wings, displaying their claws. The wide, webbed appendages seemed to envelop her. "Why is it humans are so helpless? You have nothing to defend yourself with. Even your teeth are not sharp."

"I've been kind to you," Miki said. "I've tried my best to help you."

"Only because you wanted something from me. I am not a stupid human like you."

She couldn't deny it. "You're right. I did want something from you. I wanted to help my people. The same as you want to help yours. You want to grow the best and strongest young Scythians. I know you think we're inferior, but we aren't that different."

"We are *very* different."

"If our circumstances were reversed, wouldn't Scythians do the same as us? Wouldn't they try to release the ones who had been enslaved?"

"And we would succeed!"

"My people will free some of their own today too. Maybe not all of them, and maybe some will die in the attempt. But they'll try. And they will carry on trying. On and on. You hurt us, and we fight back. What's the point? Why can't you leave us alone? I'm just a girl. My dad, my mom, and probably my sister are dead. I don't have anyone. I just wanted to do something, just one good thing with my life. Why can't you treat me like a person?"

Klghurrshhh stared at her. She turned her head, avoiding his gaze. The next thing she knew, he'd grabbed her ankle and she was sliding over the ground. He positioned her in front of him as he squatted behind her. One of his wings arched around, and the tip of a claw touched her throat.

He was just in time.

A figure appeared at the top of the wall, indistinct through the ceiling. A knife bore down and sliced the material. It began to reseal, but the figure quickly cut a square and pushed it down. The cut piece floated to the floor. The ceiling material began to ooze inward to close the gap, but the knife flashed again. A face appeared in the hole.

"Miki? Is that you?"

"Wilder! I—"

"Tell him to stop doing that or I'll kill you," Klghurrshhh demanded.

The claw dug deeper, making her gasp with pain.

It's not him, it's her. "She won't understand me. My respirator translates to Scythian."

"Then take it off."

"If I take it off I won't be able to breathe."

The claw dug deeper still. Blood trickled down her neck. She breathed in deeply and then pulled off the mask. "Wilder, it's me. He says if you don't let the ceiling self-repair he'll kill me." She slapped the mask over her face and breathed again.

"I can shoot him just as easily through the fabric, but if he lets you go I won't."

Niall appeared next to Wilder.

Miki related the message.

"I will slit your throat first."

She translated.

"Will he do it?" Wilder asked.

"I-I think so."

"She's just a kid, you bastard," Niall yelled. "How can you kill a kid?"

Miki passed the words on, leaving out the bit about him being a bastard. "Wilder and Niall are from the *Sirocco* like me. We went to Earth, but I'm not from there. My dad was. He was one of the first settlers. My mom was born here."

A pause followed. Wilder stared down through the closing hole. The second Scythian sat in the opposite corner, watching. The claw didn't move from Miki's neck.

There was movement behind her. Something hit her, propelling her forward. She landed on her knees. Klghurrshhh had kicked her.

"Climb onto my back, *Miki*. And take care not to fall, or I still might impale you."

He turned and knelt, leaning forward.

She clambered onto him, gripping the powerful shoulders. The creature straightened up and rose to his full height. She had to stand up and balance precariously in order for Niall to reach in and grab her.

As soon as she was out of the room she tore off her respirator and tossed it away. The battle was raging on all around. Scythian and human bodies littered the ground. Pulses flashed in the night and the noise of Scythian rounds echoed from the dome overhead.

"Another rope?" Miki asked.

A grapple grasped the top of the wall and a knotted rope hung from it.

Wilder replied, "I don't want to talk about it."

42

I t was impossible for Wilder to call Operation Rebirth a victory. The Resistance had been decimated in the attack—more than decimated, according to the literal meaning of the word—and it had failed to wrest control of Concordia from the Scythians. Casualty figures were still coming in but they already numbered in the hundreds of dead, permanently disabled, and seriously injured. The organization had also exhausted its supplies of equipment. Manufacturing of new pulse rifles and other weaponry was no longer possible, so once a rifle was broken or fell into enemy hands it was gone forever, never to be replaced. She had a vision of the movement finally being forced to use knives, pitchforks, and flails, as the farmers at the Vimur estuary had.

Scythian casualties had been high too, no doubt. Many domes had been successfully blasted open. Plenty of aliens had suffocated when the CO_2 flooded out. Others had died from pulse rounds. But the Scythians could replenish their numbers from outside Concordia. The call would have gone out for more soldiers, more settlers, more immigrants to the origin planet. The human population could not replace itself so easily, and the reprisals had already begun. The aliens would make Concordians pay dearly for their arrogance, for daring to challenge their masters.

More bloodshed. More deaths. It sickened her to think of it.

Had Operation Rebirth been worth it?

At least Miki was back safe and sound. Perhaps the most she could have hoped for.

She'd brought the girl to her little room in the cave complex. It wasn't really big enough for two. It wasn't, in fact, big enough for one. But it gave her comfort to have Miki close by. She would never let her out of her sight again, and she'd made her promise that if she had another bright idea about risking her life to try to learn the Scythians' secrets, she would discuss it first.

When the attack was over and it was time to regroup and debrief, she'd tried to stay upbeat for Miki's sake all the way back to the caves, but on arrival her mood had sunk low. It was hard not to despair when all you saw ahead of you was endless fighting as each side sought revenge against the other. It would never stop, not unless every last human died or accepted unending servitude. And it would be the same on Earth.

She was sitting at the cliff-side opening in her room looking out over the ocean as she morosely mulled over humanity's prospects. Faina was here too, activated. The android was another depressing problem. Faina would never be able to move around independently. She also had no role in the colony. She'd been designed and manufactured for a task that was long since over. An almost-human consciousness trapped inside a small receptacle, no one on Concordia had the skills to improve her situation even a little bit. One day soon, Wilder anticipated, the android would ask to be deactivated and buried somewhere no one would ever find her.

Faina was not quite at that point yet, however. She still occasionally enjoyed watching the seascape.

Wilder said, "I don't think I ever told you—we met the original Strongquist on Earth. The prototype the Makers built."

"Another Strongquist? I didn't know there were two. Was he the same as the one who came here with me on the *Mistral*?"

"Identical in almost every way, as far as I could tell. I didn't know the one from your ship very well."

"He was still functioning even now? He has lasted a very long time."

"The Makers deactivated him before they went into Deep Sleep. He reactivated when Niall and I entered their construction site. Do you remember it?"

"I do, perfectly. My memories do not fade as humans' do. But I was not aware of a prototype Strongquist. I would like to meet him if I could. Yet there is no possibility of returning to Earth, I believe?"

"We don't even know if the *Sirocco* still exists. If she does, I don't see how she could enter Concordian orbit without the Scythians blowing her to pieces. And the captain, Vessey, is unlikely to attempt it again. She might go back to Earth, but that would be without us. I would love to take you there. The Makers might be able to build you a new body."

"A new body would be very convenient."

"We're stuck here, unfortunately. I can't see an end to this conflict. It'll go on until I die."

"It's a pity that humans have so little to offer the Scythians. All they can provide is their labor, and the aliens can take that by force. If you had something else, something the Scythians desired greatly but only humans could provide, yet they couldn't take at their will, it would give you bargaining power. If that were the case, things might be very different."

Wilder froze.

Then she bent down and kissed Faina's burnt, mangled head. "I'll be back soon. You've just given me a brilliant idea."

"Wait," the android's voice followed as Wilder left, but she didn't hear any more. She needed to send a message via the undersea cable.

43

The air in the room was thick with tension. And it was actual air. After some negotiation in the days leading up to the potentially watershed meeting, the Scythians had agreed to be the ones to wear breathing gear. In Wilder's mind it was a very positive sign. The Fila, naturally, had to participate from an adjacent position in the ocean, visible through a glass portal. She had a feeling this place used to be the Leader's residence, and this basement room was where the Leader had discussed matters of state with their aquatic alien allies.

Three Scythians were present, taking up most of the available space. Four humans were in attendance: Wilder, two members of the Resistance Council, and Miki, who, for some reason, had insisted on coming along. It was becoming a habit.

Wilder wasn't sure how many Fila were present on the other side of the transparent barrier. With all their tentacles, they were hard to count when they got together. She guessed Quinn was somewhere among them.

She cleared her throat. "I propose that we start with the big stuff and work our way down to the details." She actually planned on absenting herself for the smaller arguments. She'd always hated long, tedious meetings involving people arguing over minutiae. "Item one:

we have something you want very much. Item two: we want to know what you're willing to give for it."

"Let us be clear about what this thing is," said the central alien.

"All right. We call it a jump drive. It's a kind of starship engine. It enables travel across the galaxy in leaps rather than via regular propulsion through spacetime."

"As the Fila do?"

"The same way the Fila travel, but this drive works for atmosphere-breathing species. Miki and I have taken part in many jumps and we weren't harmed, the same as the rest of the *Sirocco*'s crew. I don't see any reason why it wouldn't work for Scythians too."

"You are the inventor?"

"I am, though others helped with the development."

A pause followed. The aliens were probably talking among themselves.

She coughed again. "If you're thinking you only need to capture and torture me to force me to give up the design, that would be very stupid. Firstly, no agony you could inflict would make me betray my people. You've seen how recklessly defiant we are. And, secondly, I don't think that would go down very well with the Galactic Assembly. I heard your application is in progress. I ask you again, what are you willing to give in exchange for the jump drive?"

Miki nudged her and whispered, "You're too passive. Don't ask. Demand. Or they won't respect you."

"Uh, okay." She got to her feet. "I've waited long enough. You know why we're here. If you aren't willing to give us Concordia, I'm done. There's nothing more to discuss."

"We were only considering our reply," said the Scythian.

"And what is your reply?" She remained standing.

"Concordia is our origin planet. It is our birthplace. We do not wish to leave."

"Then I guess it's no jump drive for you."

"Perhaps we can achieve a compromise."

Wilder sat down. "I'll listen, but—"

"No compromises!" a Resistance leader spat. "You killed thousands of our people, enslaved tens of thousands. You need to get off our planet today."

"And many Scythians died in the recent uprising," the alien retorted. "This is how you repay our efforts in saving your colony from inevitable demise."

"You enslaved us! What do you expect us to do? Roll over and accept our fate like obedient children? How were we to know Concordia's past? How is any of this our fault?"

A Fila voice came from the speaker on the wall. "If both sides want an end to this conflict you may each need to agree to some unpalatable concessions, such as letting go of what's happened in the past. It may be impossible to forgive, but with the proper attitude it may be possible to move on."

"And what if we aren't willing to move on?" asked the Resistance leader.

"Then you are condemning yourself to repeat the same experiences you have suffered, without end and until death."

Wilder felt they were losing track. "Look, it's simple. The Scythians leave Concordia in return for the jump drive. The entire galaxy will be at your disposal. Pack up and go back to wherever you came from, and give us this one planet."

"Sounds like a wonderful idea," the Resistance leader commented.

Still, the aliens seemed to balk.

"I know," said Miki. "What if we divide the planet between us? The Scythians could live on Suddene. The climate there is much better for them. Am I right?"

Silence from the aliens.

"Out of the question!" the Resistance leader spat.

"Why?" asked Miki. "What could we possibly do with Suddene? And we could trade with them. Sell them food and stuff. Surely that has to be better than a continuation of what's been happening. Haven't enough people died?"

Now it was the Resistance members' turn for a quiet confab. Finally, one of them said grudgingly, "I suppose it might work, providing we never have to set eyes on them. Perhaps the Fila could act as go-betweens."

"I think that's an excellent proposal," came the Fila voice.

"It would be a tough situation to stomach," Wilder said. "Given the history, I mean."

The Fila said, "Compromises often are."

The Scythians conferred. The humans watched and waited. The Fila writhed.

Could the fighting finally over? The future seemed poised on a knife edge.

Finally, the answer came. "We agree."

The strain inside Wilder broke like a taut string suddenly cut. If she hadn't been sitting she might have collapsed. Could it all really be over? But, of course, it was not completely over. Not yet.

"There's still Earth. You're invading *our* home planet. Only it isn't empty. Hundreds of millions of people are living there, and you're doing the same as you did here. Taking it over. Murdering people in cold blood. We want you to leave our world alone. Completely. No half-measures. You have no right to that place at all."

"But what will you give?"

"I've already agreed to give you the jump drive. That's enough."

"That was for a half-share of Concordia."

"The land masses of Concordia," the Fila interjected.

"You can't just go around invading inhabited planets," Wilder protested. "I bet the Galactic Assembly would have something to say about it."

"Possibly," said the Fila, "but your origin planet is far from the areas the Assembly adjudicates for. It would require the submission of detailed evidence and testimonies. There would be hearings. It could drag on for decades."

"What other technology do you have?" asked the Scythians.

She frowned. What else did they have to offer? There was the Parvus's weapon, but Wilder was damned if she was giving them that. Something else? She'd won a lot of tech from the Assembly in return for... "Do you have a-grav?"

"A-grav? What is that?"

"Artificial gravity."

"You invented artificial gravity too?"

The aliens had a short discussion.

"Would you consider a position working for us?"

"I would rather stick needles in my eyes."

Miki whispered, "That's a no, then?"

The meeting took hours and Wilder was unable to sneak off. Either the Resistance leaders, the Scythians, or the Fila would drag her into the talks. But in the end she was glad she stayed. There was an unexpected revelation, and somehow it meant more than securing the freedom of all the humans on Concordia and Earth.

The news came as they were wrapping things up. A timeline for the Scythians' withdrawal from both areas of conflict, reparations, and a plan for ongoing relations had been largely agreed upon. There were a few sticking points, but they could wait for the next meeting. Wilder was itching to get out of the door. She'd had an idea for how to spend some time with Quinn.

Everyone was making a move to leave when the Fila announced, "There is one last item to discuss."

She almost groaned aloud. "Surely we've covered everything important?"

"It concerns the safe passage of human starships in Concordian space. You may wish to come to a formal agreement on the matter today, due to its urgency."

"Urgency?" Wilder asked. "But we don't have—" She sucked in air in a whoop, but before she could say it, Miki exclaimed,

"The *Sirocco*!? She wasn't destroyed?"

"The Assembly reports your ship remains stationed in the nearest star system. She appears to have sustained considerable damage and the crew has been effecting repairs. If her drive is intact, we believe it would be appropriate for—"

"Yes!" Wilder yelled. "Yes! Contact Vessey. Tell her the war's over and she can bring the ship here, and to bring the Ark too." She didn't bother asking the Scythians' permission. Screw them if they didn't like it. Only a fool would jeopardize everything that had been agreed today, and the aliens were not idiots.

Miki was weeping.

Wilder hugged her. "I'm sure Nina's fine. You'll see her soon..." She was weeping too. "She could be here in a few hours if someone flies the shuttle down. Dragan can do it."

But she didn't think Miki could hear her.

The news about the *Sirocco* meant even more than Nina and the rest of the crew's survival. It meant that they could access all the material contained in the Ark. They could reseed Lyonesse and make it beautiful again. It also meant she could go to Earth and see Cherry.

In the space of a day, a single meeting, everything had turned around. The long years of struggle, the battles, the bloodshed, were finally over. It felt too good to be true. It was, of course. In reality, many problems lay ahead. Relations with the Scythians would be hard for years, perhaps forever. Their culture seemed very different from humans'. Replenishing Concordia's ecosystem would be hard too. Such endeavors were complex and they'd lost Kes, their greatest asset in the field.

But they would try. They would try as they always had, right from the beginning when the *Nova Fortuna* had appeared in Concordia's night sky. Unknown, unforeseen difficulties would test them, and each time they would rise to the challenge.

EPILOGUE

Wilder walked down to the ocean's edge carrying her equipment. It was a warm, sunny afternoon, perfect for a dip. This part of the beach was clear. The holiday-makers and daytrippers were up the other end where the pier stuck out into the sea and the water was shallow. She needed to go into the deep water.

She put on the mask and respirator, took some experimental breaths, and then stepped into the waves. She wasn't too worried about the breathing gear failing. She had a great solution to that problem. But the translation device was a new invention, something that had never been tried before as far as she knew.

The water rose up to her chest, she dove under the surface and began to swim. She hadn't gone far before the end of a tentacle prodded her foot.

"Quinn? You didn't keep me waiting then." She faced her friend. His tentacles writhed.

Now was the real test of her device. Fila could understand human speech but humans could not interpret the complicated system of tentacle movement, water currents, and electromagnetic pulses that constituted Fila language. Until now. Maybe.

"I didn't want to be late," said a voice in her ear.

She squealed. "It works! It works! I can hear you."

"That's no surprise to me, Wilder. I was confident you could do it. Would you like to go for a swim?"

"I'd love to."

Her friend gently wrapped tentacles around her waist and arms, and carried her out to sea. Her translator only worked if it had a full view of the Fila, so she could only talk and hear Quinn if they stopped and faced each other. But, despite her excitement about her new invention, she found she didn't want to talk. She only wanted to be in this moment.

For now, the world was perfect. Word had arrived from the Assembly that the Scythians had left Earth, rebuilding progressed apace on Lyonesse, and the scientists had begun their reseeding program. Miki was spending every spare moment with Nina, and though Wilder missed her young friend, she didn't begrudge her the time one bit. The two girls were thick in their plans for Miki to run for Leader when she was old enough, and Nina was her biggest supporter.

The *Sirocco*'s repairs were nearly finished, and soon Wilder would leave to visit Cherry. She'd asked that no one told her she was coming so it would be a complete surprise. She would take Faina with her and give her to the Makers. The android had expressed unusual excitement at meeting the original Strongquist.

Quinn carried her far from the shore, sweeping through the ocean as the sun blazed down, sending ripples of light from above. She felt completely safe. Her friend's care for her had been steady and unwavering ever since they'd met.

When he stopped, she turned to face him, floating in the deep blue water. "I'm so glad we can do this. It's better than talking through a glass pane, right?"

"I feel the same. Now you're in my element. I hope we can do it often. And I will take your children out into the ocean too."

"My children?" She lifted her eyebrows. "There's nothing like that on the horizon for me. I'm much too busy."

"How strange. Aren't you aware you are growing two babies?"

"I'm what?! No, I did not know that. What the hell?" She touched her stomach.

Pregnant? With twins? What would Niall say?

THE END

Thanks for joining me for the story of humanity's first deep space colony. I hope you've enjoyed reading it as much as I enjoyed writing it. For a different take on the future of humankind, check out: STAR LEGEND

Sign up to my reader group for a free ebook *Night of Flames,* the prequel to Space Colony One, and for more free books, discounts on new releases, Review Crew invitations and other interesting stuff:

https://jjgreenauthor.com/free-books/